City of Darkness - Special Edition

UNDERWORLD GODS
BOOK THREE

KARINA HALLE

CITY
OF
DARKNESS

Cover Design: Rachel McEwan Designs

Editing: Laura Helseth

Proofreading: The Fiction Fix

Page edge design: Painted Wings Publishing Services

Shadow's End art by: Kateryna Vitkovska

Death and Hanna art by: Art by Smashley

Hanna and Sarvi art by: CebanArt

For my favorite redhead, Laura

"Pick up the sword and try again"

— ANTERO VIPUNEN

Playlist

"God Games" - The Kills
"I am not a woman, I'm a god" – Halsey
"Going to Heaven" - The Kills
"Welcome Oblivion" - How to Destroy Angels
"Death's Head Tattoo" - Mark Lanegan Band
"Always You" - Depeche Mode
"Kingdom Come" - The Kills
"Last Rites" - +++ (Crosses)
"Gatekeeper" - Torii Wolf
"Castle" - Halsey
"Meet Your Master" – Nine Inch Nails
"Runner" - +++ (Crosses)
"Welcome to My World" – Depeche Mode
"Goddess" – Banks
"Various Methods of Escape" – Nine Inch Nails
"Last Cup of Sorrow" – Faith No More
"Master of Puppets" – Metallica
"Bone House" – The Dead Weather
"Should Be Higher" – Depeche Mode
"Die by the Drop" – The Dead Weather
"Born to Die" – Lana Del Rey

"Death Bell" - +++ (Crosses)
"King for a Day" – Faith No More
"Nocturne" - Mark Lanegan Band
"Gods & Monsters" – Lana Del Rey
"Phantom Bride" - Deftones
"Lantern Room" - Torii Wolf
"Immigrant Song" – Trent Reznor, Atticus Ross, Karen O
"Sin" – Nine Inch Nails
"The Epilogue" - +++ (Crosses)
"This Place is Death" - Deftones

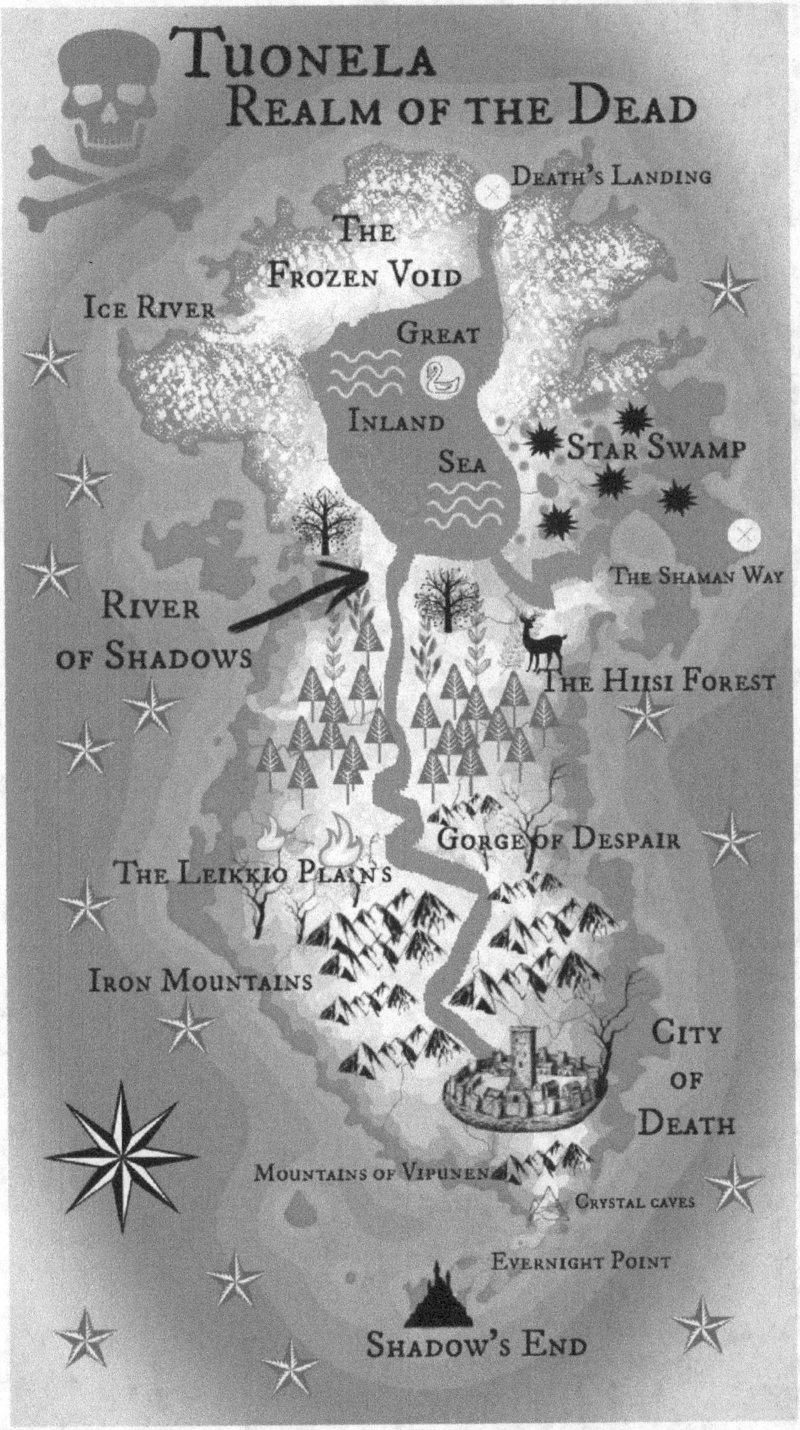
Tuonela
Realm of the Dead
Death's Landing
The Frozen Void
Ice River
Great
Inland
Sea
Star Swamp
The Shaman Way
River
of Shadows
The Hiisi Forest
Gorge of Despair
The Leikkio Plains
Iron Mountains
City
of
Death
Mountains of Vipunen
Crystal caves
Evernight Point
Shadow's End

Glossary and Pronunciation

Tuonela (too-oh-nella)

Realm or Land of the Dead. It is a large island that floats between worlds, with varied geography and terrain. The recently deceased travel via the River of Shadows to the City of Death, where they are divided into factions (Amaranthus, the Golden Mean, and Inmost) and admitted into the afterlife. Outside the City of Death, Gods, Goddesses, spirits, shamans, and the dead who have escaped the city can be found.

Tuoni (too-oh-nee)

The God of Death, otherwise called Death, and King of Tuonela, who rules over the realm from his castle at Shadow's End.

Louhi (low-hee)

Ex-wife of Death, former Goddess, half-demon daughter of Rangaista.

Loviatar (low-vee-ah-tar)

The Lesser Goddess of Death and Death's daughter. Her job is to ferry the dead down the River of Shadows to the City of Death, a role she shares with her brother Tuonen.

Tuonen (too-oh-nen)

The Lesser God of Death and Death's Son. He shares ferrying duties with his sister, Loviatar. Tuonen is also a lord in the City of Death and helps oversee things in the afterlife.

Sarvi (sar-vih)

Short for Yksisarvinen, Sarvi is a relic from the times of the Old Gods and originally from another world. Sarvi is a unicorn with bat-like wings who died a long time ago and is composed of skin and bone. Sentient, Sarvi is able to communicate telepathically. While he is a loyal and refined servant to Death, he is also vicious, violent, and bloodthirsty by nature, as all unicorns are.

Ilmarinen (ill-mar-ee-nen)

Louhi's consort, the demigod shaman she left Death for. He lives with Louhi in their castle by the Star Swamps.

Eero (ay-ro)

A powerful shaman from Northern Finland.

Väinämöinen (vah-ee-nah-moy-nen)

Death's past adversary and legendary shaman, who became a Finnish folk-hero. Väinämöinen has supposedly been dead for centuries.

Ukko (oo-koh)

A supreme God and the father of Tuoni, Ahto, and Ilmatar. Husband to Akka.

Akka (ah-ka)

A supreme Goddess, wife to Ukko, and the mother of Tuoni, Ahto, and Ilmatar.

Ilmatar (ill-mah-tar)

Goddess of the Air, sister to Tuoni and Ahto.

Vellamo (vell-ah-mo)

Goddess of the Deep, wife of Ahto. Protector of mermaids. Vellamo can be found in the Great Inland Sea.

Ahto (ah-to)

God of the Oceans and Seas, husband of Vellamo, brother of Tuoni and Ilmatar.

Kuutar (koo-tar)

Goddess of the Moon, Mother of Stars, protector of sea creatures.

Päivätär (pah-ee-vah-tar)

Goddess of the Sun, protector of birds.

Kalma (kahl-ma)

God of Graves and Tuoni's right-hand man and advisor.

Surma (soor-mah)

A relic from the days of the Old Gods and the personification of killing.

Raila (ray-lah)

Hanna's personal Deadmaiden.

Pyry (pee-ree)

Deadmaiden. Head cook and gardener of Shadow's End.

Harma (har-mah)
Deadmaiden. Head of the Shadow's End servants.

Tapio (tah-pee-oh)
God of the Forest.

Tellervo (tell-air-voh)
Lesser Goddess of the Forest and daughter of Tapio.

Hiisi (hee-si)
Demons and goblins of Tuonela, spawns of Rangaista.

Rangaista (ran-gais-tah)
A powerful demon and Old God, father of Louhi.

Liekkiö (lehk-kio)
The spirits of murdered children who haunt the Leikkio Plains. They are made of bones and burn eternally.

Vipunen (vee-pooh-nen)
An unseen giant who lives in the Caves of Vipunen near Shadow's End. The most ancient and wise being in Tuonela from before the time of the Old Gods.

Previously, On Underworld Gods

Hello, dear reader,

Thank you for your patience with this book. I know it's been a long time coming, with every issue under the sun impacting the writing and release of it. Since it's been so long and you may not have had time to re-read River of Shadows and Crown of Crimson, I've decided to do a little recap for you to catch you up to speed. Keep in mind, it won't be that comprehensive, but hopefully, it'll do the job!

Our story started off with River of Shadows.

Twenty-four-year-old Hanna Heikkinen gets word that her beloved (yet mysterious and estranged) father is dead. Heartbroken, she flies to Northern Finland for his funeral. There, she finds out that he's not dead and is attacked by two Shamans, Noora and Eero. She's rescued by Rasmus and taken through a portal under a frozen waterfall into Tuonela, the Land of the Dead. The objective? Get back her father, who has been captured by the God of Death.

Along the way, she meets Lovia, Death's daughter, sees some pretty gnarly things, and is eventually captured by Death himself. She pleads with him to spare her father's life and she will be his.

He likes that. So, he agrees and takes her to his castle, Shadow's End. There, she meets an assortment of characters, including Sarvi, the non-binary undead unicorn, Raila, her mysterious and always veiled Deadmaiden, and some other undead people. She also hears a lot about Louhi, Death's demonic ex-wife, who seems interested in raising the Old Gods to take over the Underworld and put her in charge. She wants to unleash *Kaaos*, a return to an afterlife where everything is equally horrid. "Kaaos is a ladder," as Littlefinger would say. Whoops, wrong book.

Anyway, eventually, Hanna and Death warm up to each other. And by warming up, I mean they have all the sex. Even with his mask on, it's sexy as hell (maybe sexier?). Death's kind of a grumpy dick, but Hanna can take it. Oh, and she takes it.

Eventually, he takes off his mask, and she's like, wow, he looks like Jason Momoa, maybe this isn't so bad. But just when she's getting used to the idea (I mean, she's been kidnapped into luxury, and there's a library and good food and clothes, also a little mermaid in a fishtank, whom she eventually yeets back into the sea), along comes Rasmus to fuck things up!

He takes her away from Shadow's End on the back of another undead flying unicorn. Rasmus wants to help her (genuinely) and along the way, they stay in a cave that's seriously gone all The Last of Us, with freaky fungi and a mushy lady. There, they learn some truths, such as Hanna having an evil twin and also, Rasmus is her brother. And her father slept with Louhi. Geez, Dad!

Eventually, they leave the cave, and then it turns into The Neverending Story (you know the part, I can't talk about it) and Louhi comes on the scene and is all crazy and shit, but Hanna cuts off her tongue in a sweet battle. Then, Death shows up, and Rasmus is taken by Louhi.

By the way, Death is super pissed off at her for leaving. He drags Hanna back to Shadow's End, forces her to marry him, then throws her into an oubliette. She's eventually rescued by Raila and his daughter, and then a really tense marriage follows.

With hot sex.

There are visits to the Crystal Caves, which makes you super horny, plus a voyage to the bottom of the sea to visit with Death's relatives (super not horny). Everyone is interested in who Hanna's mother could be, since the giant Vipunen has been training Hanna to fight and he told her that her mother isn't her real mother but a Goddess, Jerry Springer-style.

But the more pressing issue is the whole prophecy thing and the uprising. Death is worried about all that, so he creates a duplicate of himself using shadow magic, and then has a threesome with Hanna and himself—basically a big fuck sandwich where he's both the bread AND the meat.

Then, they all go to the Bone Match so they can dupe the public into thinking Hanna is the chosen one and can touch Death and live (did I mention he can't touch anyone with his bare hand?).

But something goes wrong. Death's Shadow Self is taken over by Louhi, Death gets killed by Salainen, the evil twin, and Hanna is thrown into a cell with him to rot.

Just when all hope seems lost, she touches the dead Death, and he is brought back to life. She can touch him! She is the chosen one! So she fucks him! And then she grows fucking WINGS, and her hair turns to fire.

And he's like, "oh shit, I know who your mother is. She's the Goddess of the Sun!"

And she's like, fucking cool. So now what?

Now what, indeed...

CHAPTER 1
Lovia
THE COLD

Nothing makes me feel more like a mortal than the fact that I hate my job.

If there's one thing I learned from my time spent in the Upper World, it's that nearly every human I've run across detests their vocation. Whether it's driving people around in cars, serving them overly-complicated coffees, or working in tiny, airless rooms often described as "offices" and "workspaces," every mortal being seems to decry what they do for a living.

I guess that's what makes what I do a little more complicated. See, I don't ferry the dead for a *living*. I don't take my boat to meet the recently deceased at Death's Landing and transport them to the City of Death so I can make money. I'm not supporting a lifestyle (I mean, what lifestyle?).

I do it because I have to, because I am the daughter of Death, a Goddess beholden to the realm, and it is my duty. In our world, duty trumps everything. You do it because it is your role in life, and don't you dare ever question it...or else.

But I *have* been questioning it. Is this all I was made for? To serve my family? Though I know transporting the dead is a noble, honorable role, it feels different when you have no choice in the matter. It feels like a sentence. It feels like punishment, like I've been held in chains my whole life. But these chains are comfortable and soft, and they do a good job of tricking you into thinking that maybe all of this, this lack of choice and freedom, isn't all that bad when you're a Goddess. Things could always be worse, right?

That's the problem with the cards life deals: they're slow to show you that things can get better, but they're laid out awfully fast when it comes to things getting worse.

Right now, I'm picking up Ethel Bagley, an elderly (by human standards) woman who had a merciful death after a bout of pneumonia. My brother, Tuonen, says he never cares to know anything about the people he's picking up, but I always tap inside myself for knowledge. I want to know something about the person I'm transporting.

Ethel is standing at the shoreline, hunched over and alone, looking so incredibly small as the ever-present mist wisps past her. This is the part that always gets me about this job—nearly everyone dies alone and, as the ferrywoman, I am the first to lay eyes on the recently deceased, seeing humanity at its most vulnerable, when the shackles of life have been taken off and they're truly unmoored in time ever after.

I sigh as the boat scrapes against the shiny black rocks of the shore. I have this strange feeling in my gut that twists and turns, but I can't figure out why. Perhaps I'm just tired and bitter that everyone in my family is in Inmost, the Hellish level of the City of Death, watching an exciting Bone Match while I'm having to deliver a little old lady to her eternal afterlife.

"Ethel," I call to the woman. "Ethel Bagley."

She looks up at me with cloudy eyes, though they seem to be clearing by the minute. Though she won't age backwards, the longer she's in Tuonela, or more specifically, The City of Death, the more she'll become the best version of herself. Her aches and pains will disappear, she'll become limber and quick, and her mind will sharpen, along with all her senses. Even those bound for Inmost will become as strong as they were in their youth, even if they might rot to their bones. Once upon a time, before my father came into power as the God of Death, they would have remained old and in pain, lost to the *Kaaos*, but my father is a fair God and, in his opinion, even the worst of the worst don't deserve an afterlife of pain. Living in Inmost is punishment enough for the most depraved.

"Where am I?" Ethel asks, looking around. "Who are you? A deer woman?"

I smile beneath the deer skull mask. We wear masks to put on an air of authority and mystery, though, honestly, I don't think it makes a lick of difference to the new arrivals. "I am here to bring you to your afterlife."

"I'm dead?" Ethel asks. They always seem surprised at first, often pushing back against the idea for a bit until they realize the truth. "But last I remember, I was..."

"You were dying. Now, you're here. Come," I say, gesturing to the boat.

"I can't climb up on that," she scoffs, crossing her arms. But even that movement seems to have surprised her, how much spryer she is than she remembers.

I hold out my hands toward her, palms up, and hum under my breath.

"*Tassa nostan sinut kuolemanjalkeisen elaman tyttareni.*"

Elderly Ethel Bagley begins to rise off the stones as I lift my hands. She moves gently through the air until she's placed delicately beside me. I don't always move the dead into the boat in such a dramatic, magical manner, but this lady looks like she could use a little fun. Plus, it usually helps them accept death quicker once they see something they'd once considered impossible.

"I must be dreaming," Ethel says, gazing around the boat. "Yep, one of them dreams I get from having too much sherry before bed."

Perhaps she'll be a little more stubborn than most.

"It's not a dream," I tell her. "You had pneumonia and died, one of the best deaths you can have. You know, aside from that whole gasping for air business."

She fixes a shrewd eye on me. "And what would you know about dying, deer girl? Have you ever died?"

She's got me there. "Well, no," I say as I steer the boat, heading to the river that will take us up through the Land of the Dead. "But I'll have you know that a death here is worse than a death there."

"You're making no sense," she mutters, the breeze ruffling her thinning gray hair that seems to get thicker as the moments tick on.

"I'm the Goddess of Death," I tell her. "Death's daughter. I am an immortal, but if I were to somehow die here, I would be sent to Oblivion, which is just floating around in the void for eons. At least you get to live your eternity in the Eternal City."

"And what's that? Heaven?"

I shrug. "It depends which level you go to."

"I hope it's not where my husband George is. That wouldn't be my idea of heaven."

I look at her in surprise. "You don't want to be reunited with him in the afterlife?"

She shakes her head, her lips curled bitterly. "I should have divorced that bastard before he kicked the bucket. Knowing him, he's probably... do you have a Hell here?"

"Something like that..."

"Then that's where he probably is," she grumbles. "Would serve him right for having an affair with Betsy McGuffin for fourteen years."

I'm about to tell Ethel that having an affair doesn't mean you'll be sent to Inmost, but I decide to keep that to myself. Wouldn't want to spoil her time here already. Besides, once Ethel meets the Magician, who will pull the card and let her know what section of the City she'll be staying in, she'll feel better about things. Once the person truly accepts their death, which usually happens on the way to the City, then the memories of their life in the Upper World start to fade away. They never disappear completely, but they don't have a hold on them like they would if they were alive. Otherwise, people would spend eternity pining for their previous life, and that doesn't sound like heaven to me.

And yet, I'm doing that to myself. Sure, I'm not dead, but I feel like I'm forever pining for a life in the Upper World. If only my father could just let me leave Tuonela and my duties and explore the human realm. I know he thinks of it with disdain (aside from the fact that they produce the coffee to which he's addicted), but he's never even been there. He has always sent others to go. He doesn't even know what he's missing.

But I do.

I sigh despondently, and Ethel looks at me. "What are you so upset about? I'm the one who's dead."

I don't normally converse too much with the recently deceased. Usually, I just let them look around the cold corners of Tuonela in silence, watching as their past life slowly loosens its grip on them.

I bring the boat along the icy shores of the Frozen Void, where a herd of white reindeer have gathered, their exposed bones gleaming in the faint light streaming through the clouds, munching on frosted bunches of red sinberries. The weather today has been pleasant so far, obviously because my father is enjoying himself at the Bone Match—which is where I should be.

"I'm just missing out, that's all," I confess to Ethel. "There's an important family event happening right now, and I wish I could be there. More than that, I wish I could do what you mortals do and take a vacation so I could venture out into your world for a bit."

"So we both don't want to be here," she says in a huff.

"Of course I want to," I say quickly, not wanting to ruin her experience. "It's an honor to transport the dead. Truly."

"I'm sure it is, but we can't love our lives all the time. That's unrealistic." She pauses. "Though, looking back, I probably should have appreciated even the most mundane times. You never know what you have until it's gone." She glances at me and gives me a one-eyed squint. "Except for George. I'm glad he's gone. And if I catch him in this world, I'll deliver him straight to Hell myself."

Sheesh. She's still holding onto her old life with an iron grip, though I have to admire the strength of her spirit.

And I'm starting to hate George now too.

We're getting closer to the City of Death, just passing out of the Hiisi Forest, when suddenly, a sharp blast of frozen air comes from above, almost like an icy hand pressing down from the sky. In seconds, the clouds gather, dark and ominous, blotting out the sun until everything is a murky shade of twilight.

To my surprise, Ethel shivers, rubbing her hands up and down the nightshirt she died in. The dead are supposed to be impervious to temperature changes.

"Are you cold?" I ask her as the wind picks up, driving snow from above that coats the boat, parts of the river freezing over before my eyes.

"Yes," she says, her teeth chattering. "Is it usually this cold?"

I shake my head. "No. You shouldn't feel any temperature at all. I don't know what's happening."

While I've gotten cold from time to time depending on my father's moods, since his moods are linked to the weather, even I'm starting to feel the icy bite of the wind, the snowflakes that have gathered in my hair and on my lashes.

What in the realm is happening?

That curious feeling I had in my gut earlier returns, twisting until I feel sick.

No. Something is terribly wrong here.

It's not just that it's dark and cold—it feels like the life has been sucked out of the land, like the very heart has suddenly been snuffed out.

And that's when I feel it in *my* heart.

In my soul.

A horrible truth I never thought could come to pass.

My father is dead.

CHAPTER 2

Death

THE AWAKENING

I never feared death.

How could I when I was the God of it?

When my whole existence was built around it?

Even though I knew my own mortality was finite, that there were ways to kill me, it's not something I lost sleep over. No God did. That was the difference between us and the mortals. Their lives were limited, and they all staggered through it in the shadow of their own death. It loomed above them like a fist, hiding behind the darkest clouds, threatening to strike them at any moment. They lived in fear of something for which there was no escape.

Foolish, I always thought, to fear something you couldn't avoid.

But then, I died.

And everything changed.

I remember being nervous about the Bone Match. I knew there was a chance Louhi could strike, and even though we had taken every precaution by using my Shadow Self, there was a risk in going out in public like we did. The last thing I wanted was to put Hanna in danger, and yet, I still found the risk acceptable enough to do so.

That was my biggest mistake. In hindsight, I should have shoved my need for power and politics aside. I should have buried my pride. What I wanted was to show my people I was still in charge, still their God, and I wanted to make an event of it. I should have found another way to do that instead of delivering Hanna right into the jaws of the wolves.

I should have picked her above all else.

But fear is a persistent creature.

Even when you think you've faced it, even when you think you've hidden from it, it will find some way to come back around. I feared the loss of my stature, the loss of my kingdom, the loss of power. I feared those more than the loss of Hanna and my own life.

Then, in an instant, I lost it all.

All those losses culminated in my death.

Death at the hands of someone pretending to be my wife.

After that, there was only darkness.

Until a voice brought me to light.

I heard Hanna tell me she loved me. Her words were a beacon in the night, in that void, in that cold space that wasn't quite Oblivion but wasn't quite this realm. They pulled me up, like I was rushing toward the surface but never reaching it.

Then, I felt the impossible.

I felt my hand, unobstructed by any glove or layer, against her cheek, my skin against her skin.

And it was like coming home.

I burst through the surface and ended up in my body, staring up at a sight I thought I would never see, feeling something I never thought I would feel.

Hanna was beside me, surrounded by glowing light. I pressed my fingers against her cheek, unsure if I was still dead or if I was dreaming. I felt her for the first time, and it was like something bright being born inside me.

I still wasn't sure if we were both alive, but it didn't matter. When she slipped my dick inside her and started riding me, I thought maybe true heaven existed after all, even better than Amaranthus.

And then, she grew.

She grew into the being I always knew she was.

She became more than just the prophecy—the one who can touch Death and unite the land. She became a Goddess.

Golden wings made of sun flares and flames extended from her back, making her dark hair turn shades of burning amber. She glowed with power, lit from within like a fuse that had been buried inside her for far too long.

She was incredible.

She was powerful.

And she was mine.

Now she sits on top of me, my cock still hard inside her, so impossibly turned on by what I witnessed—how she brought me back from the dead, how she's the chosen one, how I can touch her, how she's a Goddess—that I have a difficult time thinking straight.

From the confused look on her face, I know she can't think straight either.

"Daughter of the Sun?" she repeats my words back to me, her brows knitting together. Though her wings and remnants of the sun are gone, she glows faintly in the light of the sphere on the ground, which makes the cell around us seem even darker.

I adjust my grip on her hips, relishing the feel of my fingers bare against her soft, warm skin, my cock sliding deeper inside her until her mouth parts, lips wet. I don't think she realizes—while she was both climaxing and growing wings—that I haven't come yet.

That's alright. Her needs always come first.

"I had a feeling you were Päivätär's daughter," I tell her, my voice dropping even lower as I continue to rock her back and forth on me. "The Goddess of the Sun. The God not present at the meeting in the grotto, the one who could have infused you with all your bright light, the protector of birds...little bird that you are."

Her eyelashes flutter as she takes in my words, as I push up deeper insider her, enough that she has to lean forward, her hands on my chest, one breast popping out of her torn gown. In the back of my mind, I know we aren't dead, that we must find a way out of here and stop our impostors, but I also know the path ahead of us won't be easy, and this might be the last time I get to feel her like this.

The way I have always dreamed of.

A way I've always felt unworthy of.

"What does this mean?" she asks, her voice trembling slightly.

"It means you know who your real mother is," I tell her. "And when we get out of here, we're going to find her."

She lets out a shaking breath, throwing her head back. "And if we don't get out of here?"

"Then I'm going to make this count."

With a grunt, I grab her waist and lift her off my cock before turning over and laying her on the ground beneath me. I know it's cold and dirty in this dark cell, the only light coming from the sunmoonstone crystal, but we don't get to be picky.

"I'm going to feel you every which way I can," I murmur to her, placing my hands on her soft yet firm thighs, spreading them beneath me. Her body was sinful from the beginning, from the first moment I had her in my bed, but now, she has powerful muscle, a hint at the Goddess she is, under soft flesh that has brought me back to life.

I run my palms up over her skin, savoring her, knowing we either have all the time in the world or no time at all.

In the end, it doesn't really matter, so long as I have her.

"Tuoni," she whispers to me, her dark eyes full of something wild, something like glory. It looks like love—the way she says my name sounds like love.

And she *had* said it.

She had said those words.

I love you.

Yet, even in this darkest hour, why is it so hard to believe?

Why is it so hard to believe that someone, especially someone like her, could truly love me?

"Tuoni," she says again, reaching up to place her hands on either side of my face. "We need to get out of here."

"We will," I assure her, my eyes closing at her touch while my knuckles graze the soft hair between her legs. "But I will no longer be denied what has been denied to me my whole life."

My voice comes out rougher than I meant it to, but when I open my eyes, I only see understanding in Hanna's gaze. She knows how much this means to me.

She also knows I'm a stubborn beast.

"Then have me any way you want me," she says, her eyes damp and glittering in the faint light.

I can't help but smirk at her permission. "How I want you," I say gruffly, letting another knuckle brush closer to her cunt, causing her to moan, "is achingly slow. How I'll take you is with my own pleasure in mind. I will savor you like the finest wine. I will bask in you like a man deprived of the sun."

I place my palm against her thigh and press down, widening her cunt for me. My gaze drops to the sight, so fucking pink and gleaming wet that I'm salivating for a taste as my cock swells, wanting to shove inside her so terribly that it hurts.

Instead, I take my finger and slowly, with deliberation, run it along her wetness. The feel of her most womanly and intimate parts against my bare finger sends a shockwave up my arm and down my spine, and the silver lightning lines burn in response. But it doesn't feel like millions of mortals are dying at once—instead, it feels like I'm coming fully alive.

As I told her, I take my time. I explore her, reveling in the slickness and heat of her body. I find her wonderfully responsive clit, already thick and puffy, and tease it, eliciting a gasp from Hanna's lips that sends a thrill of pleasure through me. I glance up at her, her eyes hooded with desire, her breath coming in short little pants, and I feel my own hunger boiling up, threatening to overtake me.

But I hold back, wanting to savor every moment of this exquisite torture.

I stroke her gently at first, then faster and harder, my fingers pushing her closer and closer to orgasm each time before pulling back to start again. I alternate between teasing and tormenting, giving her just enough pleasure to drive her wild while keeping her just out of reach of complete satisfaction.

I feel the tension coiling in her body as she comes nearer and nearer to the edge. I can't help but grin to myself, to her greedy, wanton body as she tries to thrust her hips for friction. Slowly, I slide my finger inside her, and my own eyes roll back in my head at the feeling of her, a tight velvet glove that's so wet, incredibly soft and hot. I never thought I would feel her like this, never thought she would truly be mine, never thought the Creator would be so kind as to grant me what the prophecy promised.

Then, I find the raised circle on her inner wall and press my finger there firmly.

"Oh God," she says in a ravaged cry, throwing her head back, and I know that when she says that, I'm her only God.

I add another finger and thrust them in and out of her at a steady rhythm, increasing the intensity with each slick pass until she is gasping and moaning in pleasure. Her nails dig into my arms, and she pulls me closer, begging for more.

I can feel that she's close, so I add a third finger and start thrusting faster, pushing her over the edge with every movement until, finally, she can take no more, and she cries out as she shudders and quakes beneath my fingers.

"I thought you said this was all about *your* pleasure," she manages to say as she squeezes and trembles around me. The feeling of her like this from the inside out is incomparable.

I manage to chuckle, despite my raging lust. "I can't help it if you come at the drop of a hat."

I remove my fingers and run my tongue over them, savoring her taste. Without my gloves getting in the way, her flavor is pure and exquisite.

It would taste better with my cum mixed in, though.

I lick my fingers clean, all the while watching her beautiful face, her eyes heavy-lidded as she takes me in.

"And I'm not done with you yet," I tell her, though it sounds like a warning.

I grab her wrists and pin them beside her head, watching the way her body arches at the confinement, her tits rising up, one bare and the other confined to her gown until I pull it free. She groans, and her nipples point straight up into beautiful pink pebbles. I take one of the puckered tips into my mouth and suck hard, not teasing anymore. I bring my free hand up to the other breast, and I pinch and tweak the nipple between my finger and thumb, earning another moan from Hanna's lips. I take my time exploring her body, my tongue lapping at her flesh and my bare hands buzzing with electricity as I explore every curve and every dip.

I can tell this is turning her on, that she's wet again, dripping, and I leave her breasts to go lower, pushing her gown up further, pressing my tongue flat against her belly button, dipping inside to taste her. I'm hot and hard and ready to fuck, but I won't do that until she begs me. Even here, in the dark cells of Inmost, I still love to hear her beg.

I pluck at her clit with my fingers, pinching and pulling on the swollen nub, making her whimper and gasp.

My chest rumbles with desire, and I bend lower, burying my face between her legs. I inhale deeply, taking in her scent, and then my tongue replaces my finger.

She shivers and sighs, closing her eyes as I devour her. She is so soft and sweet and tastes even better than before. I lave and nip and suck her clit, then her cunt, alternating between them until I have her panting and moaning and writhing, trying to get more of my tongue on her.

I want more of her too, so I give it to her, sliding my tongue deep inside her, plunging it as deep as I can go, lapping at her and devouring her. I rub her hard against my mouth, savage and fierce.

"Yes!" she screams, and her legs jerk as her body tenses, and I feel her desire gushing around my lips. I lap up every drop, sucking and swallowing.

I come up for air, and I'm so hard that I'm twitching. When I crawl up her body, I moan as my cock presses against her soft thighs, and she helps by spreading her legs wide.

I guide my cock to her cunt and thrust into her slowly, as slowly as I licked her. I can feel every millimeter as I push into her tightness, her slick walls rippling around my cock, and I groan in pleasure, the sound loud in this dark place. I pull out and thrust in, every little movement of her body obliterating whatever self-control I've been clinging to. Her body is so hot and wet and soft and tight and I'm drowning in her softness, feeling like I'm floating on cloud.

"Fuck me hard," she says, her voice a breathless whisper, and my restraint fractures. "I want to feel it forever."

I swallow at that, wanting the same.

With a growl, I slam my cock into her, over and over, grunting at the feeling of her body, her thighs pressing against my waist as I thrust harder and deeper, until I feel as if I'm impaling her into the cold, hard ground.

"Fuck!" she cries out as she comes once again. The sound of her voice makes my balls ache, and I can feel my cock throbbing, ready to burst. I slam back inside her, harder, deeper, and I feel the cum inside me rushing up, ready to pour out in release.

"Oh, Hanna," I groan, feeling the threads of control snap. "Can you take much more of me?"

"Please!" she cries out, her whole body jerking and writhing as I thrust into her, again and again, deeper than I ever thought possible.

"I'm going to come," I say, trying to hold on a little longer, my jaw achingly tight as I fight to hold myself back.

"Come inside me," she says, whimpering her words. "Please, Tuoni. I want to feel it. Feel you."

And I will give my wife everything she asks for.

I slam into her, and her body spasms beneath me as she comes hard, again, her cunt squeezing my cock like a vice. I groan and thrust into her one more time before I come in torrents, spurting into her over and over again, filling her up with every last drop.

Fuck.

This woman.

This queen.

This Goddess.

All mine.

I collapse on top of her with a breathless cry, my cock still jerking inside her, and when I raise my head to kiss her, my hips are still thrusting out the last of my orgasm.

"Hanna," I whisper to her, but her name chokes me. Too many emotions are rising in my chest, foreign feelings that threaten to overwhelm me, to destroy me. I stare at her beautiful, flushed face in the dim glow of the crystal, and despite the fact that I'm still inside her, that I just came with the strength of a thunderstorm, I feel as if I'm walking on cracking ice, that the world might give out from under me, and when it does, I'll never be the same.

I can't let that happen to me, not yet—perhaps not ever.

You are the God of Death, I remind myself. *You have your prophecy. You have your wife. She will unite the land, the very land you have sworn to rule over. It is your destiny to put your land before all else. Even before her, if you must. It is your duty to do all you can to remain in power.*

"What do we do now?" Hanna asks, as if reading my thoughts.

I lean down and place a kiss on her forehead before pulling out.

"We get the fuck out of here and take back what's ours," I tell her.

CHAPTER 3

Hanna

THE ESCAPE

Death rises above me, his formidable frame rising like a shadow against the glow of the sunmoonstone crystal. I stare up at him, my mind still drunk from the multiple orgasms he just coaxed from me again and again and *again*. Sex with Tuoni has always been mind-blowing, and from the intense way our bodies respond to each other, I never thought that the connection between us could be strengthened.

But I was wrong. Having him touch every inch of my body with his bare hands, feeling the softness of his palms, the might of his fingers, and seeing the awe in his gaze as he worshipped me made me feel bonded to him like nothing else. The chord that has always connected us has drawn us deeper than before, our intimacy intertwined.

Because of the prophecy.

I am the one Death can touch and still live.

I am, somehow, the daughter of a Goddess.

I am the one to unite the land.

But neither of us can do anything until we're out of this prison.

Until we're out of Hell itself.

Death's lips curve into an arrogant smile, enjoying the sight of me beneath him before he reaches down and pulls me up to my feet by my elbows. For a moment, I think I'm going to be unsteady, perhaps swooning into his arms after all the tumultuous events, but instead, my feet are planted firmly on the ground. Now that the haze of my orgasms is fading, I feel strong, my senses sharper than ever.

Death's bare hand slides down over my forearm to my hand and laces his fingers in mine for a moment, a touch of intimacy that somehow manages to startle me. "I know you feel it," he says, his gray gaze flicking over my face. "Your power."

I give my head a shake, the whole thing seeming surreal—and that's saying a lot, considering where we are. "I don't even understand it. What does this mean?"

"It means you were never a mere mortal, fairy girl," he says to me, giving my hand a squeeze. "You have the blood of a Goddess in you, which means you have powers that have been lying dormant your whole life. I had suspected as much, and it seemed the giant did too."

"What kind of powers?"

"The ability to burn like the sun and grow golden wings, for one," he says with an appreciative smile. "The rest, I'm sure we'll discover."

"If only I still had my training with Vipunen," I lament.

His brows come together. "You will. This isn't over."

"Maybe not, but I need the training now, for this moment, so there can be a next moment."

"You've learned more than you think. Vipunen saw this in you. He sees all. Knowing him, he probably found a way to train your subconscious. You've got to give yourself more credit."

I don't feel any better, no matter how much Tuoni seems to believe in my abilities. I don't have my selenite knife or my sword. I feel completely ill-prepared for anything that may come my way. If some situation calls for me to grow wings again and fly, I have a hard time believing I'll be able to make that happen on command.

Hell, there's a chance it might not ever happen again. I may be the daughter of a Goddess, but there's no telling how much my mother passed down to me.

My. Mother.

My *real* mother.

Fuck, it still doesn't seem real. How could I, a former social media marketing manager sharing a tiny house in North Hollywood, be a fucking Goddess? I mean, it would be a little more fitting if I had come from the "live, laugh, love", sea moss-glugging yoga hippies in Ojai or something.

"So, if we get out of here—" I say as Death buttons up his shirt.

"*When* we get out of here," he says.

"Are we going to head straight to...the sun? Or where does my mother live?"

Why am I picturing her like the creepy sun from the *Teletubbies* but with a woman's face?

"No," Death says gruffly as he slips on his leather vest. "She doesn't quite live on the sun. It's somewhere in the ether in between, but I've never been there. Her territory and Kuutar's territory have always been outside of my jurisdiction, and I have no idea how we would get there. We will find her, but a reunion with your birth mother will have to wait. First, we have to find out what your evil twin wants."

I stare at him. "You don't know what she wants?"

"I didn't have a lot of time between figuring out it wasn't you and then her stabbing me with a shadow knife. I still have no idea how she fucking did it. I shouldn't be that easy to kill." His brows come together. "And yet, she threw you in here, didn't she? You fought her?"

"I did," I tell him. "And she was impossibly strong, even more so than Louhi was while operating your body."

His eyes widen, mouth parting slightly.

"I have to admit, it's a strange feeling knowing I know more than you do for once," I say. "What do you think happened to me before all of this?"

"I don't know; I was too busy coming back to life and touching my wife for the first time," he says with a grunt.

I ignore the warmth that spreads through me every time he says *my wife*.

"Oh boy," I say, sucking in a breath as I try to figure out how explain all that went down. "Well, let's see. I was upstairs watching the Bone Match with you, and then suddenly, you ceased to be you. I could tell right away. By then, it was too late, and you were leading me away from the crowd. That's when I realized Louhi had booted you out of your Shadow Self."

He nods grimly. "That must have been the moment your twin stabbed me. I lost connection in every way possible." His mouth twists as he stares at me, his gaze turning soft. "I'm so sorry, Hanna. I should have been there to protect you—to protect you from her, from myself."

"Same," I tell him. "I guess both of us were attacked by each other in disguise. I managed to fight off your Shadow Self, enough that some disgusting spider creature started eating him, but then Salainen showed up and told me everything."

"Such as?"

"Family history. How my father discarded her in Tuonela, how she was raised in secret by Louhi instead. How much hate she has for me. And then her plans, of course. They always tell you their plans. She will impersonate me, Louhi will somehow wrangle up another Shadow Self or resurrect the one I thought died to impersonate you, and together, they will fool the Underworld and let it run right into *Kaaos* again."

He worries his lip between his teeth. "They're going to raise the Old Gods. They're going to start a war."

"They're going to kill your family," I press.

Death looks like, well, death. His face pales, making the black around his eyes stand-out. "They won't," he says with a growl. "They can't. Tuonen, Loviatar, they're Louhi's children. She wouldn't harm a hair on their heads."

Despite everything, I think Death has a little too much faith in his demon ex.

"Even if that's true, that isn't what Salainen thinks," I tell him. "They won't be safe around her."

He gives his head a shake. "They'll figure it out. They won't be fooled. They know their father."

"But their mother knows him just as well. She'll play you like she's Meryl Streep."

He frowns at the comparison. "It didn't work on you."

"I doubt your kids will notice your smell has changed," I point out. "Louhi is going to do all she can to make sure the ruse is a success, and we're going to have to hope and pray that Salainen doesn't hurt Tuonen or Lovia in the meantime."

"Prayers don't work down here," he mutters, eyes blazing. "We need to get out of here and stop them before they reach Shadow's End."

He makes it sound so easy, as if Louhi and her crew didn't just hand us our own asses.

"And how do you propose we do that? They're long gone by now, probably at Shadow's End already. Who is to say it won't be on lockdown? Won't they be controlling your army? Won't they try and paint us as impostors the moment they see us coming? What do we have?"

He stares at me for a moment, his expression a mix of frustration and pride. "You're thinking like a queen already."

"I've been a queen for a while, if you haven't noticed," I say, punching him on the arm. Though I meant for it to be light, he winces, and I can't tell if I actually hurt him or not.

"I've noticed," he says, his eyes glimmering. "First, we get out of Inmost. Shouldn't be too hard. Unless Louhi has spies everywhere, which she might, everyone here will still recognize me as the God of Death."

"And then?"

He frowns in thought. "Then, we gather our allies before they're tricked. We head to the Hiisi Forest and seek out Tapio and the Forest Gods. He's the closest to us."

"And my mother?"

The stern expression on his face softens. "That may have to wait. We'll put out the word that you know your lineage and would like to meet, but it can't be a priority at the moment."

Part of me is relieved; the whole meeting-my-Teletubby-sun-birth-mother-who-is-a-Goddess thing will be put off for now. The other part of me is impatient—I want to know everything, including what kind of powers I might have. The more information I have, the better chance I have to protect myself during this next round.

Because Sala made a grave mistake by not killing me and locking me up with Death; she won't be so careless the next time around.

"You'll meet your mother," he says, placing his hand on my shoulder, and it's not lost on me that his hand is still bare, and I can feel the warmth of his large, soft palm. "I promise you that."

I nod and then look at the heavy door locking us in. "Who knows?

This might be as easy as you busting a move and breaking us out of here."

"Busting a move?" he asks, his brow raised quizzically.

I shake my head. "It will never cease to annoy me that you only know some slang, not all slang. I mean, kick down the damn door."

He shrugs. "As you wish."

"Oh, but of course you've seen *The Princess Bride*."

"The princess what?" he asks, but there's a knowing gleam in his eyes.

Then he turns and, with a grunt, heaves himself at the door. He collides into it with a bone-jarring thump that shakes the room and causes dirt to fall from the ceiling, but the door doesn't move.

He grunts. "Salainen must have magicked it." He looks back at me, wiping away dirt and dust that has fallen on his forehead.

I nod with a scowl. "She did; she's brimming with fucking black magic. I heard multiple locks when she closed it. Can you undo them?"

Death looks back at the door. "I'll try. Believe it or not, dark magic was always Louhi's interest, not mine. I don't have a lot of experience with it. I'm not even sure a God should be dealing with it at all, let alone the God of Death. Magic doesn't always come easily to me."

"I'm sure there are exceptions." I refrain from reminding him that he created his Shadow Self, and that magic didn't seem all that kosher.

He makes a low noise and then closes his eyes, his palms out toward the door. He's mumbling something under his breath, a chant or spell of sorts, and while the room seems to grow colder, the light from the crystal waning as if the power is being sucked out of it, nothing happens.

"Damn it," Death says. "I don't know how to overpower her magic. It's dark and strong, most likely powered by Louhi's hate."

"Add in Salainen's hate for me, and we're fucked."

He sighs heavily, running a hand through his hair as he looks me over. "Okay, then. Your turn."

"My turn? You expect me to kick down the door after you couldn't?"

He shrugs. "You somehow defeated the Shadow Self version of me; I wouldn't sell yourself short. Anyway, now is as good a time as any to see if you can conjure up that Goddess power."

"You keep saying it's a power, but all that happened was that my hair turned to flames and I somehow grew wings. If you can't open the door as the God of Death and King of the Realm, what makes you think that I can?"

"I suppose you're always surprising me. Why would this be any different?"

Hmmph. I don't share his confidence in me.

Still, it's worth a shot.

I walk over to the door, Death stepping out of the way, and take in a deep breath. I close my eyes and...

What the hell am I supposed to do? Pray to my mother? Ask the gods for help?

I sigh and try to approach this with as much gravity as I can. After all, if we don't get out of here, it's not just our lives that will be affected.

I just don't think I'll be able to help.

Stop thinking negatively, I chide myself. Pretend you're in front of Vipunen. Pretend you're in front of your mother. Ask for help. Ask for strength. Ask for the powers of the sun.

I pinch my eyes shut even harder.

Gods who can hear me, give me strength, give me light, give me the power to save ourselves.

I try to concentrate on the air in the room, the ground beneath my feet, the beat of my heart, the sound of my breath. I picture the sun radiating warmth and power from its rays, imagine it sinking into my skin and igniting something inside me. I feel something inside my core, something eternal and complex that's swirling, building, filling me with energy.

I open my eyes and point my palms at the doors as I let out a cry.

Nothing happens. The energy inside me dissipates like a candle that's been snuffed.

I glance at Death over my shoulder as I walk over to the door to check. I put my hand on the handle, but it won't budge. I press my shoulder against it for a moment, but I know it's futile.

I step back and give Death a sorry shake of my head.

"Nothing happened. I felt something inside me but...nothing came out."

He nods at me, in thought, before his eyes go over my shoulder and widen.

I whirl around to face the door again.

The handle is starting to move.

The sound of it unlocking fills the air.

Did I do that? What is happening?

Then, the door slowly opens toward us.

On the other side is a short figure cloaked in all black, a black veil over her face.

CHAPTER 4

Tuonen

THE REFEREE

The Bone Match was a success, one of the most entertaining games I've seen lately. The loser went in quite the way too; the other skeleton pulled off his own femur and, while balancing on one leg, managed to swing it like a bat, knocking the opponent's head clean off. It went soaring into the stands with a shriek that carried throughout the stadium and ended up in a spectator's arms. Naturally, everyone around him wanted the decapitated head too, and a fight to the death broke out, sending more of the Inmost dwellers to Oblivion. In the end, someone walked away a victor, numerous skulls in their possession.

As soon as the match was over, I expected my father and his new bride to make an announcement while they still had an audience. Hanna had been introduced to the crowd earlier, but I had assumed my father would later make a speech to unite the dead of Inmost to his side. It was part of why tonight was so important to him.

But that's not what happened. In fact, I can't even find my father at all, or Hanna, for that matter. The moment the victor walked away with his trophies, the crowd started to disperse, albeit reluctantly (these matches are really the only things these poor fucks have to look forward to), and their seats in the stands sit empty.

"Have you seen my father?" I ask Tapio, God of the Forest. He's just getting to his feet with his wife and daughter, a few pieces of popcorn hanging in his gray beard alongside the usual leaves and twigs. The small, sniffing nose of a mouse makes an appearance before retreating into the thicket of his hair.

"I haven't," he says with a frown, looking around me at the empty seats. "I assume we'll meet back where we first came in."

"He's not there," I tell him. "Neither is Hanna."

Tapio's wife laughs. "Tuonen, perhaps it's best you don't pry into their business too much. They are still newlyweds, after all."

I grimace in disgust at that and walk up the stairs to the landing at the top of the arena where Sarvi stands, moving their head back and forth, scouring the area.

"Sarvi," I say to the unicorn, "have you seen my father or Hanna?"

They fix their white eye on me, tail swishing. *I was just about to find you and ask you the same thing. I haven't seen them, but that doesn't mean much, does it? Wouldn't be the first time that they've made their company wait.*

Sarvi's tone is humorless; I can tell the unicorn is edgy, and I feel the same way. I can't really explain why I'm so worried when I'm sure they'll turn up at any moment, Hanna looking flushed, my father looking cocky, but I have a sharp kernel of unease in my gut that's getting harder to ignore.

Oh, there's Hanna now, Sarvi says, and I look over to see Hanna coming out of the caverns toward us.

She doesn't look flushed at all. Instead, her eyes seem darker than normal, her posture stiff.

"Are we ready to go?" she asks, a strange formality to her tone. She's asking me directly, ignoring Sarvi.

"Where's my father?" I ask.

"He's held up at the moment," she says, smoothing out her gown. "He wanted to spend some time in the dungeons finding new members for the army. He told us to go back to the castle without him."

Sarvi's tail swishes faster. *That doesn't sound like something he would say.*

Hanna shrugs and gives Sarvi a stiff smile, though I notice she doesn't look at the unicorn for too long. I don't know Hanna well at all, but perhaps there is bad blood between them.

"If you want to go to the dungeons and see for yourself, go right ahead," she says in a clipped voice. "But I want to get back to Shadow's End. I'm tired. Come on, Tuonen."

She reaches out and takes my arm, trying to lead me along, but I stop.

"I'll catch up," I tell her. "You better gather the rest of the guests."

"The rest of the guests?" she asks, brows raised.

I frown at her. "Yes. The Forest God's family."

Her eyes widen for a moment, and she nods. "Yes, of course. Them."

She turns and walks toward Tapio and his wife and daughter, who are at the top of the stairs, staring at us.

That was very peculiar, Sarvi muses. *I could have sworn Hanna decided she was anti-unicorn suddenly. Is it my breath?*

I shake my head absently, still watching her as she talks to Tapio.

"She seems different somehow," I say quietly. "But I suppose it's not that unheard of for my father to spend time in the dungeons. He has been going on about building a bigger army."

Sarvi grumbles, moving their lips in a flapping manner. *That is very true. Still, I should want eyes on Tuoni before long.*

I put my hand on the unicorn's shoulder, the cold dry bone juxtaposed against the warm, soft coat. "I know the dungeons better than anyone. I'll take a look and meet you back here. Just don't let them leave without me. Those leftovers from dinner have my name on them."

Be quick, Sarvi says. *I'd like to avoid the bowels of this place if I can.*

I take off toward the caverns Hanna stepped out of, running along the slick walls that shine in the intermittent torches lighting the way, the ground slippery beneath my feet. You'd think I would be used to the grim depravity and gore that litters the halls of Inmost, but I'm not sure I'll ever be used to this city. The matches are fun, and I more than enjoy being a ref, but I try not to spend too much time here if I don't have to. Even though I'm the Son of Death, my father taught me to enjoy the finer things in life, and this city is the antithesis of all that is good in the world.

I'm about to head down a narrow set of stone steps to the dungeon when I feel a cold blast come over me, raising the hair on the back of my neck, the stench of sulfur filling the air.

Gooseflesh seems to form both outside and inside me.

Only one person, one being, can make me feel like this.

My mother.

"Tuonen, my dear, handsome boy," her raspy voice croons from behind me, sending shudders down my spine I do my best to hide. There are very few people who sound worse the more complimentary they are, but Louhi is one of them.

I turn around and see her stepping out of the darkness, like the shadows are a second skin she decided to slough.

She's always a formidable sight—her seven-foot height, her wide black wings, her cold green eyes, the horns curling off her head like someone crossed the devil with a ram. She smiles at me, teeth sharp, the curl of her lips cruel.

I have never been what the Upper World calls a mama's boy, and that is something that has bothered my mother since the day I was born. I've tolerated her the way one would tolerate a snake slithering around in their boot. I've faked niceties, because what sort of monster hates their mother, even if she's a monster herself? But I've never loved her, and I know she's never loved me. That's pretty much the gist of our relationship.

"What are you doing here?" I ask her, and already, I feel the hair on the back of my neck growing stiffer. The shock of seeing her made me forget that she's here at all—where my father and Hanna are—and nothing good can come of that. My mother has basically had an imaginary restraining order most of my life, which has been her word that she wouldn't ever come after my father in the eons after their divorce.

Her word has never carried much weight.

"I wanted to drop in and see my relations," she says, slowly walking toward me. "Is that a crime?"

I shake my head. She's up to something. "Where's my father?"

Her gaze becomes flinty, and I notice that the earrings she has dangling from her lobes are actually two shiny black beetles that are writhing and making a clicking sound.

"You haven't come to see your mother in ages, and yet all you can do is ask about your father?" she says with a snarl. "He's down in the dungeons. I'm sure he'll be back at any moment. I just wanted to come and say hello to you before he sees me."

He'll smell you, I think. *He probably already knows you're here.*

"What do you want?"

"I told you," she says sharply, running out of patience. She comes closer now, the sulfur scent growing stronger, mixed with something bracing like menthol. I can hardly breathe as she reaches for my face and places her palm against my cheek. "I wanted to see you."

I suck in a breath as the pain of her touch sears me, something so frigid that it burns like fire, and I am mildly proud of myself for not flinching.

"What a waste, my dear son," she coos, her eyes flicking over me. "Your father treats you like a slave, doesn't he? Always doing something that benefits him, never you."

"I like being a referee," I manage to say, hating how my voice sounds in her presence, like I'm weak.

She pulls her hand away and starts to circle me like a slinking beast, her mouth smirking now. "You tell yourself that, but you only like it because otherwise, you would be ferrying the dead. That's where your sister is now, isn't it?"

I don't answer. I want to tell her that my father is trying to work out a new system to get someone else—Tapio's aimless son—to take over our job, but for some reason, I feel I need to keep that quiet.

"You know very well that if you were with me at Star Swamp, you would have the absolute freedom to do what you want. I would let you become anything you wanted, let you *do* anything you wanted."

I know that's too good to be true. My mother would never let that happen; she'd want to control me instead. What I really want is to go into the Upper World to check on a certain human I made a bargain with at one point, but that will never be in the cards with either of my parents.

"As I said," I say, squaring my shoulders, "I'm happy being a referee. Now, why are you really here?"

She gives me a hard stare for a moment, the flames from the wall torches glinting in her eyes like an inferno before she lets out a cheerless laugh. "Oh, I had heard that his new wife was making an appearance, and I had to come check it out for myself."

"You know her name is Hanna. You've met her before," I tell her. I wait a beat before I add, "She bested you and cut off your tongue."

Her lip curls in a snarl, and a malevolent, otherworldly sound comes from her mouth, like a growling beast.

"She didn't best me. She cheated." She opens her mouth as if to show me her tongue but closes it and composes herself with a flick of her head. "Regardless, I wanted to see her first public appearance as the Goddess of Death. I have to say, I was expecting Tuoni to drag her out into the middle of the arena and parade her around like a doll, perhaps make some sort of speech, but he did nothing of the sort. I do hope he's not growing tired of her, ashamed of her mere mortality. You know how your father is. Gets bored easily."

She gives me a cunning smile as she goes on. "But it doesn't matter how he feels, does it? As long as he's happy, I suppose. As long as you're happy too. I should get on now, before I start making any trouble." She pauses, licking her lips. "You're a smart boy, Tuonen. Perhaps your father knows what's best for you after all."

And at that, she turns in a swirl of black, sulfured smoke and walks away, disappearing before my eyes.

I stand there for a few moments and blink, my eyes watering.

What the hell was that?

Why was she really here?

Oh, fuck.

My father.

She had to have done something to him.

I turn around, about to run down the stairs, when I stop dead in my tracks.

My father is right below me, coming up.

"Father?" I ask, taking a step backward.

He stops in front of me, though he doesn't meet my eyes. For some reason, he's shirtless, but at least he has his pants on, though they look a little torn.

"Are you okay?" I ask.

"Yes," he says, clearing his throat and rubbing at his arm with his hand. His bare hand. No gloves. There's a huge, bloody wound there, one that looks ripped by teeth, but the more I stare at it, the more it seems to heal itself before my eyes.

"What was that? What happened?"

"Just had an altercation with one of those spider things," he says. "And before that, I was busy with Hanna, if you must know. Come along; it's time to leave."

He brushes past me—I'm careful to step out of the way of his hands—and walks down the hall.

"Did you find anyone for your army?" I ask as I jog after him.

"Mmmm, yes. Some. I'll come back some other day and be more thorough. It's important we get back to Shadow's End."

"Wait," I say, striding beside him until the hall opens to the arena. "Where's your Shadow Self?"

He looks down at me, meeting my eyes for the first time. He grins. "He's having some technical difficulties. I guess I'm not the magical genius I thought I was."

Then, he goes and joins the others, including Hanna, who almost grabs his bare hand. I'm about to yell at her to stop, but then she seems to remember and pulls her hand back, smiling at him instead.

Very fucking strange.

Sarvi looks over at me, and their voice slides into my head.

Are you alright, Tuonen? they ask.

I nod.

I'm alright.

And yet, it feels like something is terribly wrong.

CHAPTER 5
Hanna
THE DEADMAIDEN

"Raila?" I exclaim as the thin black figure hovers anxiously on the other side of the cell door.

God, I hope it's Raila.

The figure nods, and while I've never seen my Deadmaiden's face beneath the veil, I know it's her.

I'm glad that you're alright, my queen. Her head tilts to my husband. *Master Tuoni, it's a relief to know you're alive. But we don't have time to dawdle. I must get you both out of here at once.*

"But how did you know we were even here?" he asks gruffly. He pushes at the door, which grinds on its hinges as it opens further. Raila steps back into the hall, out of the way of his towering frame. "How did you know what happened?"

Raila goes silent for a moment as I step out into the hall beside her. It curves in both directions, the walls dark and slick with who knows what goop, and the only light is from behind us in the room and from a lit torch on the wall.

"Wait," I say, and I run back into the room. I snatch up the glowing sunmoonstone sphere and grasp it in my hand. "We might need this."

I look around the empty cell one last time, wishing there was something else in here that might help us, but there's nothing except his red mask. There doesn't seem to be much use for it now, but I grab it anyway, handing it to Death in the tunnel.

"Thank you," he murmurs, taking it from me before slipping it on so it's pushed up on his forehead, the iron spikes and fangs looking extra menacing in the dark of Inmost.

Quickly, this way, Raila says, heading in the opposite direction I thought she'd take us.

"You're leading us further down into Inmost," Death remarks, following her quick movements.

It is the only way, she says.

Death reaches out and yanks at her arm, pulling her to a stop.

"No. There is never only one way," he says. "Tell me what you know, or I won't risk my wife's life in your hands."

But your wife is the reason I am here, Raila says. *I am loyal to her until the end of time*. She lets out a sound that sounds like a ragged sigh, almost like a gurgle, and I'm reminded of seeing the spider thing from earlier, the one I fought off, the one set to eat Death's Shadow Self.

I can't help but shudder. That's not what Raila really is, is it? She can't possibly be a baby-eating spider monster woman beneath that cloak, can she? Then again, she did say she murdered her whole family—is it murder if you eat them?

Tuoni lets out a gruff noise of disapproval. "I don't doubt your loyalty to my wife, Raila. However, I will do whatever I can not to put her in harm's way again. Tell me what you know, Deadmaiden."

Raila's head swivels toward me. *Tuonen has left with the party back to the castle. Tuoni's Shadow Self is playing the part of Death, operated by Louhi, and Salainen is pretending to be you, Hanna.*

Death growls. "Surely, my own son can tell the difference between me and my Shadow Self. Or Hanna and her twin?"

Perhaps he can, I do not know. I don't doubt he'll figure it out sooner or later. The question is, will he be safe if he does?

"Louhi wouldn't hurt them," Tuoni says, frowning deeply. "But Salainen has no such loyalty. How do you know all of this?"

Connections, she says. There's almost a hiss to her voice. *This used to be my home, master, before you graciously rescued me. I know the ins and the outs, and I have eyes everywhere. Many eyes. Which is why I need you both to follow me. All the other ways out are being watched and guarded. Salainen and Louhi have taken no chances just in case you came back to life or Hanna escaped her cell. Everyone knows that if you are sighted here now, you are merely impostors to be dealt with.*

Tuoni grumbles his displeasure again but gives me a conceding glance. "It's up to Hanna. She's the queen you're protecting."

Great. Give me the responsibility.

I shrug, as if shrugging your way out of Hell is a thing. "I trust you, Raila. If you have a way out of here, then we're going with you."

I swear, I hear her smile underneath that black veil. *Very good. Follow me.*

She turns and starts walking down the grimy corridor. I look to Tuoni and shrug again. "Worth a shot."

He puts his hand on my shoulder and nods sternly while ushering me forward. The tunnel in this direction is narrow, so we can't walk side by side. Instead, he stays behind me with his hand holding me in place, as if he's afraid to let go. I suppose after what we've just gone through, I don't blame him.

"If anything should happen, I've got you," he says into my ear.

"I'd still feel better if I had my sword," I say.

We follow Raila down the corridor as it starts to wind around. The ground is slippery beneath my feet and tilting slightly, giving the impression that we're going deeper into the earth. It feels colder too, and damp enough that I can feel the condensation in the air. Raila had grabbed a lit torch off the wall earlier, and the flames start to dance in the air, as if being weakened by something.

Luckily, I have the sunmoonstone in my hands, and the glow stays steady.

Not that I particularly want to see what I'm seeing: centipedes the size of my forearm crawling on the walls, hiding from the light, along with thick nets of spiderwebs above and tiny skittering insects that hop about brown-red sludge on the ground. I can feel them every time they jump on my bare legs, and it takes all my strength to try and ignore them, to keep walking forward.

Down and down we go.

At first, I was running on enough adrenaline to keep me going, but the longer we walk, the more I feel it wane. If there ever was a moment for my demi-Goddess self to come through and give me wings, if not just more strength, this would be it, but I'm feeling painfully mortal. The further we go, the more my body remembers the complete ass-kicking I took at the hands of my twin.

I know you're not supposed to empathize with villains, particularly the one who literally just killed my husband, but I do.

How could my father do that to Salainen when she was just a baby? I knew my parents never had a happy marriage. I saw that firsthand. I lived through their divorce, through their epic separation. The idea of my father having an affair doesn't really shock me—I never pretended he was an angel—but who he had the affair with, and especially what he did when that magical tryst ended in pregnancy, well, that's the part I can't wrap my head around. How could he conjure up a baby from dark magic, a literal living, breathing being, and then abandon it in the Land of the Dead? Did he really think he was doing it a favor? Did he really think it would be fine? Or did he not think the baby was real at all? Was he just returning dark magic to where dark magic is born? Did he know Louhi would take care of her?

I hate that I can understand where Sala is coming from, why she hates me so much. I'd hate me too if my father brought me into this world for no reason other than to hide a lie and then cast me into another world to die or be raised by a demon.

"Be calm, little bird," Death says quietly from behind me. "I can feel your anxiety in my bones."

I nod, trying to breathe in deeply through my nose, but it only makes me cough, the air down here thin and acrid.

Oh dear, Raila says, coming to a stop in front of us.

"What?" Death growls as we both nearly collide with her.

I hear footsteps, she says. *Running, many beings.*

"They're my subjects," he says, pulling his mask down over his face. "Let them come."

Her veiled face glances over her shoulder. *They will see you and know what Louhi has told them. They will want to fight you.*

"Let them fight," he growls.

Oh boy. I clench my thighs together. What a terrible time for that to turn me on.

Master Tuoni, you don't even have a weapon, Raila chides him.

"That's never stopped me before," he says gruffly.

But while they're talking, I hear footsteps, many of them, coming faster and faster, along with some other kind of jangling noise. It takes me back to the match, and I realize it's the sound of bones clanking together as they run.

"Get behind me, both of you," Death says, grabbing both me and Raila and pulling us back. He takes Raila's torch from her and brandishes it in his hand like a weapon.

The marching sounds get closer, and down beyond the dark curve of the slimy walls, light flickers from oncoming flames.

"Here they come," Death says.

Raila reaches out with her boney, gloved fingers and gives my hand a squeeze.

Suddenly, they appear, rounding the end of the tunnel: skeletons running toward us, two abreast, shields in one hand, swords in another. They're mostly bone, though the occasional piece of dried skin hangs off them in tatters, their eyes empty sockets, their jawbones clacking as they run.

"Halt!" Death says, raising out his ungloved palm. "I am your king. Who gives you permission to be here?"

The skeletons stop a couple of yards ahead, the leader at the front cocking his head at the sight of us.

"We have been commanded to patrol Inmost," the skeleton says, the teeth snapping together. *Clack, clack, clack*.

"Commanded by whom?" he asks.

"By you," the skeleton says. "We were told that if we were to encounter you down here, along with your queen, we needed to kill you."

"What if I were to tell you that I'm the real king and the other is the impostor, a Shadow Self controlled by Louhi?"

The skeleton seems to consider that for a moment. "It doesn't matter who you really are. You're not the one promising us our freedom."

"No," Death says gruffly. "But I am the one who can send you to Oblivion."

"With what weapon? Fire?" The skeleton snickers. "If you truly were the king, you should know that fire doesn't hurt us who burn in flames every day. And if you truly are the king, you should know that we've all dreamed of the day when we could escape from this world you've imprisoned us in for eternity."

"An eternity you deserve," counters Death. "I am a just ruler."

"Just a matter of opinion," the skeleton says. "And why should you rule over us in the name of what is fair and just when the Upper World, the world we came from, has never been fair?"

The Hell-bound skeleton does have a point.

"Because only in death can there be true justice," my husband says.

"Well, we think justice is overrated," the skeleton says, looking over his shoulder at the crowd of his kind behind him. "Isn't that right, boys? Let's welcome in the *Kaaos*!"

All the skeletons raise their swords in a rallying cry that makes parts of the wall crumble away.

This isn't going to be good.

They start sprinting toward us, and I get into a fighting stance behind my husband, unsure how the hell I'm going to fight a bunch of sword-wielding skeletons. Meanwhile, from behind me, Raila starts chanting something low, guttural, and raspy, causing all the bugs on the walls and at our feet to start running away.

Well, fuck. If the insects are retreating, perhaps we should too.

Death lets out a roar as the first skeletons clash with us. I can't see over his frame, but I can tell he's swinging the torch, and he's making contact with the skeletons, the sound of bones crunching and swords rattling to the ground. One of the swords lands to the side of Death, and I quickly crouch down and snatch it up. It's heavy in my hands, but the hilt feels good against my palms, and I take a two-handed grip, all the training with Vipunen coming back to me like muscle memory. Perhaps Death was right, and the subconscious Goddess side of me learned more from the giant than I thought.

Screams fill the air, and I still have no idea what's happening until suddenly, one of the skeletons goes flying over Death's head and nearly lands on me. I stumble backward into Raila, who holds me up just in time for me to swing the sword across the skeleton's head, severing it. It bounces, and I kick it backward like a soccer ball, Raila jumping out of the way. It screams down the tunnel as it goes.

"Good girl," Death growls happily, and I feel a surge of pride and power flow through me.

"Send me another one!" I cry out. "I'll take all these boney fuckers!"

I peer around Death to see the battle just as he slices a skeleton's arm off with his sword while simultaneously grabbing another skeleton by the wrist.

That skeleton screams and then crumbles into a dusty pile of bones that seems to disappear before my eyes, and I realize what he's doing. Just as I saw him do to Surma when he tried to attack me, Death's hands have been bare, his gauntlets tucked into the back of his pants, and he's sending the skeletons to Oblivion one by one, their swords and shields clattering to the ground when they disappear into dust.

But even though Death is making quick work of slicing off heads and limbs with his sword and grabbing bone with his bare hand, they never seem to stop coming, leaping over each other, climbing up the walls.

One falls on me again, and my sword strikes its sword, the collision sending a rattling shockwave through my body. He tries to again to stab me, and I block his move, feeling quick on my feet until I notice more of them crawling on the ceiling now. It's so unfair they can defy gravity like that.

"Keep fighting them, Hanna!" Death yells at me, but now, I'm trying to fight two skeletons at once. Death quickly reaches behind with his hand, grabbing one of them by the back of the throat, and that skeleton cries as it turns to dust. I catch the hilt of its fallen sword, now having a sword in each hand, and take the opportunity to cut the other skeleton's head off.

But still, they keep coming, an endless train of armed skeletons, and both Death and I do what we can to keep them under control, but I'm not sure how much longer I can keep this up.

Meanwhile, Raila is still chanting from behind me.

"Do you want a sword?" I yell back at her over my shoulder. Her chin is down, her hands together in what looks like prayer. "A little help would be nice!"

I am helping, Raila says, and then her head snaps up. *They are here.*

"Who are they?" I ask as a skeleton drops from the ceiling and nearly takes me out. I scurry out of the way, using the slope of the walls to propel off of so I go leaping through the air on top of the skeleton's back, knocking him to the ground. I run the sword across his torso, severing him in two.

My relatives, Raila says.

"What the fuck is that?" Death asks.

My heart stills, and I look around Death to see what Raila means by relatives.

Eight long, black, giant legs appear at the end of the tunnel.

CHAPTER 6

Lovia

THE MAGICIAN

"Are you alright?" the newly deceased Ethel Bagley asks me.

I'm staring at the snowy banks of the shore ahead and the lonely dock that juts out into the river. This is usually where I would leave Ethel and tell her to follow the guided path up through the hills and across the desert until she comes to the City of Death, a journey the dead usually make on their own.

But right now, I don't trust Ethel to make it there alone. Not just because she's cold, so cold that I had to give her my reindeer skins I have lining the boat's benches, and not just because I don't trust her not to wander off alone, but because the path seems insurmountable in this snowstorm.

More than that, I feel that something has fundamentally changed in this realm. I can't shake the feeling that my father is dead. It's something I should never have to worry about, and yet, it feels true in the heart of me, like the connection I have to him and the connection he has to Tuonela have been severed at the same time.

You're being ridiculous, I tell myself. *He's the God of Death. He can't die.*

And yet, we can.

"Deer girl," Ethel says, waving her hand, "you're going to crash your boat."

I look up in time to stick my oar out and slow the boat's collision with the dock. Normally, the boat sails itself without input from me, but with everything feeling off, I'm not taking my chances.

I dock the boat and give the woman a sheepish look. "Here we are. I don't normally escort people to the City, but I think I will today."

Ethel shrugs, which then turns into a shiver. "Suit yourself. As long as we don't have to walk far."

The two of us disembark, with her following me as we walk carefully down the slippery dock. I pause once we step on the shore. The snow has covered up any sign of a trail, and darkness has fallen, making it even harder to see. I know the way instinctively, and I believe the dead know the way too. In fact, I am sure their legs are compelled to walk, no matter how they feel about marching to their final resting place, but I don't feel like taking any chances.

We walk on, trudging through the snow, hoping we're on the iron path as we climb up the hills away from the river.

Eventually, the land levels out, and I know we're close, close enough that I should be looking at the expanse of the City by now. I squint through the dark snowstorm.

The City of Death is barely visible from here. Even though the tower reaches up into the clouds and sprawls wide for miles, the falling snow obscures it, making it look like a giant, shadowy beast hiding in the distance.

"Just a little further," I tell Ethel. She holds her fur close around her neck, and I feel terrible that she's in this situation. Out of the countless people I have ushered to the afterlife, I fear her experience has been by far the worst. "Once you get inside the walls, this will all be but a dream."

"More like a nightmare," she says through chattering teeth.

I nod at that, unsure of what else I can say, and we continue our walk along the snowy path. Usually, the land here is just a dry, dusty wasteland, but in this weather, it's a different kind of bleak and foreboding. Prettier, perhaps, like the snow is wiping some sort of slate clean with its purity, but I don't trust it.

Eventually, we get up close enough that I can see the robed Magician standing outside the front gates.

"Who is that?" Ethel whispers to me. "He doesn't seem to have a face."

"He's the all-seeing Magician," I tell her. "It's he who knows what level of the afterlife you end up in."

"Ah," she says. "No wonder he gives me the creeps."

I suppose she's not wrong. I'm so used to the Magician, I don't really see him for what he is: a robed being holding a deck of cards, with no face at all but a look into the vast, dark void of the universe, complete with whirling galaxies, shooting stars, moons, and the occasional black hole.

"Do we need to bribe him?" she asks me as we approach.

I can't help but laugh at that. "I'm afraid it wouldn't help. He has his own set of morals I don't know much about."

"Ethel Rose Bagley," the Magician says in his strange voice, both empty and flat and yet deep and echoing. "Here, the cards of your life are drawn. Are you ready to accept whatever is dealt?"

Ethel shakes her head, stubborn to the end.

"I'd rather have a choice, if that's alright with you," she says.

Despite not having a face, I swear, I feel the Magician smile. A shooting star curves up across the lower half of his void face.

He shuffles the deck, as is customary, the cards flying through the air as if moved by invisible hands, until he selects one with black, velvet gloved fingers.

He looks at it and then turns it around.

A picture of a skeleton burning in fire.

"Inmost," the Magician booms.

"Is that good or bad?" Ethel asks.

I barely have time to voice my shock and displeasure before the gates of the City swing open, and black smoke, curled into the shape of claws, comes shooting out. They grab Ethel by her shoulders and snatch her back through the air in an instant. All that's left behind is the reindeer pelt I lent her, and it falls to the snowy ground as the gates slam shut.

"Inmost!" I exclaim to the Magician. "There must be some sort of mistake! She was a sweet old lady. Well, maybe not sweet, but old anyway, and—"

"She murdered her husband and his lover," the Magician interrupts me.

I swallow hard, my eyes still wide. All that talk about her ex, and it turns out, she's the one who killed him. No wonder she's been so worried about running into him in the afterlife.

"Surely if you repent for your crimes and sins, you'll at least go to the Golden Mean," I say to the Magician, feeling the need to barter for Ethel's doom.

"She hasn't felt remorse a single day in her life," the Magician says plainly. "She has gone where she belongs. As the ferrywoman, you should know better than to get involved with the lives of the dead. I'm surprised you felt the need to accompany her here to begin with."

"I know," I say. "It's just that I was feeling...well, it doesn't matter. But this storm. The cold. She was so cold, and I felt bad that her afterlife was going this way. Don't you feel it? Don't you think this storm is odd?"

"I feel nothing."

Of course he doesn't.

"There's something wrong," I say, staring into the inky abyss of the Magician's face.

"Indeed, you're right about that," he says.

I blink. "I am? What do you think it is? Is it my father? Do you know if he's, he's..."

"The Bone Match is over. Your father left this place not long ago," he says. "Heading back to Shadow's End."

My heart soars. "He's alive!"

The Magician doesn't say anything for a moment. If he had a face, I think I would see him close his eyes in thought, but there are only spinning galaxies and waxing moons.

"He is alive," he finally says.

I exhale a shaky breath, my hand at my chest. "Thank the Creator," I say before I pause. "Wait, you agreed that something is wrong."

He nods. "Yes."

"So what is it? Is it connected to this storm?"

"The storm will end soon," he says. "Then, a new storm will begin.

You better get back to your post, Loviatar. The dead never stop coming."

I stare at him for a moment, wishing I could read something in that universe of a face. "What do you know, Magician?"

"I know everything and yet nothing," he says mildly. "But I know that you need to get back to your post, for your own good. Take that as a warning if you must."

"A warning?" My heart starts to race again.

"If you know what's best for you, you'll stay as far away from Shadow's End as you can. Do not leave your post unless someone comes to relieve you. The dead will rise up, and you need to be there."

I frown at his choice of words. "But Tuonen will eventually take over again. We trade."

The Magician doesn't say anything for a moment. Then, he lets out what can only be described as a sigh, the sound of wind blowing through caves. "I am a subject of both your father and the Creator," he begins. "I have an important role, as do you. It is thanks to the two of us that the City of Death and the afterlife for mortals continues. If things were to change, if our roles were to become obsolete, I'm not sure what I would do."

"Why are you telling me all this?" I ask carefully.

He laughs grimly, like he knows a joke I don't. "Because it's important you stay alive. Even a Goddess can lose. Trust no one, Loviatar, not even your family." Then, the Magician pauses, his voice dropping to an eerie register. "Especially not the ones you love."

CHAPTER 7
Hanna
THE SPIDER PEOPLE

"Raila!" Death bellows as he brings his sword across another skeleton's head. "Did you invite the spider creatures?"

They're only here to help, Raila says from behind me as I dodge a skeleton who launches himself over Death's shoulder and nearly knocks me down.

"Are you sure?" I ask, ducking as the skeleton swings its sword at me. "Because the last time I saw one of those creatures, it was about to devour Death's Shadow Self whole."

They knew he wasn't the real Tuoni, Raila says. *They will obey me and the king.*

Fucking hope so, I think.

I crouch low—not an easy feat when you're wearing a gown and holding two heavy swords—and kick out hard with my boot so that the skeleton's leg breaks off at the knee and he collapses to the ground. Death quickly reaches back and grabs the skeleton by the hand, picking him up and flinging him through the air as he dissolves into dust that rains down on the advancing army.

The spider things are advancing as well, long, spindly yet thick black legs crawling along the sides and ceiling of the tunnel, reminding me of when I was child, sitting on our dock on the lake, seeing dock spiders crawling up through the cracks. They seemed huge to me at the time—if only I knew I'd be battling human-sized versions of them in the distant future.

Except, I'm not battling them, not yet. I watch as they crawl over the skeletons, demolishing them in their wake, breaking them into many pieces. They seem to be doing as Raila had hoped, definitely making it easier for Death and me to win this siege. But what happens once the spider things reach us? Will they obey Raila and Death? I don't feel like I can bet on it, not now, not when the skeletons have already turned against him.

Besides, I saw these gross things devour a baby. Maybe I'm being too judgmental, but it's definitely clouded my opinion about them.

The skeletons keep coming. A couple more get past Death, and I make swift work of them, Vipunen's training seeming to pay off. The more skeletons I take down with my swords, the more confident I become. I know that if Death asked me how I was doing, I'd probably pull a Captain America and tell him "I can do this all day."

But eventually, the skeletons die out in a pile of bones and ashes, and all that we're left with are a dozen giant spider things at the end of the tunnel, staring at us.

Alright. This is *way* worse than the skeleton army. Earlier, I had done my best not to look at the spider I came across in the tunnels, especially since there was a bigger danger at hand, but now, I don't have much choice. The spiders are black and hairy, with a row of shining eyes down their backs, human-like hands at the end of their legs. Their heads are oblong with a hole in the middle, a mouth filled with rows of silver, needle-sharp teeth covered in fine hairs.

It makes me want to vomit.

I glance over my shoulder at Raila. If that's what she looks like under that veil, I pray to God she never lifts it. I'll be much happier pretending she's just some regular murderous woman under there.

"Well," Death says gruffly to the spider people, lowering his sword slightly. "I thank you for your help."

Raila makes a series of unsettling chirping sounds.

"Are you translating for them?" I ask her. "Do they not know English?"

I am asking them for safe passage, she says.

"Asking?" Death says, his chin lifted with an air of importance. "They do realize I am their king? I shouldn't have to ask; they should know to give."

Yes, but as you saw with the Inmost dwellers, things have changed here, Raila says. *I am explaining the best I can that you are still their king.*

She goes back to making that chittering sound, and I exchange a glance with Death. He's not amused, his mouth setting into a firm line before he turns to face the spiders again. This time, he raises his sword.

"Let us pass, and there will be no trouble," he commands. His voice is gruff and steady, and if I were them, I wouldn't risk his brand of trouble.

But the spiders don't move.

Raila lets out a raspy sigh and walks past us so that she's in front of us, facing her kin.

She starts chittering again, louder now, throwing out her hands.

And yet, the spiders don't move.

Finally, one in the middle starts tapping a leg against the ground, the weird, human-shaped hand slapping the surface. Then, the rest of the spiders join in until the slapping sound fills the tunnels and dust from the ceiling begins to fall.

"What's happening?" I ask, my chest growing tight along with the grip on both swords.

This isn't going as I'd hoped, Raila says, sounding unsure for once. It makes her seem human, and for once, I don't like it. *They are having a rebellion of their own. They say that Louhi has promised them a new life running free on the surface...feasting on anything they see. It's too tempting for them.*

Death growls. "How the fuck has that she-devil been turning everyone in Inmost against me?"

She has her ways, her networks, her spies, just as I have mine. I should have known, master, that this was her plan. For that, I am sorry. I thought my relatives would have listened to reason.

Death grunts. "Reason. There is no reason anymore. Guess we'll have to fight our way out of it."

Raila turns to face us. *Please. Allow me to make sure you can pass. At the very least, I can get the queen to safety.*

"I'm not going anywhere without my husband!" I cry out.

"And I'll slaughter every creature I see before I let my wife walk off with you," he sneers.

You'd risk her life on that? Raila questions.

I can tell my husband is two seconds away from driving his sword across Raila's hidden neck, so I quickly reach out and put my hand on his arm to calm him.

"Let's try to get past them first," I implore him. "If they don't let us through, then we'll lay waste to them." I look to Raila. "I'm sorry if they're your kin, and I'm grateful they came when you called and helped defeat the uprisers, but if they don't let us through, then we don't have a choice."

I understand, she says quietly.

She turns to face the spiders again, throwing her hands into the air, the chirps coming out loud.

"What are you saying to them?" Death asks.

I'm promising things, she says, then continues chittering.

"What sorts of things?" His hand tightens around the handle of his sword.

Promises you won't keep but might let you live, she says.

And at that, the spider people stop stamping their feet.

Silence fills the tunnel.

We stare at them.

They stare back at us. Or at least, it feels that way, considering their eyes are on their back.

Then, the one at the front slowly starts to move to the side.

The others follow suit, half of them curling up on the walls and then the ceiling so that they're building an arch of giant spiders we must walk under.

"Don't look up," I mutter.

Come along, Raila says. *Quick now.*

She starts walking toward the tunnel of spiders, like some nightmarish attraction you'd find at a horror night theme park, and Death goes behind me, nudging me slightly. I grip my swords as tight as possible and walk with them both pointed up. If any of those fuckers drop from the ceiling on me, I'll gut them.

I instinctively hold my breath as we walk underneath, hurrying along after Raila, feeling as if the spiders might drop or leap out at me at any moment. From the way that Death is close behind me, I know I'm not the only one creeped out by this turn of events.

We hurry through without the spider walls collapsing from above, and I don't dare turn my head to look behind us.

Then, I hear it.

A heavy thump.

Raila stops dead in front of us, and I nearly run into her. She doesn't turn around at first but immediately starts chittering loudly.

"What's happening?" Death asks.

Raila turns around, as do we.

Behind us, the dozen spiders have gathered, moving slowly toward us.

"What are they doing?" I ask, my voice coming out in a squeak.

Raila shakes her head and moves past us so she's between us and the spiders and holds her hands out at them. *They've changed their mind,* she says, her voice barely a whisper in my head. *Go.*

"What?" Death asks.

They don't believe you'll uphold your promise, she says quickly. *They're going to kill you both. Go! Go, now! Run and follow the tunnel to where it forks and take the left passage until it comes to a door drawn in the dirt with a single obsidian knob. Open that door and leave!*

"Raila, we aren't leaving you," I say, reaching for her shoulder.

I'll hold them back! she yells, shaking me off and marching toward the spider creatures. *Go! Now! Please, my queen!*

At that, the spiders start running toward us. Raila looks so small and powerless in front of them; there's no way she can hold them all back.

I hold out my swords. I don't want to go. I don't want to leave my loyal Deadmaiden behind. I want to fight.

But Death is grabbing me by the waist and pulling me along the tunnel. I try to fight him off, but he's too strong, and soon, the tunnel curves. The last thing I see before we disappear in the bend are the spiders descending on Raila, followed by a haunting scream I pray doesn't belong to her.

"We have to keep moving," Death says.

"You're running from a fight!" I yell, squirming in his grip, my feet tripping as we go. "We can't just leave her."

"She knows how to take of herself. She knows how to deal with them. We don't."

"But they're *your* creatures! They live in your City of the Dead!"

"I'm the God of Death," he says gruffly as we round another corner, the tunnel still tilting downwards. "But not the God of the world they came from. I don't know how to defeat every creature we come across. And while I know I would probably win against them, I'm not risking you, not when we have a chance to escape. You are my queen, my woman, my world, and I am not letting you go."

That would be epically romantic if he weren't physically dragging me.

"Now, am I your king?" he practically growls, his grip on my waist growing stronger, as if he's waiting for me to wriggle out of his grasp.

"You are my king," I admit.

"Then you will obey your king," he says. "I know that most days, you'd rather do anything but. However, right now, you will obey me, and I will get us both to safety."

Even though I hate the idea of leaving Raila behind, I keep my feet moving, my steps higher, until he has enough faith in me to let me go. We both keep running down the tunnel, and I'm growing more conscious of the fact that the spiders might be running after us. The thought is so paralyzing that when we do come to a fork in the tunnel, I can't remember which direction to go.

"Which way was it?" I ask, breathing hard.

Death looks both ways, and for a horrible moment, I fear he forgot, too. Finally, he nods. "This way."

We take the tunnel to the left, the passage now sloping upwards. It grows colder the higher we go, the ground slippery with frost until steps start to appear in the dirt.

"This can't be right," Death mumbles as we climb. "We should be going down still, not up."

I have no idea what to think; I just pray to my mother Goddess that this tunnel doesn't have a dead end with no door. We'd be sitting ducks.

But finally, we see the end: the door in the dirt at the top of the iron stairs with a single obsidian handle.

"This is it!" I cry out. "This is what she said to look for."

Death grunts and reaches out with his bare hand, hesitating for a moment before he places his palm over it.

He turns the black handle and pushes open the door an inch, then presses his shoulder against it until it opens the rest of the way.

On the other side of the door is another tunnel, this one level.

And there's light at the end of the tunnel. Not a metaphor or platitude—literal light.

"This must be it," I whisper.

"Possibly," Death says. "The passageway I know of runs straight to the caverns. My mountain lair."

"Castle Greyskull," I comment.

His eyes squint under his mask. "It's a journey of several days in complete darkness. This light, though...it seems to lead right to the outside."

"So let's go!" I tell him. "Anywhere outside is better than here. And what if Raila can't hold the spiders back?"

He nods slowly. "Alright. I'll go first, but we'll have to close this door so we aren't followed. There's a good chance once it closes, we'll never be able to go back in this way."

"Can't go back to Hell? What a shame."

He gives me a wry grin and then turns to close the door shut. It groans on its hinges, and the moment the door becomes flush with the dirt wall, it disappears before our eyes, like it was never there at all.

"No turning back," he says.

"No turning back."

We start walking quickly down the tunnel toward the light. It gets brighter and brighter, and for a moment, I think perhaps we've taken a wrong turn and are heading up to Amaranthus instead, the light is so white and glowing.

Yet, the closer we get to the end, the more familiar the light seems.

It's daylight.

We come to the end of the tunnel and peer out. It's daylight alright, a cloudy, cold, snowy white day.

We're standing on top of a forested hill, the snow thick on branches of pine, the smell of balsam in the air. I immediately take deep gulps through my lungs, the fresh air never feeling so good.

"Where are we?" Death grumbles suspiciously, looking around. From where we are standing, the only view we have is of the trees, though, through the rows, you can see how the forest slopes downward.

"I have no idea," I say. "You mean to say you can't recognize a forest from the trees?"

He shakes his head and speaks in a low voice. "Perhaps we're not too far from Shadow's End, near the Iron Mountains. We'll have to get to a more open vantage point for a better look. The last thing I want is for us to be ambushed by Louhi when we least suspect it."

He turns around and sighs.

I follow his gaze. The tunnel we just stepped out of is now a solid rock face, like there was never anything there at all. I kick at the rock with my boot for good measure, but it doesn't budge.

"Looks like we're stuck here no matter what," I say.

"It won't take long for me to find some allies," he assures me, pushing his mask up on his head. "There are many spies for the Forest Gods. The next bird I see, I'll be able to pass a message off to Tapio and tell him what's happened. Hopefully, I'll get my bearings soon and figure out where we are and where we need to go next."

I nod and follow him as he starts trudging through the snow. We walk a while through the strands of trees, but we don't come across any animals at all, no tracks in the snow either. It's just us in the trees. Normally, I feel like there's a million eyes watching me here, but that's not the case now. I feel like we truly might be alone, and there's a strange comfort in that.

Finally, we come to a bit of a clearing, where a rock juts out over a gentle drop. Death climbs up on the rock and then pulls me up alongside him.

Below us is a valley of pine trees, a glimpse of a rushing river before it rises into a hill on the other side. Not quite the Iron Mountains, though. More like iron hills.

"Smoke," he says, and I look to see a puff of smoke coming up from the tree line below. "Someone has lit a fire."

I squint at where it's coming from. A metal pipe. From a roof. "Is that a...house? Whose house is that?" I ask him. "It looks so normal."

I hear him audibly swallow. "I don't know," he says quietly. "This doesn't make sense. None of this is familiar."

And that's when I notice the thin gray line between the river and the rising hill on the other side. At first, I thought it was a crack in the rocky face of the hill, a place where snow hasn't gathered.

But then, I realize what I'm actually looking at.

A road.

And not just any road.

A paved road with a blue SUV driving down the middle of it, exhaust rising from it and hanging in the air.

Oh. My. God.

"Tuoni," I say slowly, watching as the car drives off into the distance. "I don't think we're in Kansas anymore."

CHAPTER 8

Death

THE VOLVO

"Kansas?" I repeat absently, staring down at a kingdom that's not mine. It sure looks the same in some ways: the tall pine trees, the thick snow. But the air has a different smell, not as pure, and the cold feels, well, cold. Even the faint sounds of birds and animals are muffled, as if they are hiding themselves from us, and no animal of the dead has ever hidden themselves from their king.

"I'd joke about you not getting a Wizard of Oz reference," Hanna says breathlessly, her voice filled with awe, "but I don't think we'd find it funny."

I make a noise of agreement because for once, she's right. Not about the *Wizard of Oz*—I've seen that film—but because there's nothing funny about any of this, the fact that I am a stranger in a strange land, that I am watching a blue automobile drive along a road before disappearing around the corner of a hill.

I am in the Upper World.

We are in the Upper World.

A place I've always secretly yearned to go, a place that has fascinated me since I was a young lad. A place where I've sent my servants in my stead, and I've sat back in jealously as they recounted their tales of where they'd been and what they saw. A place I could only visit through the grainy screens of the movies I've played or in the fresh cups of roasted coffee.

I should be thrilled that I am finally here.

But instead, all I feel is fear.

Because I am no king here.

I am merely a god with no power, a god that this world has no idea they serve.

And it's fucking cold.

"What do we do?" Hanna asks me, her body starting to shiver the same way mine is. "Do we try to find a way back in through the rocks? Maybe there's another tunnel."

I stare at her for a long moment; the wildness of her brown eyes, the furrow in her brow. "Curious," I say. "How fucking curious."

"What?" she asks, slightly aghast.

"You would rather turn around and try to find a door so you could take a tunnel straight back into the place you know as Hell instead of taking another step in the world you know as your own."

She blinks at me as snow starts to fall from the sky, gathering in her hair and on her lashes. "How do we know this is my world? What if it's another universe?"

"It's your world, fairy girl. Only one in the universe looks like this."

A knowing look comes over her face, and she rubs her lips together. "Okay, but we need to get back into Tuonela. We need to find another portal to the Underworld. Maybe not to Inmost, but we need to get back to stop Louhi. You know that if that world descends into chaos, this world does too."

My Goddess. I don't think she knows what she's doing to me, hearing those words from her lips, her devotion to my kingdom, to me. It makes my heart do strange things, swelling and simmering in my chest, like it's caught on fire, my ribs barely strong enough to contain it.

"You think I'm crazy, don't you?" she asks, her eyes searching mine.

"At the moment, yes," I tell her, taking her face in my hands. "Luckily, we're a match made in Amaranthus."

I kiss her deeply, her lips cold against mine. She shivers again, and while I can't tell if it's from the weather or my kiss, I know we need to figure out the next steps.

I pull away. "Since this is your world, I'm leaving you in charge. I was the king there. You are the queen here. I have no idea what to do or what to expect, other than what the movies have taught me. I guess our first mission would be to go to the road. I make a car stop, then we take the driver hostage with our swords and tell him to take us some place where we can buy warm clothes."

Hanna eyes widen, and she breaks out into a laugh. "You want to take someone hostage? What movies have you been watching? If we do that, we're going straight to jail. Then what?"

"Will they clothe and feed us in jail?"

"Well, yes, but—"

"I don't see the issue. Solves one part of our problem."

She shakes her head, looking incredulous. I don't know why; it seems fairly sound to me. Eventually, I'd find a way out of jail, I'm sure of it. That one guy did it with a poster of Rita Hayworth on his wall.

"*Tuoni*," she says, using my name like a weapon. "We don't have money. We need clothes. I think the best thing we can do is hurry down to the house, the one with the fire. I'll see if I can steal us something to wear and some food."

"Oh, so you're against taking hostages, but not stealing?" I snort.

She ignores that. "While I do that, you could check out his vehicle. Maybe he's got his keys in it. We can take it to the nearest town."

"Again with the stealing."

"Borrowing. We'll return it," she assures me, her teeth starting to chatter.

There's no time to keep arguing, not when her lips are turning blue. I take off my vest and slip it over her before I take her arm, noting the swords in her hands and the one that slipped through my pant loops.

"Do you think we need swords in this world?" I ask.

She nods. "I think it's how we're going to get our money."

"By threatening people," I say with a nod.

"By *selling* the swords," she says, exasperated. "Man, you're lucky I'm here. You wouldn't last a day before you end up in federal prison."

"Is that a special prison?"

She sighs. "Back home in California, yes. Here? I don't even know where this is. But I suppose we'll find out soon."

She starts walking down the hill, using both swords as balancing poles of sorts. I get in front of her, just in case she takes a tumble, but she seems to be competent.

Fortunately, the hills here are small, and soon, the ground is level. We hurry across a snowy field, conscious of being seen in the open, though so far, other than that passing car on the road and the house nestled between the trees, we haven't seen signs of anyone.

Once we hit the cover of the trees, we slow down, carefully making our way toward the house so we aren't discovered. The house itself is small, made up of dark wood planks, but inside, there's a warm glow.

"I'm going to sneak up to the windows and look inside," Hanna whispers. "You stay here."

I don't think I like taking orders from her, especially in a potentially dangerous situation. But I manage to bite my tongue and stay where I am, though I don't take my eyes off her, my sword ready to be drawn at any moment.

She leaves her swords behind in the snow and then gets into a crouch and walks low toward the house. I hold my breath as she reaches the wood siding and slowly peers over the edge of the window, looking inside.

Her head pokes up higher, looking all around the interior before she turns and quickly hurries back over to me.

"I just see one man asleep in his armchair by the fire. He has a cup of coffee beside him, but he hasn't had any of it. I think he's out for the count."

"So then we break in and hope not to wake him," I say, picking up her swords from the snow.

"No," she says, shaking her head vigorously. "We'll get caught. It's best we take the opportunity to steal his car."

Again with the stealing.

"Seems silly that humans would keep their keys in the car if people like you can just steal them," I say as we start creeping along the edge of the house, keeping to the trees.

"Well, most don't, but this guy seems to be in the middle of nowhere. I don't think he expects many people out here. With any luck, the keys are in the car, and we can drive off without waking him."

"Do I get to drive?" I ask.

She lets out a sharp laugh and then quickly covers her mouth. "Sorry. You're serious?"

I shrug. "I am a god. Do you think I'm unable to operate a motor vehicle?"

"Because you just called it a motor vehicle, I'm going to say no, you can't."

"What? That is what it is. Is automobile better?"

Hanna just shakes her head and trots along in front of me until we round the corner of the house. There, at the side of the building, at the head of a wide trail, is a low, gray car covered in a dusting of snow.

"Vol-vo," I say, reading the name at the front of the car. "So they name their transportation here too. I think I had a cousin called Volvo. Goddess of earthworms or something."

I glance over at Hanna as she goes for one of the doors, her mouth twisted in such a way that I can tell she's trying not to laugh again. "Volvo is the name of the car manufacturer, not the car itself."

"So it's not like Sarvi?"

"It's nothing like Sarvi." She tries the door handle, and it opens. She shakes her hand. "Fuck, that's cold. The heater in here better work."

I try the same on my side and then throw my swords in the back-seat before I crouch down and step into the vehicle. I barely fit, my frame nearly too wide for the seat. "Who do they make these for, children?" I grumble as I try to shut the door, my shoulder pressed up against it.

Hanna laughs but doesn't say anything. She quickly reaches for some flaps on the roof and lifts a section between us before she nods at a small door that my knees are pressed up against. "Can you open that and see if you find any keys? You can move the seat back by the levers underneath."

I reach down until my fingers grasp metal rods, and I push and pull at them until my seat slides backward with a loud clack. It gives me just enough room to open the small door and rummage around.

"Only papers, no keys. Wait." I grab something small and pull it out. It's shiny, flat, and thin, and I proudly display it to her. "I have it. The key!"

"That's a stick of gum," she says with a sigh. "Fuck, maybe I have to break into his house after all."

I peer at the stick of gum. Ah, I see now—the metal part is just paper that peels off. I'd seen people eat gum in the movies, so I take the green, flexible material out of the silver paper and pop it in my mouth and swallow it. It doesn't go down very easily, and the mint flavor is barely detectable. Quite disappointing.

"Tuoni," Hanna chides me. "You're supposed to chew gum, not eat it."

"Not eat it...ever? What is the point of it then?"

She thinks that over, tucking her hair behind her ear. "You know what? I have no idea."

She shivers, and I realize that perhaps I can do more to fix this situation than I thought. Magic works in Tuonela. Perhaps magic works in the Upper World too.

I place my hands on the steering wheel and start chanting an old spell about making things work again, mixed in with an adage about bringing things to life.

Then, the car *does* come to life with a sudden roar that shakes us in our seats.

"You did it!" Hanna cries out. "You started the car!"

"Of course," I say with a rise of my chin. "I'm a god."

She rolls her eyes. "I'm going to be hearing a lot of this, aren't I?" Then, she grins, a slightly maniacal look that makes me a little worried. "Let's go."

CHAPTER 9

Death

THE PAWN

Hanna suddenly starts jerking levers around, and Volvo starts moving backward, sliding on snow as it goes. I place my palm on the roof of the vehicle to keep myself from knocking into Hanna as she's driving.

Once the back wheels hit the main road, she spins the wheel, and the automobile straightens out as it roars again, louder this time, heading down the road and away from the house.

"How do you know which way to go?" I ask.

"I don't," she says, adjusting her grip on the wheel. "I just remember the car from earlier was coming from this direction. It could have been heading nowhere, but you're always coming from somewhere."

"That's poetic," I remark.

She laughs. "Don't sound so impressed. If I'm not careful, I'll drive us both into the ditch. I've never driven in winter conditions before. Maybe you should put your seatbelt on."

"You afraid I might die?" I question.

"Good point," she says while she reaches over and clicks in her belt. "But Goddess of Death or not, *I'm* not taking any chances. Now I just have to keep this car going fast enough so we leave plenty of time between us and that man discovering his car is gone. Once he does, things won't be so easy."

She reaches over, fiddles with some knobs on a console, and hot air comes out. "Heat works, so at least we won't freeze to death, no pun intended. And there's almost a full tank of gas. Can you take a look in the back and see if there are any blankets or clothes? He might have an emergency kit; I would assume you would in this area."

I twist in my seat to look in the back. The three swords are lying on the backseat, but beneath them seems to be a finely woven bag with handles. I pick it up and bring it to my lap, trying not to look at the road as the vehicle weaves back and forth.

Inside the bag, I find a puffy red coat, some thick socks, bottles of frozen water, some sort of sustenance in the shape of bars, a black knit cap and gloves, plus a few other strange plastic items.

"There's a coat, socks, hat and gloves," I tell her. "I don't know what the rest is. Do you want them now?"

She shakes her head but doesn't take her eyes off the road. "I'm warming up. What about you?"

"Do you think anything would fit me? I am starting to think you don't have God-sized people in your world."

"Only a few," she says with a small smile. "If this was LA, I could get you The Rock's tailor."

"Why would a rock have a tailor?"

"It doesn't matter."

We drive along for a bit longer, passing only a couple of vehicles, until we come to a fork in the road. There are a few signs, plus a big one with words that don't make any sense with some numbers.

"The signs are in Finnish," Hanna says as she brings to the car to a stop, though the engine is still running. "So I'm still in Finland! That's what I was hoping."

"Makes sense," I say. "I can read them, too. Then again, I can read every language. I just haven't put it to much use other than in the Library of the Veils."

She glances at me. "Since we're here, you know what we have to do first then."

"Aside from getting the money?"

"We have to find my father."

Oh. *Him*.

I purse my lips. "Are you certain about that? I erased his memory, Hanna. He's probably living some happy little life here with no knowledge of what happened in Tuonela. He might not even be in Finland. Perhaps he got on one of those aeroplanes and flew somewhere."

Her face falls at that, and I immediately feel bad.

"I didn't erase who you were to him," I say quickly. "I just erased what happened. That's all. It was for the best. You know this."

She clears her throat as she kneads the steering wheel. "We'll have to find him anyway. But before we can do any of that, we need money. We need to find a pawn shop and figure out where we are."

"What will we do with a pawn?" I ask her. "Oh, I think I understand. We buy a pawn to use, and he will somehow get us the money."

"A pawn?" she repeats, giving me a bewildered look that I've seen more than enough times already. "Like in chess?"

"Like in the world," I explain. "A pawn is someone you use."

"Well, here, it means a place to sell off your wares and get money in exchange. Let me know if you see any stores with that sign. I'm going straight for the closest town."

She brings the vehicle onto the left road, and we drive along for some time before buildings and houses start to appear. At another sign, she pulls the automobile off the main road and onto another one that narrows between buildings. We lack proper towns in Tuonela, other than the ones in the Golden Mean and Amaranthus, so the fact that I am in a moving vehicle and going through one has me nearly glued to the window, watching this world go past.

There are people here, dressed in heavy coats, walking on paths between the road and the buildings. Some of them are carrying bags, while others disappear through doors. I see the names of what I assume are food establishments, shops for various things, and places with pictures of coffee cups.

Coffee.

"Coffee," I manage to say. "We must get coffee."

Finally, I'll know what it's really like to have a cup of the stuff here in the Upper World, where it's grown and made.

"We will get coffee," she says. "First, we get money. Look for any stores with the word pawn or buy and sell."

Though the town doesn't seem very big, I eventually spot a sign that says "Deposit Sell and Buy Shop" and point it out. Hanna brings the vehicle to a stop right outside.

Then, she grabs the coat from me and slips it on, along with the knit cap. She eyes the mask on head. "You sure you want to wear that?"

"It can be my hat," I tell her gruffly as I open the door and step outside the vehicle, reaching into the back to grab the swords.

I immediately cough. The air here is filled with not so pleasant things emitted from the cars as they pass. It tastes like the fires and smoke of Inmost.

Hanna closes the door and comes around to me, wearing the coat and hat. She looks presentable, if not a little cold, since her legs are bare. At least she is wearing boots. "How do we turn off the car?" she asks me.

"Turn it off?" I frown.

"Yes. If I had the keys, I would turn it off. Otherwise, you're polluting unnecessarily and wasting gas—fuel."

"It seems everyone is already polluting unnecessarily," I point out with another cough. "Let us leave it running. We shouldn't be long."

Frankly, I'm afraid that if we turn the car off, I won't be able to bring it to life again.

Together, we step inside the shop. It reminds me of Shadow's End in a way, the space filled with every conceivable item from the Upper World. The shopkeeper must have great nostalgia for his land and be a collector like I am. I could spend all day in here, marveling at it all.

"There he is," Hanna whispers, nodding at a gangly man with thinning, gray-brown hair and a pinched face standing at the end of the room. "Let's agree right now that the swords should go for about, oh, I don't know. I wish I had a phone so I could Google resell prices on swords. They're rare, aren't they?"

"To this world, yes. Back in Tuonela, all in my army have one. How much do you think they're worth?"

"It's more like how much money do we need? A couple of thousand at least. Should you do the talking, or should I?"

"Do you speak Finnish fluently?" I ask.

"No, but most Finns speak English better than I speak Finnish," she says under her breath as we approach. The man gives us both a startled look, eyeing us with suspicion. "On second thought, you do the talking. Men like him are always going to rip off a woman."

"No one is ripping you off," I growl to her, but she gives me a look that says I might be taking her words too literally.

"Good day to you, human from Finland," I say to the man, speaking Finnish. "We have swords we need to...*pawn*."

The man squints at us. "You have what?"

"Swords," I say, placing them on the glass counter with a loud clatter. "The finest swords you'll ever see in all the Upper World. I await your fair offer."

I cross my arms and stare at him. The man taps them lightly with his dirty nails, not looking the least bit impressed.

"I'll give you five hundred euros for all three swords," the man says with a sniff.

"That's preposterous!" I cry out, nearly slamming my fist into the glass counter.

The man raises a brow at my reaction. "It's just a bunch of swords. The metal is worth something, but that's it."

I gasp, leaning across the counter to stare him right in the eye. "This blade is dual-hardened in the fires of Vipunen's cave, made from the finest of Tuonelian steel, and smithed by the giant himself! The pommel is cast from the bronze crown of a fallen god. Each one was created for the soldiers in my Army of the Dead."

The man stares at me for a moment, as if I'm the one acting strange and irrational.

"It's a Viking replica sword," the man says with a tired sigh. "The real one is from the eleventh century, from an archaeological dig not far from here, hanging in the museum in Helsinki."

"These swords are from no centuries," I tell him. "They are timeless. They are infinite. They are godly."

"I'll give you six hundred for them if you throw in that mask." He jerks his chin at the top of my head.

"What is he saying?" Hanna asks me, tugging at my shirt.

"He's trying to cheat me," I say to her.

I narrow my eyes at him.

You cannot cheat a god, I think, the words burning through my veins, enough that I feel the silver lines of death faintly pulse. *You can only submit to them.*

"You will give us our asking price," I tell him, deliberation behind every word. "You will give us five thousand euros for the swords."

The man goes stiff, his mouth clamped together, his eyes taking on a blank quality. It's like all the lights inside his head just went off.

"What did you say?" Hanna whispers to me. "What happened?"

But then the man shakes his head slightly and blinks. "I will give you your asking price. Five thousand, was it?"

"It was."

I reach out my hand to shake on it.

He's about to shake mine, but Hanna quickly grabs my wrist and pulls my hand back. "Let me shake on it," she says with a loaded look at my hands, and I realize I haven't put my gauntlets back on. I step back quickly and grab my gauntlets I had tucked into the back of my pants, slipping them on while Hanna shakes the man's hand.

He still seems a bit dazed as he goes over to the cash register and pulls out the money, counting it.

I can't help but stare in awe. While I'm not surprised—I commanded him to do something—I am enthralled by the sight of what they call "cold, hard cash." He flips through the thin, colored papers and then hands them over to Hanna.

"Here you go," he says, switching to English. "I hope the both of you have a pleasant day."

Hanna eagerly takes the money and tucks it into her coat pocket. Then, she hurries over to me and takes my arm, leading me out of the store, I suppose before the man has a chance to change his mind.

"What did you do to him?" she asks again as we step out into the cold.

"Nothing." I shrug. "I just told him our price and that he must take it. It turns out, I'm rather influential."

Her eyes dance as she looks at me. "You mean to tell me we could have asked for anything?"

"It's important not to get greedy," I tell her. "Greediness and godliness do not go together."

"But you like it when I'm a greedy girl," she says rather coyly.

Fuck. I swallow hard, my cock flaring. "When do we find a private room for ourselves?"

She laughs. "After we get clothes and a phone. But let's do it in the next town, just in case the owner of the car has the police looking for it here. That way, when we get to Helsinki, we'll at least look presentable."

We get back into Volvo and drive off.

CHAPTER 10

Hanna

THE OUTLAWS

We're on the outskirts of a town called Lahti. While Death is glued to his window, staring at the sights of the flinty ski hills and buildings and traffic, I'm trying to figure out our next move. Being in Tuonela may have hardened me in some ways—nearly being killed by your evil twin and fighting skeletons will do that to you—but I haven't turned into a master criminal. I know hijacking a car is wrong, and I feel more terrible with each mile I'm burning up in this Volvo.

But I also know that our situation is unique, and that's putting it mildly. I think if we can look presentable enough, we can take a bus or train into Helsinki without much fuss. Getting a hotel room without any ID might be a different problem, but I'm hoping that whatever magic Death used on the pawn shop man might come in handy again.

"So, where again do you think your father is?" Death asks. "In Helsinki?"

"I'm not sure," I say, chewing on my lip as I take an exit off the highway and into the town. "I don't know where he ended up when he left Tuonela. And with his memory erased, I'm not sure if he'd go back north to the resort he was working at in Ivalo—"

"The resort he was found dead in..."

"Yes, that. Might be another complication, with Eero and Noora still being alive," I say with a heavy sigh.

There's something else. The other day, I used the portal glass—the crystal sphere Bell gave me—and in it, I saw my father. But it was green in the background, not white with snow, which makes me wonder what year it is exactly. Either way, I have no idea of his whereabouts.

"Or he could be in Helsinki," I go on. "At the very least, I know people in the city. I have an uncle, Osmo, my father's stepbrother, who I think is still there. I would assume he'd know. Hopefully, he's in town and can meet us."

I should have found it odd at the time that Osmo wasn't at my father's funeral, but of course now, I know the whole funeral had been faked.

Once we're in Lahti proper, I find a large thrift store that would be best for one-stop shopping and a place to buy cell phones across the street. I promise Death that we'll get a coffee in Helsinki, and he pouts like a petulant child who isn't getting his way.

I have to admit, as fucking weird as it is to be back in my own world, I'm adapting to it quicker than I thought. Meanwhile, Death is completely out of his league here, a fish out of water for the first time, and while I'm sure his machoism is finding it emasculating to not be in charge, I'm loving it. It's nice for once to not be in the dark about things. It's also nice to be the one showing him things about my world, instead of the other way around.

I park the car in the parking lot at the back of the store and make Death turn off the engine, this time with his magic.

"This is where we'll leave *Volvo*," I tell him. "I'll write a note, telling people the car belongs to a man to the east of here who might be looking for it."

"You can't send a messenger pigeon or raven back to him to let him know?"

I can't help but smile at his sincerity. "No. Hopefully, someone will report it to the police, and eventually the guy's report will match up and the two will be reunited."

"I am sure Volvo will be happy to be back with his master," he says.

He starts chanting some words and lays his hands along the dash before the car abruptly turns off. He looks impressed with himself. I just hope that whatever magic he may end up using in the future doesn't attract any unwanted attention. I know we already turn heads with the fact that he's an impossibly large man with silver lines for tattoos, walking around Finland in the winter without a jacket. The crocodile devil mask doesn't help either.

Somehow, I manage to convince him to carry the mask instead of wearing it. Then, I open the glove box and pull out the man's insurance papers. I tear out a blank one, find a red Sharpie in the side console, then write out the note to put on the dash. Then, I take the Sharpie and write down the man's address on the back of the receipt from the pawn shop.

"What are you doing?" Death asks. "Are you sending ravens after all?"

"I'm writing down his address so I can send him some money through the mail. It's safer than leaving it here in the car. I don't trust people, or the cops."

He grunts. "I wouldn't trust cops either. Inmost is full of the corrupted ones."

"Right," I tell him, waving the Sharpie at him. "So keep that in mind when it comes to causing trouble. The more we stay out of their way, the better. I don't care what country we're in."

I place the receipt in my pocket, put the insurance papers back in the glovebox, and finally, place the note on the dash. Then, we leave the car and stride toward the front of the building. Luckily, the lot is fairly empty back here, and no one has seen us who could potentially connect us to the car.

"You're a good woman, you know that?" Death comments warmly as he grabs my hand and holds it tight.

I look up at him in surprise. "What makes you say that?"

"The fact that you're going to send the man money for borrowing his car and taking his coat."

"It's the least I can do, really," I say with a shrug. "I know the world is hard and cruel; I don't want to add to it if I can help it."

"A true queen," he murmurs, giving my hand a squeeze.

Damn. He's giving me butterflies I wasn't prepared for. There's something about having a literal god admire you that does something for your self-esteem.

Don't forget, you're part god too, I remind myself.

But the funny thing is, even though I've never really felt it, the more I'm in this world, the more that being a goddess feels like a fever dream. How can any of *that* be real?

And this man walking beside me. This God. This King of the Underworld. How can he be real too?

I shake the thoughts from my head. The more I think about the two worlds colliding, the more it will do my head in. I barely understood the movie *Inception*; I don't think I'll start with this.

Hand-in-hand, we walk around the corner of the building. We pass by a couple on the street who look at Tuoni aghast, or at least as aghast as a Finnish person can look, their faces stoic with only a hint of an eyebrow raise.

The overhead bell rings when we walk into the store, and the employee by the cash immediately notices us, giving us a cautious nod.

"Hej," I call out in my best Finnish accent.

"Hello," the employer says in English. "Welcome."

I look over the racks until I spot the men's section. "There," I say to Tuoni while I snatch up a basket from the door. "Those are the men's clothes. You're going to want to start with the ones labeled with an XL. Or an XXL. Or an XXXL. The more Xs, the better for you."

"I take it X is good," he says with a cocky grin.

I nod and slap his shoulder. "Absolutely."

I watch as he strides off toward the row of clothes, walking every bit like a king or a warrior, before I hurry over to the women's section. I make quick work of it—I was a champion thrifter back in the Valley—and in Lahti, the prices remain reasonable. It's not all threadbare fast fashion. I find a pair of fleece-lined leggings and skinny jeans that I can tuck into winter boots, both with long enough inseams for my legs, and then I grab a few sweaters, thermal Henley shirts, a slim black parka with a faux-fur lined hood, plus a pair of sneakers and plaid winter boots lined with shearling. The only other things I really need are bras, socks, and underwear, but since I'm not about to thrift for those, I figure I'll hit up a department store in Helsinki when I get a chance.

When I'm done piling everything into the basket, I notice Tuoni hasn't found anything. I walk over to him with my haul, and his eyes widen when he sees it.

"So what they say about women and shopping is true," he muses.

"And what they say about men and shopping is true too," I counter. "Can't even decide on a shirt."

It's then I notice one of the employees creeping closer to us, the same way one might approach a skittish foal.

"Can I help you?" the employee says in English.

"Yes, my good mortal," Death says without a hint of awareness of what he's saying. "Do you have any furs or pelts, or perhaps a good pair of trousers that might fit a man of godly stature?"

Somehow, I manage to swallow down my laughter, watching as the employee tries to take it all in stride.

"Uh, let me check with the manager," he says before walking quickly to the back.

"Such expedient service," Death comments, holding up a Hawaiian shirt and then snarling at it before he shoves it back in the rack. "Perhaps they recognize me as a god."

"Or just a customer," I tell him. I pull out the Hawaiian shirt again and hold it up to him. "This could actually fit you, but you'd look like a partying, surfing playboy."

Or Jason Momoa.

"Surfing?" he asks with a brow raise. "Like in the Elvis movies?" He stares at the shirt as if considering it, then shakes his head. "I can't. I have an image to uphold. I'll save the partying for when we return to Shadow's End."

Return to Shadow's End.

Just like that, I had forgotten our plan: to find our way to a portal back to Tuonela, to return to the world and life I had there.

A strange look comes across his pewter eyes as he stares at me, and his brows come together in a frown, as if he knew I'd forgotten our plan already.

Just then, the employee comes back, carrying a bunch of pelts and furs in his skinny arms. "Will any of these do?"

"Wow, yes," I say, clearing my throat and taking some of the furs from the guy's arms. They all smell like a grandmother's musty closet.

"There's a mirror over there," the employee says as he places the rest of the items into Death's arms. "And if you want trousers, they'll be in the next aisle."

Then, the guy scurries off to the other employee at the register, as if he thinks Death is going to toss him clear across the store for bringing him the wrong things.

But Death looks happy with his lot. He brings the pelts over to the mirrors and piles them on top of an old, embroidered armchair for sale, bringing them up to his neck and draping them over his shoulders. Most of the pieces look like they're supposed to be rugs or something to hang from the wall, but a couple of them look good on his shoulders, and a few more actually tie together at the collar like a proper fur cape.

"What do you think?" he asks, eyeing me in the mirror as he strikes a very noble pose.

Honestly, it looks no different than what he wears back in Tuonela. "Looks fit for a king," I tell him. "And the God of Death, since you're wearing dead animals around your shoulders like that."

"Perhaps you should look more like a Goddess of Death," he says, taking one of the furs and putting it over my shoulders. He nods his approval. "There you go. This should be in your wardrobe when we return."

I stroke the soft fur, knowing I shouldn't be so hypocritical when I'm wearing leather boots. At least these foxes or minks died a long time ago and are probably running around the Hiisi Forest as we speak. Providing there's still a forest left, if Louhi hasn't raised the Old Gods and released a world of chaos yet.

He reaches out and adjusts it at my collarbones. "You forgot, didn't you? About where we need to get back to. About your life there by my side."

I give him a placating smile, not wanting him to think that. "No, I didn't forget. We'll get back there no matter what. I know what's at stake."

His eyes soften, looking almost melancholy. I don't like that expression at all. He looks resigned.

"Let's find you some more things, and we'll be on our way," I quickly add, taking off the fur and placing it on the chair. "The sooner we can get a phone and transport to Helsinki, the better."

"Don't forget the coffee," he adds.

"You won't let me forget," I tell him. Lucky for him, even if we get to Helsinki late, the cafés will still be open. The Finns drink the stuff at all hours.

I head over with him to the next aisle, find a pair of large black jeans that should fit him; even if the inseam is too short, his boots will hide it. Then, I grab a gray Henley that will be too tight for his otherworldly muscles but might work as an undershirt, plus a black knitted sweater that's been overstretched. I want to find more, but he says one outfit is all he needs until he gets back. With his gauntlets and the furs, I'm sure he'll be warm enough here.

I grab a leather purse and a couple of nice duffel bags to carry everything in. Then, I pay for everything with the cash and ask the nervous employee the best way for us to get to Helsinki. He tells me that there's a railway station a few blocks away with trains leaving to the city often.

"Farewell, dutiful mortal," Death says as we leave the store, and then we head across the street to the convenience store that sells Nokia phones and cards. It's not long before I'm loaded up with a good internet plan, and we're making our way down the street to the train station. We still don't have any ID, but at least with the train, that's not an issue when it comes to getting tickets.

It's only when I sit down on the bench at the station, waiting for the next train to come in, that I unlock the phone to look at the internet.

I stare at the date, not blinking.

It's not the year I thought it was.

CHAPTER 11

Tuonen

THE WRONG GOD

Something is wrong, something is wrong, something is fucking wrong.

The entire ride back to Shadow's End, the words kept repeating in my head. It didn't help that I was at the back of the line, the last rider in formation, with the carriage carrying the Forest Gods who were our guests for the night, my father and Hanna on Sarvi at the front, which left me alone with my thoughts.

It also didn't help that the moment we stepped out of the City of Death, a snowstorm swooped in, the temperature dropping enough that even I felt cold. It wasn't long before snow covered the iron path that led from the city toward Death's Passage, and I was straining to see through the oncoming blizzard. Every now and then, I swore I heard and saw something lingering behind me, moving shadows in the whiteout, but that could have just been my paranoid nature. Finally, the dark of night swooped in, and I could barely see anything at all.

By the time we pull up to the castle, my hands are numb—and I'm wearing gloves. I remember seeing my father walking out of Inmost without his gauntlets on, the way that Hanna was moments from grabbing his bare hand. Did she forget she can't touch him, that she can only touch the Shadow Self?

A complicated thought comes into my head as I dismount my horse and hand him off to one of the Deadhands.

Is it possible my father before me, the one I saw walk out of the dungeons, isn't my father at all?

But why would I be looking at his Shadow Self? Did my father decide to stay in Inmost for some reason? Why would he do so without telling me? And wouldn't Hanna notice it's not him?

Unless she also knows.

Perhaps the two of them had something planned.

But if that's the case, why is it a secret from me?

I watch as the two of them enter the front doors of the castle, now hand-in-gloved-hand, smiling at each other in a way that's both smug and cunning.

That would explain a lot, them hatching a plan no one knows about. Wouldn't be the first time my father has done things without telling me. I suppose I should be happy that he shares such intimacy with my new stepmother.

And yet, I'm still not satisfied. The feeling still lingers.

"Come along, Tuonen," my father calls from the doorway. He glances at me over his shoulder and meets my eye. There's something there, something like love and familiarity, that his Shadow Self could never have mustered.

Still, I remain on edge as I walk after him and head inside the doors.

"Do you feel up to entertaining our guests?" my father—or someone who looks like him—asks me. "Hanna and I are rather tired and would like to retire to the bedroom."

"I'm rather tired myself," I admit, stifling a yawn. Normally, I don't mind being an entertainer, but not tonight.

"I don't ask much of you," he says, disappointment in his eyes.

Well, *that's* definitely like my father.

"Oh, come on, Tuoni," Tapio says, putting his hand on my shoulder. "Your son just did an excellent job refereeing the match. I don't blame the poor boy for being tired. Besides, we're all tired. We don't get out of the forest much."

My father shrugs. "Suit yourselves. I'll see you all in the morning."

"We might be off before you wake," Tapio says. "Need to get a head start, find Nyyrikki, have that talk you proposed."

My father just nods, his expression blank, as if he has no idea what Tapio is talking about. I look at Hanna, expecting her to at least be smiling since she was so adamant about getting the Forest God's son to help take over my ferrying duties, but her face is also impassive, like we're speaking another language.

Another fucking weird thing.

"If I don't see you, have a good journey," my father says with a nod.

Then he turns and heads up the grand staircase with Hanna.

I stand there with Tapio and his wife and daughter, watching them go up the floors until they disappear from view. In the distance, I hear the sound of his chamber door shutting.

"Something seem strange to you?" I ask Tapio, keeping my voice low.

I expect Tapio to brush me off or make some flippant remark about how my family is always strange, but instead, he leans in slightly, speaking in a hush. "If it's alright with you, Tuonen, we'll be heading back this evening to the Hiisi Forest."

I look at him in surprise, that strange foreboding wrapping around my chest like a snake. "Why?"

He tugs at his beard and shakes his head. "I really can't say, but I think it's for the best. We don't want to overstay our welcome."

"You wouldn't..." I begin.

Tapio gives me a steady look. "Your father and Hanna seem like a match made in Amaranthus," he says, a stony edge to his words. "I am curious what brought on that snowstorm earlier. He's been a great mood this entire evening, until then."

That's what it is, what was bothering me. Tonight was a big night for my father, something he's looked forward to for a long time. It went great. He seemed more in-tune with his wife than ever. They made their first public appearance. They impressed the citizens of Inmost. So why did the weather change to something so cold and drastic?

What happened when he was in the dungeons, coming out with a wound that healed itself? And what changed so that by the time we got back to Shadow's End, the storm subsided? I know if I looked out the window right now, I'd be looking straight at the Goddess Kuutar on the moon through a clear sky.

"Please take no offense," Tapio says to me. "And please take care of yourself, Tuonen. I have a feeling I can't shake and need to council with the other gods."

"What is the feeling?" I ask, almost pleading.

"I can't put it into words any more than you can," he says and gives my shoulder a squeeze again. "But if it all ends up being nothing, which it very well may be, I'll make sure my son gives you and your sister some relief with the ferry boat. I believe he will treat it like an honor and give him purpose where he hasn't had much before."

"And if it ends up being something?"

He gives me a grim smile. "Then perhaps the ferry boat is the best place for you to be. You know where to find me."

He walks off, his wife and daughter nodding their solemn goodbyes as they head back out the doors and into the night.

I sigh, standing in the middle of the great hall, wondering what the hell I should do. There's no way I can go to sleep, especially now that Tapio seems to have confirmed that something is wrong, even if he doesn't know what it is either.

But it's enough for him and his family to leave Shadow's End late at night, after an already long day, and that's enough for me.

I decide it's time to tell Sarvi. The unicorn is nothing if not loyal to my father, but they're also logical to a fault. They'll be able to tell me I'm overreacting, or that Tapio was foolish to leave like he did. They know my father better than anyone at this point.

But as I roam the halls of the castle, I can't find Sarvi anywhere. I suppose it's possible they went to bed too.

I go upstairs, checking the guest bedrooms where the Forest Gods would have stayed before I head to my own bedroom. Despite thinking I'll spend the whole night awake, I fall asleep almost immediately.

I wake up to hear my father screaming in rage.

I immediately spring to my feet and run across my bedroom, opening the door to see my father walking out of the guest bedroom, shaking his head, his hands in his hair, muttering angrily to himself. He's shirtless and barefoot, wearing low-slung pants.

With a knife in his hand.

I shrink away from the door a little and watch as he disappears down the hallway.

I glance out the window at the night sky. Though some clouds have moved in suddenly, it's still dark out, and I think dawn is a few hours away.

He must have discovered that the Forest Gods had already left.

But why would he sound so angry and feral, a sound I rarely hear from him?

A sound that's too familiar for some reason.

And why would he have a knife?

What did Tapio know?

I throw on a jumper and head out into the hall, slowly and quietly shutting my door behind me.

It's time to find Sarvi.

I go to the end of the hall, where the circular staircase winds up to Sarvi's room at the top of the castle. Even in the dead of night, the black candles along the wall flicker and burn, dripping onyx wax below that never seems to add up. Magic.

I knock quietly on Sarvi's door, hoping the unicorn is in there. I don't hear anything until it suddenly swings open, a velvet rope in Sarvi's bony jaw pulling the door.

Tuonen, the unicorn says with a shake of their head, *what are you doing here? It's the middle of the night.*

"I know, I'm sorry. It's important I talk to you." I pause. "And it's important you don't tell anyone about this. Can I trust you?"

They stare at me, tilting their head slightly. The flickering flames from the hallway dance in their one eye, making their black mane gleam with gold.

Finally, a faint nod. *Come on in, Lord Tuonen.*

Though Lord isn't an official title of mine, I do appreciate it when

Sarvi uses it—makes me feel like I actually amount to something in this world.

I step inside, the door closing behind me, and follow the unicorn across the room, their hooves clicking on the shining obsidian floors. They lead me over to the single armchair draped in black furs and meant for human guests. Though I've never been to the Upper World like Lovia has, I know enough about their culture from her and from the dead I've ferried to the city to know that Sarvi's chambers would be considered heaven for goths.

I sit on the arm of the chair, not wanting to get too comfortable.

What seems to be the problem? Sarvi asks, tailing swishing.

I clear my throat. "I don't think the father I went to Inmost with is the father who came back."

Sarvi's nostrils flare on a deep inhale with air that never fills lungs, for Sarvi has no lungs, because Sarvi isn't alive. They're not alive, but they can die.

What makes you say that?

"I saw him come out of the dungeons, not wearing gloves, a wound on his arm that healed before my eyes, and moments later, Hanna almost touched his hand before she realized her mistake."

I'm sure it was instinctual, Sarvi says. *Reaching for her king's hand for comfort.*

"But my father would never make such a careless mistake as to forget his gloves and not warn her and everyone else about it. He did no such thing with me."

I see. You're right. It's always on his mind.

"Then, when we left the city, a snowstorm swept in. I'd never felt bitter cold like that before—have you?"

The unicorn shakes its head.

"Why a storm when my father has seemed happier than ever?"

I did question that myself, Sarvi muses. *He was astride me during the storm, and he seemed jovial, perhaps even happier than earlier.*

"You must have been inquisitive?" I prod. "Did you try to read his thoughts?"

I would never do such a thing, Sarvi says haughtily. *You know me better than that.*

I stare at them steadily before finally, they give their head a shake. *I tried. He had blocked me. Hanna, too. I figured they needed privacy, so I didn't push it.*

"Uh huh. Then we got home, and Tapio mentioned leaving in the morning to talk to his son about taking over my duties as ferryman. Neither Hanna nor my father showed any emotion whatsoever that Tapio agreed to this. I at least expected it from Hanna, but staring into her eyes, it was like there was nothing there at all. Just a void."

That could mean anything, Sarvi says.

"Then Tapio pulled me aside and told me he had plans to leave immediately, that he thought something was wrong, that he and his family shouldn't stay the night here."

Sarvi's head perks up. *Really?*

"Yes. He seemed afraid for them—afraid for me too. He couldn't put his finger on why, but the feelings were there all the same. He said he needed to council with the other gods. He too noticed the change in the weather."

So, the Forest Gods are gone?

I nod. "They left, and just now, I was woken up by a scream. My father's scream. I'd never heard that sound come from him before. It was shrill, immature, sounding more like a child who didn't get his way. Reminded me of..."

Reminded you of what?

"Before I tell you, perhaps I should tell you why my father screamed. I looked out my door and saw him leaving the guest chambers where Tapio and his family would have stayed overnight. He thought they were leaving in the morning. He came to pay them a visit just now, in the middle of the night, and was upset that they were gone."

Feeling insulted, perhaps...

"He was carrying a knife."

Sarvi stills. *A knife. Are you sure?*

I remember the way the torches on the walls reflected off the blade. "I'm sure. The way he carried the knife wasn't like him either. The way he walked, frustration rolling off him. I think he meant to kill Tapio."

Why in hell would he do that?

"Because of the way he sounded. Because right before he appeared in the dungeons of Inmost, I had run into my mother."

What? Sarvi's eye goes wide. *She was there, at the match?*

I nod. "She said she wanted to see Hanna's first public appearance, but she disappeared before my father came up from the dungeons."

Silence fills the room. Sarvi turns and slowly walks over to the glass doors that look out onto the landing on the castle wall where they often take flight. Outside, the faintest hint of dawn lightens the horizon over the Mountains of Vipunen.

Louhi has taken over Tuoni's Shadow Self, Sarvi says after a moment. *But where is Tuoni? And how does Hanna not know?*

I get out of my chair and join Sarvi at the window. "I believe my father is still in Inmost with Hanna. I don't think that's Hanna at all. Perhaps it's another Shadow Self Louhi conjured from her own magic."

Or perhaps...something—or someone—worse.

A chill runs through me. "We have to go back to Inmost."

Sarvi eyes me sharply. *No. I will go back to Inmost. I am quick. Both of us going would rouse suspicion. If your mother truly is impersonating the king, she'll be paying far more attention to you than to me.*

"If something has happened to him, do you think you'd be able to help?" I ask gently.

Sarvi thinks about that for a moment. *I'll pay Tapio a visit since he's already suspicious, see if he's learned anything from the other gods. Something like this, perhaps it's better not to do anything alone.*

They're right about that.

We have no idea what we're up against.

CHAPTER 12

Death

THE SECRETIVE MAN

"I've missed a year," Hanna says breathlessly, staring down at her phone. I have a hard time understanding what she means; the sight of the phone in her hands is so foreign to me that it feels like I'm walking inside a film, that I'm still back at Shadow's End watching something, and I'm not really here.

"You missed a year?" I repeat, shifting in my seat beside her on the bench at the train station. I'm constantly aware of how much space I'm taking up in this world. So is everyone else, it seems. People stare at me in barely disguised awe, a mixture of wonder and fear. I don't know if the fear is because I look strange to them, darker skinned with silver lines, long hair, furs draped around my shoulders, which don't seem to be the fashion here, plus my height and stature. Or is it because they instinctively know that I am Death? Perhaps not the one that comes for them, but the one that welcomes them. Do they know, deep down, that I am their king when they go to the afterlife?

If only I had access to the Library of the Veils right now. I could look inside the books of their lives and learn something about each and every one of them.

"Yeah," Hanna says, her voice dull now, tapping at the screen on her phone. "My father's funeral was in February, and now, it's the first week of January."

"I told you that time moves differently on the other side. To be honest, I'm surprised it's only been a year and not more. Does that affect anything with your father?" I pause, weighing my next words. "Or does it more affect your life here?"

The one you could go back to. The one I would be powerless to keep you from returning to.

She doesn't answer me, just keeps reading something with a slowly growing look of horror on her face. Finally, she puts the phone in her coat pocket and cradles the big bag in her lap. "People think I've gone missing," she whispers, and I notice her eyes growing wet. "People say I was last seen getting off the plane in Ivalo. There was a search party for me, for my father. He hasn't been seen either." She looks at me. "Tuoni, everyone thinks I'm dead. They think my father is dead too. How can I find him if we're both ghosts?"

This is affecting her greatly; I can see that. I want to ask her why it matters if everyone thinks she's dead—after all, is there not a great honor in death?—but I don't think she'd like that question.

"As you know, your father is *not* dead," I tell her. "We would know if he had entered Tuonela again, so that means he is alive somewhere."

"But he hasn't come forward. He hasn't been seen."

"Then he must be in hiding."

"Which makes him harder to find."

"Perhaps, perhaps not. We haven't tried yet. Don't let your mind get away from you before we've even started."

"Ugh, my poor mother," she says, putting her head in her hands, her long, messy hair spilling over her. "She thinks I'm dead. She thinks she lost her only child."

"She is not your real mother, though."

"It doesn't matter," she cries, her voice muffled.

I think about that for a moment. "But if there is no body to be found, then how can they say you are dead? I know enough that your body stays behind in this world while your second self, your soul, steps into my Underworld."

"People give up hope after a year. They lose interest when they become a cold case. Well, except for the people who watch the cold case shows."

"Perhaps you will be on a cold case show then."

"I don't want to be on The Cold Case Files!"

My queen is so hard to please. I thought everyone wanted to be on TV.

"Then perhaps you should send your mother a message, let her know that you're alive and well but currently...indisposed."

"Indisposed doing what? That I ran away to join a cult?"

She lifts her head, her hair sticking to the trails of tears on her cheeks. My heart sinks at the sight of such sorrow and torment inside her. I reach over and brush her hair out of her eyes, wishing I wasn't wearing my gauntlets so I could feel her.

"Is joining a cult considered a good thing in this world?" I ask, keeping my voice soft.

She shakes her head, her lower lip quivering.

"Then no," I say. "Don't tell her that. You'll think of something."

I lean in and kiss her, trying to be gentle. But the feel of her lips, the rush of energy that seems to surge from her and through to me, straight to the marrow of my bones and the depths of all that is dark and unknown inside me, makes me want to take her away from this, from here. I want her beneath my body, gasping at my fingertips. I want to take away the uncertainty and pain that this world is already bringing her. I want her to see the goddess that she is.

But then, the ground starts to shake, and I think it's more than just my heart. I pull away in time to see a train pulling into the station. It's the only thing that could have distracted me at this moment: my first time getting on a train.

Hanna gets up and grabs her bag, but I take it from her and pick up mine, watching her for cues on how to deal with the train ride. She waits until it comes to a stop, and after people leave the train, we follow the crowd onboard.

I have to admit, the train is not what I would have thought. In the black-and-white movies I've watched, the train has always seemed grand and opulent inside, with wood furnishings and fine linens, and the outside was always black metal, something loud and menacing, something that would easily fit in the land of Tuonela.

However, as Hanna takes me to our narrow seats and I'm once again squished up against a window, I'm disappointed at how clean, boring, and sterile this train is. The chairs are upholstered with thin, scratchy fabric, and the walls are plastic.

"Well, what do you think?" Hanna asks as the train pulls away from the station.

"I don't like it," I admit. "It's so cheap looking, and it moves silently. Where is all the noise and the shaking and the steam?"

She laughs, and it sounds good to hear her spirits lifted slightly, even if it's at my expense. "Those kinds of trains aren't so popular anymore. They're old-fashioned. These ones are electric and much more efficient."

"I think when we return to Tuonela and get everything with Louhi sorted, I should look into installing a train. Not a plastic thing like this, but the old-fashioned kind, with big metal gears and loud whistles. Perhaps we could transport the dead from the River of Shadows to the City of Death that way, maybe even take them on a tour of the land before they settle in for eternity. There's so much of my kingdom the dead never even see."

She puts her hand over mine and gives it a squeeze. "That is a lovely idea."

The train into Helsinki goes quickly. I spend my time staring out the window at the passing trees and frozen lakes, at the buildings that get higher and closer together the further into the city we go. Hanna seems glued to her phone, researching her own disappearance. The entire ride, I think she's touched on every emotion, from crying over the heartfelt messages people left on her so-called wall to disappointment over how quickly people seemed to forget her.

Of course, I figure those people are all idiots, possibly blind, because I don't know how anyone could forget Hanna—not her body, not her mind, and not her spirit. But I don't tell her that—it seems she needs to work her way through these emotions on her own. I could never pretend to know what she's going through; I doubt anyone could. I might be the God of Death, but I assume it's not every day people think you're dead when you're not.

This creates a bigger problem for me. If Hanna lets her mother know she's alive, will that make Hanna want to stay? Will seeing the messages from those she loved make her realize all she's lost? Will being in this world make her realize that this is where she belongs?

Does she belong here?

Or does she belong at my side, with me, ruling the Underworld?

My heart does something strange. It feels like it's freezing in place, no longer beating, and I have to press my fingers against my chest to warm it up. The thought of Hanna not being my queen is so painfully cold and sharp, it takes my breath away. She belongs with me, every single inch of her; I know that in the depths of my being. She is the queen of the prophecy, the one to touch Death, the one to rule and unite the land. She has been promised to me.

But for how long? I always assumed that if she was the true queen, she would be with me for the rest of eternity. But what if the prophecy ends? What if she's only supposed to be in my life to unite the land and was never promised to stay until the end?

"Tuoni?" she says softly, bringing my thoughts back to the present, this strange fucking present.

I glance at her and realize that though my worries feel like a burden, I must push them aside for now. That's what a true leader does. That's what a god does.

"How are you feeling?" I ask her.

She gives her head a shake while sucking in her lower lip. "I have no idea. I feel like the kid at the start of Flight of the Navigator."

I stare at her to imply I have no idea what thing she's talking about, as per usual, and she goes on, looking chagrined. "Sorry. I'll stop that. It's just, it's beyond weird to have a whole year gone, just like that. It's not just that everyone thinks something terrible has happened to me; it's knowing I just lost a year of my life..."

She trails off and looks away.

I swallow the brick in my throat. "In Tuonela, you will not age, at least not for eons. In Tuonela, you have all the time in the world. *We* will have all the time in the world."

And when we return, this will no longer be your problem, I want to say, but I don't.

She nods at that, but that frozen heart feeling comes back, the fear that I'm slowly losing her, whether she knows it or not.

"Oh, I think we're here," she says, looking out the window just as the train starts to slow. We get up, and I grab our bags from the metal rack overhead, standing in line with the rest of the passengers as we wait for the train to come to a stop, ignoring their curious looks.

The train station is busy, the busiest place I've seen yet, though it doesn't hold a candle to how chaotic and crowded it gets during a Bone Match. I follow Hanna as she makes her way through the throngs of people with their suitcases and bags until we step out onto a street.

Strange looking, long vehicles with rods protruding from the roof trundle on past through the snow. The light is low now, the way I am used to, and it seems everything is colored in shades of blue and gray. Nighttime will fall soon, and I know I'll feel more at ease in a city of darkness.

"Do you know where you're going?" I ask her.

"To find a good hotel that doesn't cost an arm and a leg and hopefully has someone working the front desk you can easily manipulate." She glances up at me. "Remember, we don't have any ID, and we need ID here to make a reservation. We also need credit cards, which we don't have. You'll have to convince them that we're allowed to pay with cash, no ID." She pauses and gives me a coy smile just before we cross a street made of icy stones. "But if that works, perhaps you can convince them we don't have to pay for anything at all."

"What did I say about being greedy?" I say. "We'll pay the rate, fair and square."

"But we could stay in a hotel we can't afford," she says. "A place fit for a king."

"I'll be the judge of that," I tell her, stepping out across another road.

This time, Hanna gasps. "Tuoni! No!" She grabs my arm, tries to pull me back, and I notice the red automobile that I stepped in front of doesn't look like it wants to stop.

In fact, the vehicle keeps coming, and I lock eyes with the man behind the wheel, his mouth open in a yell, his hands spinning the wheel back and forth.

I'm starting to think the man isn't going to stop his vehicle.

"Halt!" I yell, throwing my hand out toward the automobile.

I feel the silver lines pulse against my skin, and it looks like they're coming out of my glove, faint twisting threads that shoot through the air toward the vehicle like a million strikes in a lightning storm.

The vehicle comes to a complete and sudden stop two feet away from me.

So does the man.

He slumps over in his seat.

"Oh my God," Hanna cries out softly. "Did you kill him?"

I stare at the sight in wonder. I've never been able to kill anyone by sheer will before. I have to touch them with my bare hands on skin.

Hanna goes over to the man's window and knocks on it. The man stirs, looking up at her with dazed eyes.

He says something. Probably a curse word.

"He's not dead," I say. "I probably stunned him. Just in time too, I think."

I'm still fairly certain I can't die in this world, but I'm not about to take my chances if I don't have to.

Now, the man is quite awake and honks at me, making me jolt, and Hanna runs over, grabbing me by the arm. "Come on, before we cause a scene."

She pulls me down a narrow street, away from the cars, as if she's trying to hide me. "Cause a scene?" I ask. "If there was a scene, he's the one who caused it. Imagine, not stopping when a god steps in front of you." I scoff.

"You're not supposed to step out in traffic, especially when there's snow and ice on the road," she chides me, hurrying me along. "You could have been killed."

"I doubt that," I say. "Though perhaps that's one way I could get back to Tuonela."

"Don't even think about it," she says. "You'd probably end up in Oblivion. I think you almost killed him, though. I didn't know you knew how to do that, whatever that was."

"Neither did I. Perhaps I have different powers and magic here than I do back in Tuonela."

"Well, you're about to put the power of your charm to the test," she says as we come to a stop in front of a building with HOTEL on the sign. "Are you ready?"

I shrug. She looks a little nervous, as if our ploy won't work, but at least now, I know I can make the front desk clerk go unconscious if needed.

We step inside to the beat of music I'm certain I've heard Lovia listen to before, and Hanna takes the lead. We walk past a busy looking food establishment that seems to be more about serving drinks than meals, across a tile floor to a counter where a very austere blond man with glasses stands.

"Can I help you?" he asks in English.

"Yes," Hanna says, giving him a smile I don't see her use too often. "I was wondering if you had any rooms available. We'd like to stay three nights."

"Let's see," the man says, clicking on his computer. I'm curious as to what he's doing, so I lean over the counter to try and take a look. But the man shields his screen, as if he's working on something secretive, and gives me a dirty look while Hanna pulls at my furs.

She then proceeds to kick me lightly with her boot. I suppose you're not supposed to look at the secrets on the other side of the desk.

"We have a few," the secretive man says and then looks at me up and down. "I take it you need a king-sized bed."

"Of course," I say proudly. "I am a king. It's about time that someone recognized that. So many mortals in this city do not."

I'm still annoyed about that driver not stopping for me.

"Uh huh," the man says, blinking slowly before clicking away at the computer again. "King-sized bed it is."

I give Hanna a look to say *see? I knew it would be fit for a king*.

"Alright, I'm just going to need some ID and credit card for payment," the man says, looking at me then Hanna, then back to me again.

"We don't have a credit card, but we do have cash," Hanna says, taking out a wad of it from her jacket pocket and placing it on the counter.

The man curls his lip, as if the sight of money displeases him. What a foolish fellow.

"I'm afraid we don't take cash," he says with a sniff. "We need a credit card and ID."

Hanna kicks me again, signifying it's my turn to say something.

"My good mortal...man," I say to him, and he pushes up his glasses in a nervous gesture. "Where I come from, cash is treated like the treasure it is."

"And where is that?" he asks.

"Tuonela."

"Tuonela?"

"The Underworld."

He purses his lips as he looks at Hanna, who avoids his eyes. "Listen, we reserve the right to turn away guests who might not be a good fit for this hotel, and—"

I reach over the desk and grab the man by his collar while Hanna nervously looks around to see if anyone is watching.

I don't care if they are. I lift the man up until I know his feet are dangling off the ground and stare directly into his beady eyes.

"You will accept the cash. You will accept the fact that we do not have this ID. You will give us a room fit for a king. And you will do so without any trouble."

The man starts to slump in my grip, his eyes glazing over slightly.

"Tuoni, someone is coming," Hanna whispers frantically.

I release the man just in time for someone to walk behind us and disappear around the corner.

The secretive man sways on his feet for a moment and then splays his hands against the counter. He gives his head a shake and then reaches for the cash. "Yes, of course. A room fit for a king. That will be no problem."

I give Hanna a shaky, albeit triumphant, smile while he counts out his portion of the cash and hands the rest back to Hanna. He does some more clicking on his computer and hands me a slim yet hard piece of paper.

"Room 354," he says to us. "I hope you enjoy your stay."

CHAPTER 13

Hanna

THE SHOWER

The front desk clerk hands Death the keys, and I immediately take them from him. The last time he thought something was a key, it turned out to be a stick of gum, which he then promptly put in his mouth and swallowed.

I give the clerk a grateful smile, watching him carefully for signs that his brain might have been permanently scrambled, or that he's playing along and is about to call the police on us once we turn our backs. After all, Death literally had him by the throat.

But the clerk only smiles at us, dazed, before his attention goes back to the computer, as if nothing out of the ordinary just happened.

Imagine the power, I think to myself as I touch Death at the elbow, guiding him toward the elevators. *He can get anyone to do anything. We could rule this whole entire world.*

For the first time since I discovered I lost nearly a year of my life and that everyone I love thinks I'm missing or dead, I feel empowered, but I know that feeling won't last long.

How can it?

The world might feel the same, with not much change happening on a global scale in the time I've been in the Underworld, but I feel as if I've been in a coma, just waking up. To have time taken out from under your nose is probably the most unsettling, unnatural feeling one can have.

I've felt unmoored before. When I had to go into recovery for my eating disorder when I was a teen and drop out of dance, I felt like I lost my place in the world. I watched as my old friends went on in their classes, progressing where I should have, while I was stuck on the sidelines, battling my mind and body. I lost my identity. I didn't know who I was anymore if I couldn't dance, if I couldn't be the person my mother wanted me to be.

Then, when I graduated high school, I briefly moved to San Francisco for an internship at a fashion app start-up. Even though it was still in the same state and a long day's drive from LA, I felt totally alone. I didn't know a soul, and the job wasn't what I thought it would be (unpaid internships are a capitalist scam). I ended up quitting the internship long before I told anyone, because I was too afraid to be seen as a quitter. I just wanted to go back to where the world was familiar to me. It turns out, I didn't hate stability and comfort as much as I thought I should.

And now, well, now, the world has never seemed more at odds with my existence. I feel like a literal ghost, someone who died and came back to life in time to see that the world has moved on, as it always does.

I suppose that *is* what happened, though. I *did* trade my life for my father's. I essentially gave myself to Death, in two different but literal ways. I was never supposed to come back here like this.

Neither was Tuoni.

Which is apparent when he reaches out and actually *knocks* on the closed elevator doors.

"Tuoni, no," I say to him with a quick shake of my head.

"Ah yes, we need a key," he says.

I sigh softly and push the button for the elevator. At least he's taking things in stride, much better than I am. He probably feels just as unmoored as I do, yet I don't think he's too concerned about not getting back to Tuonela. I suppose it's hard to lose confidence when you're an immortal god. He has spent his existence getting everything he asks for.

The elevator dings open, and I step inside before waving for him to follow me. He does so with great suspicion, his brows furrowed together. The elevator shakes a little from his weight as he looks around.

"Surely you know what an elevator is," I say to him, pressing the button for our floor.

"Of course," he says with a scoff.

Mmmhmm. I try to hide my smile.

We make our way to our room, which is nice, if not small in the way most European hotels are.

"This is what they consider fit for a king?" he asks, looking around with a shocked look on his face. "I would hate to see a room fit for a queen."

I laugh and sit down on the edge of the bed, testing the firmness. "The bed is king-sized," I tell him. "That doesn't mean the room is."

At that, my stomach lets out a loud growl, hungry as hell. I guess the last time I ate would have been the dinner at Shadow's End. "I know we're exhausted, but I'm starving," I say.

He looks at me on the bed, and his eyes turn molten as he tosses the duffle bags on the floor. "So am I."

He's on me in a second, and I'm giggling under his weight, pressed into the bed as he kisses my neck.

"I'm serious," I tell him, pressing my hands up against his chest to meet his heated gaze. "I need to eat before I have the strength to do anything, whether that means thinking or fucking."

His mouth curls into a carnivorous smile. "You don't need strength. You can just lie there, and I'll do all the fucking."

"I want *food*," I tell him. "Or you're going to have a Hangry Hanna on your hands, and you don't want that."

"Is Hangry Hanna the same as a Hungry Hanna?" he asks with a wag of his brows.

"No, she's terrifying," I warn him.

"I might like that."

"You won't. Besides, you can finally get that coffee you've been harping me about."

His eyes light up. Hmmm. Seems coffee and sex are of equal importance to the king.

He gets up and brings me to my feet. I grab my duffel bag and head into the washroom to do my business and freshen up.

While I'm washing my hands with the round bar of hotel soap, I glance at myself in the mirror and nearly faint. I look dirty and slightly deranged, dark circles under my eyes and a rat's nest for hair, coated with who knows what kind of filth from Inmost. My eyes themselves don't even look like their normal brown. There's a slightly golden sheen to them, or it may just be a trick of the bathroom lights. It makes me look otherworldly and decidedly not normal. Looking back now, I'm not sure if everyone was staring at Tuoni or at *me*.

Okay, maybe I need a shower first, then food. Then sex. Then thinking about the next step.

I open the bathroom door and shout into the room, "I'm going to take a shower first."

"Can I join you, or do you need privacy?" he asks, appearing before me, already shirtless in only his pants and bare feet.

Well, there goes the whole food before sex thing. "You don't mind showering with someone who will literally have dirt streaming off her?"

A low rumble sounds from his throat. "I'm the one who fucked you into the dirt, remember?" He steps inside the bathroom and glances around with a raised brow. "Besides, it will be my first shower. I need you to show me the ropes."

Of course. I hadn't thought about that. Living in Shadow's End is like living in a mixture of Ancient Greek and Medieval times—he has always bathed in a tub, and we've never bathed together, though our little tryst in the Crystal Caves came close.

"Alright," I say to him as I start taking off my clothes. I nod at his pants. "You'll need to remove those, unless you want them wet."

He gives me a smug smile and unbuttons them before stepping out. His cock is half-hard and already making my pulse quicken.

I bend down and turn on the tap, waiting for the water to warm.

"Like a waterfall," he murmurs, stepping up behind me until I feel his cock at my ass. I move back into it in a slow, teasing manner while his bare hands coast over my hips. I can't help but shiver already at the feel of his palms as they glide over my skin, as his fingertips press into my flesh. I don't think either of us will ever take the fact that he can finally touch me like this for granted.

I step into the shower, the warm water cascading over my body, then turn around to face my king.

The expression on his face darkens with lust, his eyes taking in the rivulets running over my breasts, over my stomach, between my legs. I feel a little self-conscious, even though I probably shouldn't, but it *is* our first shower together, and we're rarely naked in front of each other like this. Usually, he's pushing my dress up and fucking me without even taking his pants off. I'm rarely so on display or vulnerable.

It doesn't help that the water is dirty at first, though it's not long before it's running clear and the last reaches of Inmost have been washed away.

Not that he seems to have noticed. He lets out a guttural noise of want and steps into the shower stall. Suddenly, the space feels very small, his size all-consuming. His cock stands even more at attention, bobbing slightly as the water hits it. A fucking beautiful but never *not* intimidating sight, if I must say.

"Little bird," he whispers to me, taking another step closer until I'm pressed back against the wall. "I'm not sure you know just how beautiful you are."

My breath hitches at his words, words that threaten to unravel me, and I press my palms against the cold tiles of the wall in an attempt to keep myself upright.

Our bodies brush against each other as we maneuver in the confined space, our breaths mingling with the sound of steadily falling water droplets. I notice the way he looks at me, his eyes never leaving my skin as the water drips from my body. I feel his desire intensify, as if he's absorbing every detail of me.

I do the same to him, watching as the rivers roll over the silver lines across his body, the way the water drips off the tip of his ever-growing cock.

I reach out and trail my fingers over the length of it, feeling its hot, pulsing rhythm against my palm. He lets out a low groan, his eyes closing in pleasure. I can't help but feel empowered by his arousal, the way my touch ignites an uncontrollable response in him. Seeing him becoming undone by my touch is one of my favorite things, a true power I've always had, even before I found out I was part goddess.

With a sly smile, I reach down for the bar of soap, quickly tearing it from the plastic and lathering it in my hands before using it to trace delicate patterns on my skin, as if I'm creating art for him and I'm the canvas. My eyes never leave his as I touch myself, running the soap over my breasts, down my abdomen, between my thighs.

He steps closer, his cock rigid and pulsing in front of him, unable to resist the sight of my wet hands on my own body. I reach out again, this time running my fingers over the sensitive tip of his shaft, feeling his body tremble as his eyes roll back in pleasure.

"You don't seem to care so much about food anymore," he rasps.

"I guess I was craving something else instead," I tell him, giving his cock a hard squeeze.

He lets out a deep groan, his hips bucking forward slightly in response.

I carefully drop to my knees, my eyes locked with his.

He lets out a ragged breath, and I can feel the hot pulse of want against my soap-slick palm as he nods for me to continue. I lean in and press a soft kiss to the tip of his cock, letting my tongue trace the slit before dipping inside and tasting the salt of it. He groans loudly, the sound reverberating in the small space, his hands running through my wet hair as he pulls me closer to him.

I take him fully into my mouth, savoring the wet, soapy taste of his skin as I wrap my lips around his thick length. He gasps, his hand finding its way to the back of my head, guiding me in my exploration.

I suck and lick him, each movement calculated to send jolts of pleasure through his body, knowing exactly what I need to do to get the response I want. His hips buck again, his breathing becoming raspy, his fists tightening in my hair as he fights to maintain control.

"Wait," he says gruffly, his chest heaving. "I don't want to come yet, and I will if you keep doing that."

I smile to myself and release him from my mouth, standing up and facing him once more. The desire in his eyes is molten with the need for release building between us.

"You're always making me come twice," I tease him. "Maybe it's time I return the favor."

He responds by grabbing my hips, lifting me up onto the slick tiles of the shower wall. I wrap my legs around his waist, locking him against me, and with one powerful thrust, he enters me, filling me completely as I gasp at the sensation.

"Fuck," I whisper, feeling so thoroughly full and complete.

So grounded.

In the chaotic turn our lives have taken, in the lost time and becoming a literal ghost in the only world I have ever known, having him inside me feels like the only thing holding me together.

He might know this too from the way he's savoring me.

He begins to move inside me, slow and deliberate at first, as if lingering on the feeling of my body surrounding him. But soon, his rhythm quickens, deepens. Each thrust sends waves of pleasure coursing through me, and I cling to him desperately, my nails digging into his shoulders, holding on to him, like if I don't, I might be lost and never be able to find my way back.

His hands grip my hips, guiding me as he thrusts deeper and harder, our bodies slapping together with each powerful stroke. My breasts bounce wildly, our skin slick with water and soap. I arch my back, meeting each thrust with abandon.

A wave of need crashes over me as I feel myself growing closer to the edge, the sensations building higher and higher. The water from the shower seems to merge with our sweat, a hot, wet cocoon around us, sealing us away from the rest of the world, a world that doesn't feel like mine anymore, a world that has moved on without me. All that matters at this moment is the desperate need I have for him, this connection that seems to transcend all boundaries, if not time.

As Tuoni continues to thrust into me, I can feel him swelling even more, his body growing more and more taut. My own climax is just a breath away, and I know that together, we're going to shatter.

With a moan that echoes off the tiles, I feel his body tense, his cock pulsing inside me one last time before he releases himself. A wave of warmth floods me, and it pushes me over the edge. Pleasure courses through my veins, washing away any fears and doubts that might still be lingering, replaced instead by the raw, unadulterated bliss of this intimate moment. I come hard, my cries filling the space, my soul feeling as if it's in orbit.

As we collapse against each other, our breathing slowing, our bodies still joined together, the water cascading down around us, I know this is what we both needed. This connection, this passion, this release. It's more than just sex to me; it's a bond that transcends any obstacle, any distance, any uncertainty, and in this moment, I'm grateful to have found it here, in the warm, strong embrace of the death god's arms.

It might be the only thing I have right now, the only thing keeping me from spiraling out of control.

And so we simply hold each other, our hearts beating in sync, our bodies still connected. The water continues to fall around us, steady and pure, pulling me back into the present, into the now.

As we finally break apart, I see the satisfaction and contentment in Tuoni's eyes, the warmth in the silver. There's silence between us, only the sound of the shower and our breath that slowly returns to us. There isn't much to say when our bodies have already said it all.

Finally, he pulls out of me, and we get to work cleaning up. He shampoos my hair, and I do the same to him, adding conditioner after. By the time we finally turn off the faucet and step out of the shower, I feel like a whole new person.

He takes one of the towels and wraps it around me before he ties one around his waist in a rare display of modesty. Perhaps this world is rubbing off on him already.

And that's when I remember.

This world.

My world.

And everything we have to go through to get where we need to go.

It all seems impossible.

"Hanna," Tuoni says, reaching his warm fingers under my chin and tipping it up so I meet his gaze. "One step at a time. Let's get food first, shall we?"

"Am I that easy to read?" I ask him, grabbing a towel for my hair.

"Only when you're in despair," he says, holding my hand to his mouth and placing a kiss on my knuckles. "If we had more time, I'd fuck it right out of you, but I think you need to eat first. I don't want to meet this Hangry Hanna."

I can't help but laugh. "No one does."

CHAPTER 14

Hanna

THE PICK-UP LINE

It doesn't take long for us to dry our hair (yes, I used a blow-dryer on Tuoni for the first time—he wasn't a fan, no pun intended) and to change into our new old clothes and head down into the lobby for dinner. I don't really feel like roaming the streets of Helsinki looking for a restaurant when the one in the hotel seems okay to me. Besides, we'll be able to charge it to the room and hopefully get away without paying for it in the end.

The place is busier than I expected, but the hostess is able to seat us at a round table in the bar area. Despite how modern the hotel looks, the bar is all dark wood and darker corners, the perfect place for two escapees from the underworld to plot their future.

Death looks around appreciatively. "This is my kind of establishment. Perhaps I shall open a joint like this in Tuonela. Maybe a meeting place for the gods."

"Anything is better than having to dive into the bottom of the sea to get to a grotto," I point out, looking over the menu.

He doesn't say anything to that, and when I glance over the menu at him, he looks deep in thought, his eyes seeming to change from dark silver to stormy grey as he stares at the wall.

"You're worried about the gods," I say, sure to keep my voice low in case someone hears us talking like religious fanatics. "You think Louhi will do something to them as well."

He nods slowly and brings his gaze back to meet mine. "Until recently, it would have never crossed my mind. I knew that only I had the power to kill the Gods, but since Salainen proved she had the power to kill me, I don't think any of them are safe." He sighs, and I can see the weight on his shoulders. "I wish I knew what was happening, that there was some way to know if at least my children are safe."

I reach across the table and place my hand on his, wishing he wasn't wearing gloves, but knowing it's for the best when we're around other people. "I hate to sound corny and new-agey, but what does your heart tell you? Your heart will always know."

He seems to think about that, or perhaps he's wondering what *new age* means. "I think," he begins slowly, "my heart is a little confused at the moment. It doesn't feel like I have it under control."

There is meaning in his words, a heaviness, and I can't decipher if this is a good or bad thing.

"But," he goes on, giving me a faint smile, "I think Lovia and Tuonen are alright. For now. As for the rest of my family, I don't know. I have worries."

Just then, the waitress appears at our table. I do the talking, lest Death start questioning who this woman is, since he's never been to a restaurant before, and I get us two dark ales to get us started while we look over the menu.

"What is this?" he asks, peering at it. "This looks like what Pyry writes out when I'm having a dinner party, but I've never seen so many options in one night."

The menu is very Finnish, lots of game meat and fish and hearty stews, and my stomach curls in on itself in hunger. I want to order everything, then figure I might as well. We don't know how long it will be until our next meal. We have to plan for the fact that anything can and will happen.

I'm fairly certain I know Death's appetite well, especially since a lot of his favorite dishes are smuggled from this world anyway, so when the waitress comes back with our beers, I order an assortment of meals, everything from reindeer and pheasant to turnip stew and a shrimp sandwich. Even if I can't finish it all, I know he can.

"What should we cheers to?" I ask him, lifting the mug of ale.

He lifts his and stares at me deeply. For one magical, strangely wonderful moment, it feels like the two of us are out on a date, a couple still in their honeymoon period, all sparks and fire, still getting to know each other while having a basis of familiarity. A normal couple visiting the city of Helsinki during a dark winter, a couple of this world.

What would that be like?

What if, instead of finding our way back to Tuonela, we could stay here?

Why do I have to be the one to give up everything?

But guilt follows that thought.

I know why. I know he has his family. On the other hand, Lovia loves this world more than her own, and I think Tuonen would fare well here too. What if, instead of returning, we could somehow get his son and daughter out of the Underworld and into this one? If Louhi is so focused on becoming the ruler of Tuonela and retaining her status as the Goddess of Death, why shouldn't we just let her have it?

Because she will induce Kaaos, and the afterlife will never be fair, I remind myself. But maybe there's a point to it. Or maybe we can just join the rest of humanity who don't know what the afterlife actually entails. Most people don't even know there is one.

I don't dare tell Tuoni this, though. I keep my thoughts to myself.

"We cheers to you," he says, his voice grave. "My queen who has given up so much to be with a king she doesn't serve." He clinks his glass against mine.

"I serve you," I tell him imploringly.

I love you. But the words stay hidden, as if I'm too afraid to say them again.

"No, Hanna," he says with a soft smile in juxtaposition to his stern features. "You were bound to me by promise and obligation. If anything, I am the one serving you. At least, that's how it should be. The dead serve me, and you are not dead. You are a living, breathing, fairy girl, half-goddess herself, the most alive creature I've ever held in my hands."

My heart does summersaults at his words, at the sincerity in his voice and the intensity in his gaze until he looks away. He has a sip of his beer, and his eyes practically roll back into his head in pleasure.

"Now I think I'm in Amaranthus," he says with a sigh of satisfaction before he swallows.

I take a sip, not expecting to be all that impressed, but it tastes amazing. I suppose I haven't had proper beer in a long time, because this beer hits different (I would never tell Tuoni this, but the beer served at Shadow's End can be rather flat sometimes).

It also seems to go straight to my head, which is just as well, because we both down the beer. When the waitress comes by with our appetizers —Finnish squeaky cheese on rye bread—we order more beer.

And more.

It's not long before the two of us are feeling pretty buzzed—at least I am—and are stuffing our faces with food. I thought my appetite would be satisfied early on, but I keep on eating. Maybe going from Underworld to Upper World takes a toll on your body, or maybe I've just had my share of horror and exhaustion over the last however long it's been. Days? Time ceases to behave when you know how easily it can be taken from you.

As the night goes on, the fuller the bar area gets. I know I should be trying to figure out how to contact my father, doing full-on Google searches, perhaps reaching out to my relatives, but with that comes so much baggage I can't face at the moment. Every time I open my phone, I'm reminded of what a ghost I am. If I Google my father, I'm afraid I'll see another article about how I went missing. It's so much of a headfuck that my sober brain can't handle it, let alone my drunk one.

Death seems content, though, drinking and eating with a voracious appetite. I've never really seen him drunk, so this might be the closest he'll be to it—his eyes are heavy-lidded, his shoulders relaxed, with a mouth that's quicker to smile. It's odd to see him in this light, in such a modern setting as a bar filled with beer-swilling patrons.

Once again, I find myself pretending that he's a mortal man I met on Tinder, or perhaps through a mutual friend, or maybe he was an instructor at one of my capoeira classes. Here, in this world, his eyes could be grey. The silver lines of death covering his body could be tattoos. His long hair, beard, and dark lashes could paint him as mysterious, rugged, wild. His height and muscles could be attributed to genetics.

And yet, he doesn't belong here, not even a little bit. Even the people in the bar know this, and it's not because of the things I listed that could be explained in this realm—it's because he exudes the supernatural prowess of a deity. He's a god walking the Earth, something that should never be, and that draws the attention of people like a moth to a flame, even if they don't know it.

This isn't your world, Tuoni, I can't help but think.

And I'm not sure if it's mine anymore either.

I'm not sure where I belong.

"Excuse me," a guy with a British accent and a skinny mustache says to me as he approaches the table. He's probably in his late twenties, part of a group of businessmen who have taken over a few of the standing tables in the middle. They've been boisterous and loud this whole evening and keep looking over here at us, which I've been ignoring.

I give the guy a pointed look. "Yes?" I probably sound a little rude, but I think being in Tuonela has hardened my edges. Also, I'm always wary when a guy approaches me out of the blue.

Meanwhile, Death is staring at the guy curiously, though the line between his brows deepens when he realizes the guy won't look at him.

"I was wondering if you could tell me: if you're here, who's running heaven?"

My eyes widen, and I bite back a laugh. "Are you serious?"

Is this guy not only trying to pick me up in front of Tuoni, but with the cheesiest pick-up line in the world?

"What do you mean?" Death says gruffly, enough that the guy finally looks over at him. "Have you mortals already heard the news about my ex-wife? She's running heaven at the moment, though it won't be heaven for much longer."

The mustache guy's face scrunches up in drunk confusion. "Your ex-wife?" he begins before he shakes his head and gestures to me. "Nah, mate, I'm just trying to tell this woman that she's so gorgeous, she takes my breath away."

Death is about to say something else, but I beat him to it. "He's not being literal," I say to Tuoni. "He's just trying to pick me up." I give the guy a loaded look. "And he should know that cheesy pick-up lines don't work on a married woman."

"Oh," he says with a slow raise of his brows. "You're married? Sorry, I didn't see any rings."

"He gave me a crown instead," I answer before I have a sip of my beer. I wave him off. "Now, run along to your friends."

The guy jerks his chin back, and his flirty gaze turns into a scowl before he heads over to his drunken, laughing cronies, who have been watching the entire scene unfold.

"What the fuck just happened?" Tuoni asks. "A pick-up line? I would never let him pick you up."

"He didn't mean it literally. He was hitting on me." I pause, unsure if he's also going to take that phrase literally or not. "He was trying to sleep with me."

Suddenly, Tuoni's fist curls around his mug so tight, the glass shatters in his hand.

I gasp, watching as the beer spills across the table. Luckily, he's wearing his gloves, so he wouldn't be cut anyway, not that it would probably matter with him.

Everyone else turns to look, and our waitress hurries over with a towel and a tray for the glass.

I apologize profusely on Tuoni's behalf, even though he's just sitting there, eyes sparking with rage, his jaw tense as he wiggles it back and forth.

"I should kill him," he seethes under his breath after the waitress leaves.

"It's fine," I tell him. "I'm used to it."

"You're used to it?"

"I mean, not to toot my own horn..." He blinks at me, and I clarify, "Not to sound conceited, but yeah, I get hit on from time to time, especially in a bar where men are drunk. It happens to all women."

"Is that why they all keep staring at you? Do they all want to sleep with you?"

I shrug. "I don't know. Maybe. Or you. You seem to be attracting the most attention in this place. Or wherever we go. Perhaps they wanted to see if they could best a god, steal his woman out from under his nose."

I was joking about that last part, but from the fire in his eyes and the way his nostrils fare, I realize I need to tread more carefully with Mr. Literal here.

"They're just being guys," I say quickly. "I know how to handle them."

"A knife to the throat, I hope," he says, nodding his thanks as the waitress brings over another glass of beer, one she tells us is on the house. Obviously, she thinks the glass was faulty, because what man could break a thick mug with his bare hand?

"If it comes to that," I tell him. "The sad thing about learning self-defense is that you can actually use it when the time comes, and that time usually does come."

"I know. I've seen you put it to good use already. I just didn't think you would need it in *this* world."

I sigh. "Yeah, well, you might have a skeleton army uprising going on back at home and usurpers and vengeful exes, but in this world, mortals aren't much better. Don't you ever wonder how so many people end up in Inmost? This is where they learn to be bad people."

He grumbles at that, palming his beer as he thinks it over. "I've never seen anyone hit on you before. Threaten you, yes, and I made sure they were never able to do it again. But try and sleep with you? No. That doesn't happen in Tuonela, not under my watch."

I laugh softly. "That's because everyone is under your watch. Who is going to try and sleep with me in Shadow's End? Your son?"

The light in his eyes darkens. "Why would my son?"

"I'm using him as an example. Your son wouldn't, but he's also the only slightly human being there. Sarvi's not trying to get their horn in my pants, that's for sure."

His lip curls up slightly, and I can tell he's trying to picture it.

"Well, you have no reason to be jealous," I go on, though, truth be told, I'm tickled pink that he is for once.

"Jealous," he says slowly. "What a strange emotion. I'm not sure I've ever felt it before."

"Maybe you've never had anything you..." I trail off before I say *love before*.

I can't finish the sentence, because the truth is, he doesn't love me. I know that much. The fact that when I told him I loved him, he didn't say it back hasn't left the back of my mind, nor my heart, having wormed its way deep inside like a cavity. It's a constant reminder that though our feelings for each other may be genuine, they aren't equal.

"Everything has always been mine," he finishes. "Including you. Here, it's like that doesn't matter. In this world, it's like any man can come and try to take you away from me."

Butterflies take flight in my chest. "No one is taking me away from you. You have nothing to worry about."

He nods at that and takes a generous sip of his drink, but I can tell it's troubling him. I'm all for making a guy jealous, but I don't want them to be sad about it.

I finish the rest of my beer and then excuse myself to go to the restroom, which is located around a dark corner, in between the restaurant and the hotel lobby. It's not until I'm walking that I realize how drunk I am, weaving slightly as I go. It could also be that my body is just absolutely tired after taking beating after beating in Inmost. Either way, I think I have to slow my roll, because the last thing I want is to wake up tomorrow with a hangover. I've already lost a year of my life here; I'm not losing another day if I don't have to.

After I'm done, I look at myself in the mirror above the sink. I look a lot better than I did earlier, but I'm wondering if I should stop by a store tomorrow to get some makeup and skincare. We were lucky enough that the hotel had mini teeth cleaning and vanity kits in the room, but it would be nice to have at least a hairbrush.

I tuck my hair behind my ears and step out of the bathroom.

I run right into the drunk mustache guy.

"Oh, sorry," I apologize, stepping out of the way.

But the guy just steps in front of me again, blocking the way back to the bar.

"Is that guy really your husband?" the guy says, slurring his words. "Or is he an overprotective friend who doesn't like it when men talk to you?"

I'm about to tell him to fuck off and shove him back against the wall when I see Tuoni approach out of my peripheral.

Death moves like a flash of silver lightning.

Tuoni's hand shoots out, and he grabs the guy by the throat, throwing him back against the wall, holding him a few feet above the ground so his head is almost touching the ceiling. Unlike what he did with the front desk clerk, I think Tuoni means to kill this guy.

"Stop!" I cry out, keeping my voice down so we don't attract attention. "Don't kill him."

"Where's your knife to the throat?" Tuoni growls at me, squeezing the man's neck tighter until the blood vessels in his eyes burst.

"I could have taken care of this," I say, pleading now. Oh God. Oh fuck. I'm about to witness a murder, aren't I? "Let him go, or you're going to kill him."

"I am the God of Death," he seethes.

"You are, but right now, if you killed this man and sent him to Tuonela, there's no telling what might happen to him there. What if it's already reduced to *Kaaos*?"

"He deserves that *Kaaos* then."

"No," I say, grabbing his arm. "He's just a fucking idiot who doesn't deserve to die or rot in hell just because he hit on me. He'll get what's coming to him one day, I'm sure of it, but not today. We don't kill people here on a whim, even when they fuck up."

Death grumbles but finally loosens his grip.

The man slumps to the ground.

Dead.

CHAPTER 15

Death

THE CHOICE

"He's dead," Hanna cries out, dropping to her knees beside the pick-up line boy.

"He isn't," I say with a sniff. "I would know."

For further assurance, I wave my hand at him, and the man coughs, which makes Hanna exhale in relief. Then, I pull her up, giving the guy space as he slowly gets to his feet.

He puts his hand at his throat and rubs it as he eyes the both of us with blood-shot eyes.

"You tried to hit on her, and she fought back," I tell the man, putting *command* into my voice. "Make sure it doesn't happen again."

The man gets that glazed look in his eyes, which I now know is the sign that I'm making them do and think things under my will.

The command works. He nods.

"Apologize to her," I tell him.

He looks at Hanna. "I am so sorry. I don't know what came over me."

"Tell her you'll never behave that way with any woman again," I tell him.

He nods profusely. "I promise I will never behave that way with any woman ever again."

"Very well," I say with a flick of my hand, trying to keep the anger I still feel bubbling inside me at bay. "Go back to your friends, leave this place, and don't speak a word of this to anyone."

The man nods, his hand still rubbing his throat, and then scurries around the corner into the bar.

"Tuoni," Hanna says to me slowly as she turns to face me. "I didn't need—"

I don't give her a chance to speak.

I grab her face in my hands, and I kiss her.

Hard.

So hard, I hope I'm imprinting myself on her soul.

She freezes at first and then slowly melts into me, her arms wrapping around my neck and her tongue sliding into my mouth. The taste of her is like a balm to my insecurities, a reminder of what I've been longing for and fighting to protect. The anger and jealousy I have inside me doesn't go away; it remains there like a fire about to rage out of control.

Seeing that man hitting on her like that, seeing how desirable she is to the men here, makes me feel like she's just sand slipping through my fingers. I'd always gotten that feeling with her, like she was only going to be a temporary part of my life, even after she married me and became my queen, even after she was able to touch me.

Even after she told me she loved me.

I've always felt—feared—that I could lose her at any moment.

And now that we're in this world, her world, and I'm the outsider here, I feel like I'm hanging on to her devotion and affection by a thread. That man, as puny and mortal as he was, thought she should have been with him instead of me...what if, one day, she comes to that conclusion? What if she already has?

This jealously thing is a viper inside me, venomous and biting, and before I can control myself, I'm whirling her around in my arms and kicking in the door behind her.

It's a bathroom without a bath, the air smelling of chemicals, and I practically throw her inside, the need to plant my seed deep inside her overpowering me.

She is mine.

"Lock the door," she says with a gasp and, from the wildness in her eyes, I know she's feeling this too.

I take off my gloves then turn and close the door, quickly locking it before I stride over to her and grab her by the back of the neck, my other hand going to the stretchy waistband of her thin pants.

As I yank her closer, she lets out a surprised gasp, but there's a spark in her eyes that matches the fire raging within me. The heat between us is palpable, the air crackling with tension and desire. My hands slip under her pants and undergarments, urgency and possessiveness guiding my movements as I reach down to find her warm and slick.

"Fuck," I say through a moan as Hanna's hands roam over my chest, her touch igniting a frenzy of need deep within me. I feel like a man possessed, consumed by the fear of losing her and the overwhelming desire to mark her as mine in every way possible.

I slide my fingers inside her, and she moans softly, arching her back towards me. I feel the walls of her tight heat clenching around my fingers as I move them in and out, her eyes locked with mine in a silent plea for relief. Her nails dig into my shoulders, and I reach down and pull her pants and underwear down to her knees, wanting more than anything to rip them right off her, but vaguely aware that she went through great effort to procure them from the store.

So, I flip her around, her hands pressed against the cold surface of the sink, and push her legs apart as far as they will go. It's going to be a tight fit.

She glances up at my reflection in the mirror, her mahogany hair in waves around her face, her cheeks and neck already flushed. Her desire is a storm raging within her, and I want to be the tempest that breaks her open, that makes her mine in every way I can.

"Don't stop looking at me," I tell her as I undo my pants and guide my cock against her entrance, teasing the curve of her ass first. "Don't stop looking at your king. Don't fucking forget who rules you in this world and the next."

"Never," she whispers, but that whisper breaks off into a gasp as I take a deep breath and thrust into her, feeling the tightness of her body, the slickness of her desire, the warmth that envelops me.

She moans softly, her round bottom rising back to meet each thrust. I can see the fire in her eyes, the possessive hunger that matches my own.

This is not just about lust, but about claiming and possessing what I fear losing.

Is it possible she fears losing me too?

My hands grip her waist, pulling her closer, as I drive into her with increasing urgency. Her moans grow louder, and I can feel her muscles tightening around me, her release drawing near.

Her eyes start to flutter, her mouth opening, her tongue shining like candy.

"Tell me who I am to you," I command, and she brings her gaze back to meet mine in the mirror. The intensity in her eyes feels like a bolt of lightning between us, holding us in place, heart to heart.

"You're my king," she whispers, her voice shaking.

The words are a key, unlocking something I've been too afraid to let loose, that cage inside me, the one I've never been able to shake.

I thrust into her harder, feeling her tighten around me.

"Say it again," I demand, my voice low and gruff. I thrust once more, my hips slamming against her. "Tell me you'll always be mine, that you'll never wear another man's crown."

"I'm yours," she cries out on a moan, fighting to maintain eye contact with me. "I'll always be yours, my king. No other will ever touch me, no other will ever have a place in my heart. I wear your crown and no one else's."

Her words send a wave of possessiveness coursing through me, and I lift her up, holding her hips as I continue to thrust into her, deeper and harder with every stroke.

Her heart. She told me she loved me back in that cell—had that been a lie? Had that been a false plea to bring me back to life?

Do I really have this woman's heart, even now, in this world?

"You told me you loved me," I manage to say, so painfully aware of how weak it makes me sound. "Did you mean that? Do you actually love me?"

Her eyes widen, her mouth dropping open at another hard, deep thrust, and before my heart sinks, she nods. There's a mixture of fear and devotion in her gaze, a plea for understanding.

"I meant it," she says through a gasp before she swallows thickly. "I love you."

My heart presses against my ribs until I'm sure they'll break. "Even here, even now?"

"Yes, here, now, always."

Those words release the storm inside me, and with a roar of triumph, I thrust into her one last time, the pleasure and relief coursing through us like a tidal wave. We convulse together in the dim light of the bathroom, her body arching against me, my moans and her cries filling the space.

When I finally pull out of her, she collapses onto the cold surface of the sink, her ass exposed, her hair tumbling around her face. I reach down and carefully pull up her pants and underwear. Then, I grab her shoulder and make her turn to face me, tucking her hair behind her ear and wiping the sweat from her forehead with a tenderness that surprises me.

"You're my husband," she whispers again, the words soothing to my soul. "That hasn't changed."

Why do I have such a hard time believing it? Hanna has never shown me anything but devotion and affection. She's never given me a reason not to trust her—not lately, anyway.

"Why am I so scared you'll change your mind?" I whisper to her. Each word feels raw, bare, vulnerable. Each word terrifies me.

She gives me a tired smile. "Because even though you're a god, you have the emotions of a mortal, and us mortals only fear two things: death and love. It means you're far more human than you ever thought."

"I'm not sure I like that," I admit, tucking my cock back in my pants and buttoning them up.

"Yeah, well, we don't like it either," she says with a sigh. "I think we spend most of our lives trying to run from it in some way, even when we know it's really the thing we want most. Love, that is. Not death."

There's a melancholy to her words, and I'm unsure if it's because of me or not. I can't even begin to imagine the stress she must be under. I just don't want to add to that stress if I can help it.

"How about we go back to the room?" I say to her. "I think I'm finally full."

She laughs softly, an angelic sound. "Sounds good. We'll go back to the table and make sure we've settled up first. Hopefully, that mustache guy will still be on his best behavior."

My jealously flares again at the mention of him. I thought I fucked that emotion out of my system, but I guess not. What if the longer I'm in the Upper World, the more I'll start feeling all these emotions, as if they're some sort of contagious disease?

Fortunately, when we step back into the bar, the man and his group of friends are gone. Just as well; I'm sure the sight of him would probably cause me to do something else Hanna would frown upon. When you know you can punish or manipulate people with impunity, morality starts to crack.

Hanna makes sure the waitress has gets paid and then we get on the strange elevator ride and go back to our floor. I have to wonder if an elevator in Shadow's End would make sense. It would make traveling to Sarvi's room a lot easier, if only I could figure out a way to operate one. Steam engine, perhaps? Maybe I could bottle lightning during the next storm and find a way to use that as electricity.

But all those thoughts of Shadow's End bring a darkness back to my heart, as elated as it's been this evening.

By the time we get back inside our hotel room, turn off the lights, and crawl into bed, I already feel pulled under by worries again.

"It's going to be okay," Hanna says to me with her head on the pillow, reaching over and brushing a strand of hair off my forehead.

I capture her hand in mine and kiss her fingertips. "I'm supposed to be the one telling you that."

"Then we can take turns," she says with a soft smile.

I sigh heavily and stare up at the ceiling, the enormity of where I am and what we need to do to get back home feeling heavy. "We need to get back," I say quietly. "Tomorrow, we need to go to wherever you first went through the portal, the one your father would use."

"We will need my father for that. We need to find him first."

"Even if we don't, we need to try anyway." I roll my head to the side to look at her dark eyes. "I know you want to find him, and you will, I just..."

"What?"

"Perhaps it would be best for you to stay behind with your father and let me go back to Tuonela."

Her face blanches, and she flinches like I've just struck her. "What? No!"

"Hanna," I say, my voice low with conviction. "This is your world. You entered a marriage bargain with me in exchange for your father's life. I don't want to hold you to me anymore. I don't want to be that burden."

Her mouth drops open for a moment as she sits up. "Tuoni, please. I just told you I love you."

"I know you love me—"

"You don't know!" she cries out. "And you don't..." She trails off and shakes her head, holding the sheets over her naked breasts. "No. I am with you because I choose to be."

"I don't understand why you would choose this. I look around, and I see your world. I see all the things you've had to give up. Don't you see the things you gave up because I captured you, because I forced you into marriage? I made you become a queen; it wasn't your choice."

"But I like being a queen now," she says adamantly. "I think I might even be good at it. I'm the chosen one, for god's sake."

"Not the sake of this god," I tell her. "You had a life before me. I didn't let myself think about it, but now, I see it. I see it when you look at your phone, at your mother and your father and your friends. Your old city, your old job. Before you met me, you would have had plans and dreams. You would have imagined meeting a nice man, getting married to him, having his children, living in a nice house by the ocean. Those were your dreams."

She looks away. "You know nothing of my dreams."

"I know that you had ideas of how your life might have gone, and then I took that all away from you. I took you from your home, your world, and I bent you and shaped you until you fit into mine. I can't..." I take a deep breath, my heart pounding. "I can't live with myself if I know I've prevented you from living the life you should be living. I can't afford to be so fucking selfish all the time."

She's quiet, looking down at her hands, and deep in the darkest parts of me, I fear I struck a nerve, that maybe she didn't think that way before, but now she's thinking it. Feeling it. Considering it.

Oh fuck, what have I done?

I want nothing more than to take back those words. Perhaps I could use my mind control on her too.

"Is that what you want?" she asks quietly.

"Me? No," I tell her. "I don't want you to go. I don't want to lose you. If I lose you, I lose everything."

"Because of the prophecy," she says with a slow nod.

"No," I say, reaching out and putting my hand at her cheek, forcing her damp eyes to meet mine. "I lose everything because *you're* my everything."

Her mouth quivers, and she blinks at me, a tear spilling down her cheek.

"Fuck, the last thing I ever want is to make you cry," I say to her, wiping the cheek away with my thumb, reveling at the feel of it against my bare skin. "But you're so damn beautiful when you do."

I exhale heavily, my heart still heavy. "Listen, Hanna, my queen. You will never stop being my queen, nor will you stop being my prophecy, but I no longer wish to keep you bound to me. I want to let you go so you can be free to fly, to be that little bird you are."

She places her fingers around my hand and holds me like that. "And I appreciate that you're giving me that chance, but I'm not taking it. Because I don't want to. Because I love you. My plans for my life? All I wanted was to find my purpose and find someone to love and, with you, I've found that. No matter how you try to spin it, there is no way I can just move on with whatever life I have left in this world knowing that my mother is the Goddess of the Sun, knowing that the balance of the afterlife rests in me uniting the land, that my heart truly belongs to yours. It's too late for me now. I'm with you until the bitter end, Tuoni."

Fuck. Now *I* feel a wet burning sensation behind my eyes. Damn these mortal emotions. "You have no idea how much I've needed to hear that. To know that."

"Well, I'm glad I've made you see otherwise," she says. "You can't get rid of me that easily."

"I would never try to get rid of you."

But as I lay back down beside her and hear her slowly drift off to sleep, my mind starts to plan. It starts to race.

I don't want to let Hanna go. I selfishly want her at my side as my lover, my wife, my queen, for all of eternity. But I don't know what the future holds, and I don't know what her part in the prophecy is. They said the one who can touch Death is the one to unite the land, but there has to be a way for her to do that without coming into danger. I know we were lucky in Inmost, but when we step back in Tuonela, if it's already descended into *Kaaos*, I'm not sure how much luck we'll have left. I want to keep her safe. I want to keep her alive.

I need to figure out a way to do that.

CHAPTER 16

Tuonen

THE DUNGEON

I didn't go back to sleep after I visited with Sarvi. We decided that the unicorn would fly to the Hiisi Forest to see Tapio in the morning, and we stayed up talking, figuring out what could have possibly happened to my father and Hanna. Unfortunately, none of the scenarios we came up with were anything but horrifying.

As a result, I'm tired as fuck, and when I'm tired, I'm not at my best. I'm in my room, afraid to leave. My father—ahem, my *mother*—knocked on the door once to ask if I would be down for breakfast, something my actual father would never do, since eating around the table together as a family is something to be saved for special occasions, not for shoveling toasted grains into one's mouth in the morning hours.

But I managed to mumble a reply through the door that I was tired from the match and wanted to sleep in. If I had said that to my actual father, he probably would have kicked down the door and told me to smarten up and act like a god ("Gods don't get tired! Straighten up!") but now that I know it's my devil mother, she's a little softer.

It's all an act. Or maybe it's not. Maybe my mother does have natural motherly instincts when it comes to her children. She's never really showed them, but perhaps during this charade, they're coming out.

Either way, she left me in peace.

If you can call this peace.

I need to get in touch with Lovia. She's down on the river, ferrying the dead to and from Death's Landing. With everything that's happening, will Tapio have his son take over for us? If he does, then Lovia will be free to come back here—but what if she's walking into a trap? What if the best place for her is remain in the north with the rest of the gods?

I can only hope Tapio has told her his suspicions about the situation, and I hope Sarvi can find them both and tell them the truth.

There is no sun at the moment, hidden behind thick clouds that cover the tops of the mountains, the sea below calm and dull. There's nothing particularly unusual about this weather—the gloom has always followed my father. But since he met Hanna, the sun has been out more and more each day. The old man must really be in love or something.

But to see the clouds again is troubling. The winter storm is gone, but this static gloom and darkness doesn't bode well for my father being alive and well.

How did Louhi dispose of him? I thought no one could kill my father. If my mother always had this power, why didn't she use it earlier, from day one, or whatever day she decided she suddenly hated my father and wanted him dead?

None of this makes any sense. When Sarvi mentioned that Hanna had a twin of sorts, they noted that she might have some sort of powers or dealings with dark magic, but no dark magic should ever be able to take down my father.

Unless my father isn't as strong as he has led us to believe.

Unless none of us are, including me.

And now, I'm feeling very, very afraid. A useless fucking feeling, but it's still there, still sinking into my bones, and I don't know how to deal with it.

My mother wouldn't actually hurt me, would she?

Would she hurt Lovia?

Maybe I should go visit the giant Vipunen. I know Lovia is the one who has had more training with him, but he's been an overseer of my father since the very beginning. From the way my father tells it, Vipunen was there to help him become the God of Death after his own parents cast him away.

I decide it's time to take action in whatever way I can. I don't know what chance I have against my mother or Hanna's twin, but I can be a good son and a good brother. I can get Lovia out of danger, I can save my father. Might be the only chance I'll ever have to prove myself.

I slip on proper clothes: boots, trousers, knits, and furs. My hair looks like it hasn't been brushed in a long time, and when I style it into place, my fingers graze the sharp points of my horns just poking up beneath the hairline. My horns and my tail are constant reminders that I am the son of a demon woman, but thankfully, my horns only protrude when I'm experiencing some sort of excitement or emotional turmoil, which is rare for me, and my tail stays hidden in my pants.

But I don't want my mother to suspect anything is wrong at all. If my horns grow anymore and become visible, she'll become suspicious.

I decide to slip on a black knit cap over my head, just in case.

Then, I head out into the halls.

Normally, there would be voices floating about, perhaps my father talking to the servants or to Sarvi and Kalma, or the Deadmaidens in the kitchen, making lunch, but everything is so eerily quiet. You could hear a pin drop.

I climb up the stairs to Sarvi's room, but there's no one there. The doors to the landing are open, a cool breeze blowing back the curtains, but Sarvi is still gone on their journey.

When I come back down, I nearly run into Kalma at the foot of the stairs, the torches on the wall casting his decaying face into sickly shadows.

"Tuonen," Kalma says in his craggy voice. "You're finally out and about."

"I was just checking on Sarvi. Have you seen them?"

"The unicorn left a few hours ago. I saw them in the sky when I was in the garden." He pauses. "Your father wasn't very pleased to hear that the unicorn left without telling him."

I swallow hard, trying to ignore the tightness in my chest.

"You alright?" he asks, squinting at me.

I nod slowly. Kalma has always been a kind man and a great advisor to my father, but I can't tell if he's in on this or not. Surely if he knew my mother was operating my father's Shadow Self, he would do all he could to get my father back. He must not know the truth.

I open my mouth to try and tell him, but my instincts prevent me from making a sound. There's something about Kalma's gaze, a blankness and sheen to his eyes, that makes me think he might be under some kind of spell.

"I'm fine," I say carefully. "I'll go check on Sarvi when they get back."

I brush past him as I walk the rest of the stairs.

"But Sarvi did get back already," Kalma says. "Your father went and got them back...somehow."

Somehow. My father can't fly.

But my mother can.

I frown, that uneasy feeling back in my veins, sticky and cold. "So where is Sarvi?"

"In the Sect of the Undead," Kalma says with a grave nod. "Your father is about to raise the Old Gods with Hanna by his side."

My eyes go wide. "He's about to do *what*?"

Kalma smiles, his face increasingly vacant. "Such a glorious day, isn't it? A glorious day for the Old Gods to return."

He shuffles up the stairs to Sarvi's room, his robes dragging behind him.

I waste no time.

I look around for a weapon that could possibly do any harm to a demon, but anything remotely useful would either be in the crypt itself or in the Library of the Veils, and even I don't have access to that room.

But if Sarvi is back and being held in the crypt, that means I have to act fast, never mind the part about the Old Gods. I just hope that's something Kalma was exaggerating.

I take off, running down the hall and the levels of stairs, taking them two at a time until I finally get to the stairs to the crypt and the dungeons. The hallway is shrouded in darkness, lit only by glowing blue torches placed at even intervals along the stone walls. The floor is made of smooth, polished black marble that reflects the flickering light, giving the illusion of walking on water. High arched ceilings stretch above, adorned with intricate carvings of skulls and bones.

Here, I come face to face with Hanna.

For a moment, I think maybe I've been wrong about the whole thing. Perhaps this isn't an imposter or twin at all, and maybe this actually *is* Hanna. Maybe this was Hanna's plan all along. After all, her father was a powerful Shaman. Maybe they arranged for him to be kidnapped and for Hanna to take his place, a way to infiltrate the Underworld right under our noses.

But even though I don't know Hanna well, I know a girl from the Upper World when I see one, a mortal stuck in this world, part of a noble bargain. My father is smart, smart enough to see when someone is playing him, and the way Hanna acts around my father tells me she has true feelings for him.

That also means Hanna wouldn't fall for my father's Shadow Self.

Therefore, the person who's standing in front of me with Hanna's face isn't her at all. Especially not when she smiles, with teeth sharper than they should be.

"Tuonen," the not-Hanna says. "I've been looking for you."

"Is that so?" I ask, taking a step back.

"Yes," she says, still smiling. She reaches out and grabs my arm, her dagger-like nails digging in through my top. "You're looking rather delicious today."

I swallow hard, wondering if punching her in the face would get me in trouble.

I try to take my arm from her grasp, but her nails dig in deeper until I feel them draw blood.

"Let go of me!" I bellow, finally ripping my arm from her hold, though her nails create a long tear in the fabric.

She just continues to grin at me and then takes her nails, wet with my blood, and slides them across her tongue.

Her black tongue.

"Hanna!" I hear my father's voice bark from down in the crypt. "Bring my son to me."

Oh fuck.

I'm about to turn and run when suddenly, everything starts to spin a little. My arm feels like it's on fire, and then it feels deadly cold, like ice is creeping up it, taking over my limbs. I stare down at where her nails dug into me and see black swirling underneath my skin, like my veins have been injected with smoke.

Immediately, my horns punch through the cap on my head, and I feel myself doubling over as the cold blackness starts to take over my body.

"I was just subduing him," not-Hanna calls out as she reaches up and grabs me by the horns, forcing my body to twist as she leads me down the narrow, winding stairs to the cellar.

I grind my teeth together, trying not to cry out, to show any fear. I feel like that might only anger my mother as not-Hanna leads me past the wine cellars and dungeons into the crypt and the chapel of the Sect of the Undead.

Down the aisle, lined with pews and snakes and statues with bleeding eyes and razor crowns, is my mother in my father's body, standing at the altar.

With horror, I see she's not alone.

Sarvi is beside her, manacles over each hoof, weights on both wings, and a large collar around their neck, the chains leading to the ceiling. On the altar's table lay jars and potions next to a broadsword with glittering red gems on the hilt.

"So, this is where we got married," my mother/father says, nodding at not-Hanna as she brings me down the aisle toward her. "Pity I wasn't invited to the wedding."

I try for a moment to fool her, to pretend I have no idea what's going on.

"Father," I manage to say. "What's going on? What did Hanna do to me?"

My father's eyes narrow at me, and for a moment, they glow green. *She* is coming through.

"Oh, Tuonen," he says, though it's turning into Louhi's voice now. "You are such a terrible liar. It's hard to believe that you're my son. Your father has corrupted you too much with his goodness."

If neither Sarvi nor I were in such a predicament, I would have laughed at that. I don't think my father is known for being the epitome of good, but I suppose, compared to my mother, he will always have that distinction.

I knew my mother was bad, but seeing her like this, knowing the truth, I realize I've deeply underestimated her.

Still, I try.

"I don't understand," I say, trying to twist away from not-Hanna's grip on my horns, but the ice in my veins barely lets me move. "What are you doing to Sarvi? They're your most loyal servant."

"I haven't done anything yet," my mother says with a raise of her chin. "And you know that horse isn't my servant. They're nothing but a spy, operating on your behalf. I saw Sarvi take flight. Didn't take me long to fly up after them and bring them down. With Sala's help, of course. I couldn't do any of it without the help of my adopted daughter, who is a better child than you or Lovia will ever be."

I grind my teeth together. "Why are you doing this?"

"Because," she says, "it is time to take back what is rightfully mine. My father married me to Tuoni because he wanted the demon blood to rule again one day. All I had to do was bide my time, but Tuoni grew bored of me. He cast me aside. Can you imagine getting married, putting in the days, the weeks, the eons, and then having that marriage severed?"

"You took on Ilmarinen," I point out with a groan, the cold pain still rolling through me. "You made him your new husband."

"I had no choice. I needed him for my magic. Now, he's obsolete, depleted, with nothing left to give. What better time than now to put my plans into motion? The Old Gods have been depending on me to raise them, to build an army to do their bidding. And that's just what I'm going to do." She pauses and smiles. I don't see my father's face anymore; the more I look at her, the more it looks like my mother's demon features. "And you're going to help."

"I will not help you," I manage to say.

"But I need the horn of a living god," she says, pouting. "And you have such lovely horns, Tuonen."

I stiffen. She can't be serious.

"Use your own," I tell her.

"I already have. It wasn't enough. Though I suppose I could get it from Sarvi here," she says, looking at the unicorn. Sarvi's head snaps up briefly, though it's quickly weighed down again by the iron collar.

"Sarvi is a servant," I tell her. "Father's most loyal one. They are not a god."

She lets out a caustic laugh. "You really don't know anything, do you, Tuonen? Sarvi is a god in their own right; a god of servitude. We're all gods down here."

"Except for me," not-Hanna says with a whine.

"You are a goddess," my mother says to her fiercely. "You are my daughter."

"Not by blood," I point out.

Not-Hanna immediately twists my horn, sending more ice and pain cascading through my body, enough that I crumble to my knees. "Mother, please, stop her!" I call out.

"Hmmm?" Louhi says. "See, there you are. *You* are my blood, and yet, I barely feel anything for you. Isn't it funny, the way things work? I can give birth to you and feel like you've been nothing but a waste of space, licking your father's boots your entire life and spurning me, and yet, here is Salainen, not of my blood, but definitely of my spirit. She was discarded, and I took her in, made her a queen. It was so selfless of me, don't you think?"

"Take my horns then, if you must," I say to her, grinding out my words. "But let Sarvi go."

A low, guttural sound comes from her, and the snakes in the room all hiss at once.

"That's why I know you're no true son of mine. You have a bleeding heart, just like your sister and father. It's so...*messy.*" She picks up the broadsword and holds it in her hand, brandishing it in front of Sarvi.

"I will take your horns, Tuonen, and I will take Sarvi's too. There is such a thing as punishment, something your father's side of the family doesn't know much about dishing out. I caught Sarvi trying to leave, and it's through Sala's magic that I was able to glean *why* they were leaving. It was because of you. You wanted to warn the Forest Gods and your sister about me. You wanted to cry for help, like a fucking baby."

She moves her sword to her other hand then back again. "If only you had kept your mouth shut, son. If only you had trusted me a little more. You could have kept up the charade. I would have kept it up for as long as you let me, but you worried about your father too much, didn't you? You immediately suspected me. Talk about playing favorites."

"Where is my father?" I ask, though I'm afraid of the answer.

"He's dead," she says sharply, and it's like a dagger in my heart. "Sala killed him. She's a Godkiller, you know, someone you would want on your side. Sala killed him and then tossed Hanna in the cell with him. They'll rot together in Inmost, the lovers they are. The last thing Hanna will see will be the Inmost dwellers running loose as they swarm to the surface to join the rest of the Bone Stragglers in my army."

"You will pay for this," I growl at her, fury rising inside me even though my heart is shattering like glass.

"Ha!" she says with a smirk. "I've already paid. I've made my sacrifices; I have since day one. Do you think I wanted to marry your father? I didn't. I did it to please my own father and to service the family line. And today, I will finally reap the rewards of all that I waited for. I shall start by bringing him back from the dead."

Who? Sarvi asks, voice shaking.

"So the unicorn finally decides to speak," she says. "If you had been paying attention at all, you would already know."

Rangaista, Sarvi says through a gasp.

"Yes. My demon father," she says with a nod. "One of the oldest of the Old Gods. Both of you will be instrumental to the process."

At that, she swiftly raises the sword above Sarvi's head.

"No!" I scream, breaking free of not-Hanna's grasp.

I run down the aisle, but it is too late.

The sword comes down.

Not on Sarvi's neck, but on Sarvi's horn, slicing it in half.

Sarvi lets out a brutal scream, and the half-horn clatters to the floor.

I holler, running full speed at my mother just as she turns the sword toward me.

I can see my own death, see that I'm about to be impaled and sent to Oblivion, and that will be all that I will ever know.

But at the last minute, my mother moves the sword out of the way.

She quickly brings it up and across, severing my own horns at the tips.

The impact knocks me off my feet, and I fall to the ground, just to see her catch the tips of my horns in her hands. She then picks up Sarvi's horn and takes them to the altar.

I never thought my horns would hurt if they were cut, but the pain is so excruciating, I can barely think, barely breathe. It may be even worse for Sarvi, whose screams still fill the crypt, burning my ears.

I writhe on the ground and glance up at the unicorn. Sarvi has collapsed to their knees, head hanging on the ground, twitching. I don't think this injury will kill me, but I don't know about Sarvi. It's possible that removing that much of the horn is akin to losing a limb.

"You'll want to be quiet, or you'll lose your wings too," my mother snaps at him. Then she nods at not-Hanna. "Make sure neither of them do anything stupid."

"Should I take them to the dungeon?" Not-Hanna asks.

"Wait," she says. "I want them to see how the Old Gods become the new gods. I want to them to see the downfall of their underworld as they know it."

This would be the time to run. If only I could just get up and run or attack my mother and kill her, kill Salainen, put an end to what they're about to do.

But the pain has me in a chokehold. I can't do anything but lie here and squirm and watch as my mother places a gold cauldron on the altar's table.

She starts to chant, pouring in various liquids from multi-colored vials, stirring them together with Sarvi's horn. My vision starts to blur, becoming grey at the edges, her voice going so high that the glass vials and containers start to shake and then, so low, the crypt itself starts to rumble.

At one point, the liquid in the cauldron starts to cast green shadows on her face, and in those shadows, I see the false face of my father fade. I see hers emerge.

And yet, it's not my mother anymore. She's becoming someone else, something else, something she's always kept hidden behind her already deadly façade.

The air is becoming heavy and musty now, smelling of dirt and decay. As the ritual progresses, the smell of death becomes stronger, filling my nose with a sickening stench, and it gets harder to breathe.

The taste of magic lingers in the air, sharp and metallic, almost tangible on the tongue. It's as if the very air is charged with darkness, ready to be unleashed.

I will be the witness.

My mother is making sure of that.

Finally, she picks up my horns and a dagger and starts shaving off bits into the cauldron. Sparks and smoke emerge, floating up through the air, and my mother bellows, arms held out to the sides.

Then she laughs and laughs and laughs.

The statues of dead saints that line the aisle begin to move. They lift their legs, marble and stone come to life, and walk to the altar with heavy, shaking steps to stand behind my mother. Their eyes gleam with a malevolent light as they raise their arms in a synchronized motion, their mouths opening in eerie unison. Their voices drone on and on until I have to press my hands over my ears, until it becomes louder and louder, impossible to keep out. It's no longer just words, but this frantic buzzing sound, like a million insects coming to the surface.

The ground beneath us trembles, sending cracks snaking through the ancient stones of the chapel floor, and parts of the ceiling start to fall, dust billowing into the room.

I lie frozen in terror and pain, unable to tear my gaze away from the surreal scene unfolding before me. My heart pounds in my chest, each beat echoing in my ears like a drum of impending doom. I feel as though I am on the precipice of something unimaginable, something beyond the realm of human or godly comprehension.

As the chanting reaches a deafening crescendo, a blinding light erupts from the cauldron, illuminating the chamber in a sickly green glow. Shadows twist and dance along the walls, taking on grotesque forms that seem to leer at me with malicious intent.

And then, with a final, ear-splitting shriek that pierces the air like a knife, the ritual reaches its climax. The ground tremors intensify, threatening to swallow us whole as the very fabric of reality seems to warp and twist around us.

The cracks in the aisle split open, right down the middle, just feet away from me.

A large, long arm emerges from the crack.

All black fur with long, red claws.

It's then I feel my horns being grabbed again, this time closer to my head. I yelp, trying to move out of the way, afraid I'll be dragged to the creature waiting in the fissure, but instead, not-Hanna is dragging me away from the altar, to the back of the crypt.

"You'll meet your grandfather some other day," my mother says to me while all the statues behind her grin in unison. "Better to introduce you slowly. I wouldn't want him to eat you all at once."

And at that, I'm taken straight to the nearest cell and thrown in there in a heap. The last thing I hear before I pass out is the sound of the cell being locked with a key, and then a deep, animalistic growl coming from inside the crypt.

CHAPTER 17

Lovia

THE OLD GODS

The bell should be ringing, I think.

But there is no sound.

I sigh, putting my head in my hands. I don't know how long I've been sitting on my boat, waiting at the dock, but it feels like forever. Time has been acting funny today, no matter how you look at it. Is this even still the same day? Or is it the next day? I seem to recall night falling, but it felt like it was only for a second.

At least the weather has calmed down. It's back to being still and gray, much like it usually is with my father. Perhaps the Magician was right, and my father did leave the match in one piece. He's probably back at Shadow's End right now, and, if it's the next morning, relaxing in bed with Hanna and a coffee.

But even though the weather is no longer as deathly cold and stormy, I can't seem to shake the feeling that something is wrong. It didn't help that the Magician's words were so unsettling and cryptic.

It also doesn't help that the bell hasn't rung once since I've returned to the boat. The last dead to enter Tuonela was Ethel, the senior serial killer, and there hasn't been anyone since. Sometimes, we don't even hear the bell ring—not every newly dead knows they're supposed to ring it—but even so, we instinctively know when the newest members of Club Dead are waiting for us.

And yet, for all the time that has passed, there hasn't been anyone.

It's beyond unusual. It's actually a little disturbing.

Where are the dead?

I should probably head down the river anyway, I think. Go past the forest and maybe say hello to the Forest Gods. Drop by my Aunt Vellamo in the Great Inland Sea. Perhaps go for a swim and give my mermaid friend Bell a visit. Or just make my way to Death's Landing, because, eventually ,someone has to die. It's just the way the world works.

I sigh again and look around. No point sticking around here. I guess part of me wants to go back to the Magician and talk to him some more, but he's got his job to do, and I've got mine.

Still, he can't do his job unless I bring him the dead.

I adjust the mask on my head and think about leaving the boat. But if I see the Magician now and the bell does ring, I'll just be further away. I'll have another talk with him when I drop the next person off.

I pick up an oar and push the boat off the dock, standing at the bow as it starts moving swiftly down the river, the cool misty breeze in my hair. I close my eyes and breathe in deep through my nose, the smell of the water usually invigorating.

Instead, I cough, my eyes suddenly burning as I smell a putrid, decaying stench. I know this the Land of the Dead and all, but for the most part, it doesn't smell like it. This is something rotten and sulfurous.

And wrong.

For a moment, I'm reminded of my mother.

I quickly twist around, expecting to see her somewhere, the glint of her horns, the cloak of her wings.

But I don't see her.

I see something else instead.

On the riverbank in front of me, the earth starts to move and crumble down into the water. It looks like something is trying to push itself up through the dirt. A giant earthworm, perhaps?

Yet as I stare at it in trepidation, my heart beating faster, I get the feeling that it's not something so harmless, and I start to steer the boat over to the opposite side of the river.

Just as something pushes out of the ground.

Horns.

A head.

Not just any head, though.

It's a deer skull, very similar to the one I have pushed up on my forehead.

Except the head coming out of the ground has to be the size of my entire body, the horns adding extra height, and as the dirt falls away, the horns suddenly catch fire. A flaming skull.

"What in the realm?" I breathe, watching in horror and confusion as the rest of the creature emerges.

It's not a deer at all. It's like a giant elk-human hybrid, a twenty-foot-tall creature of bones and sinew, finding its footing on top of the river bank. It looks impossibly strong and menacing, radiating energy not from this world or from any world I've known.

Eldritch horror. I've heard that phrase a few times, particularly when it comes to books, but I've never really understood what it meant.

Until now.

Until it turns its head towards me, and though it has only empty sockets for eyes, I know it sees me.

And it wants me.

Oh *hell* no.

I immediately grab my sword, holding it at my side while silently willing the boat to move faster. Thankfully, the boat seems to pick up speed, and the giant deer creature on the riverbank doesn't come after me. It just stares in my direction, and I get this feeling of crawling, buzzing insects in the back of my head.

What the fuck is that? I think, afraid to take my eyes off it. I watch it carefully until the boat goes around a bend in the river, and it disappears from view.

My whole life in this land, I've never seen something like that before. I haven't even heard about anything like that, not unless someone was talking about the Old Gods...

I give my head a shake.

No.

There is a rational explanation for that thing. The Old Gods are dead, and they aren't coming back, not unless someone raised them.

Someone like my mother...

Thud.

Suddenly, the boat comes to a stop, and I go flying down against the bow, nearly dropping my sword in the water. I straighten up and look around wildly. Did I hit a log? A sandbar? The boat isn't moving at all.

I look over the edge of the water, but I don't see anything in the murky darkness.

Wait.

A flash of something white and red.

Bones?

Blood?

Please don't tell me today is the day one of Vellamo's sea serpent monsters finally decides to have fun with me. I have immunity with the creatures of the sea, and normally they're not found this far up the river, but—

Thud.

The boat shakes violently, and I almost lose my balance.

I whirl around, my sword drawn.

I see six white claws wrap around the end of the boat, each claw the size of my forearm, then another six claws beside it, digging into the wood and making it splinter.

I gulp, the sword starting to shake in my hand.

Vellamo! I call out in my mind, hoping she can hear me. *I need a little help. One of your sea creatures is misbehaving!*

But then it pulls itself up.

And it's not a sea creature at all.

It's a giant beast with the face of a snouted creature, a row of serrated teeth at the end, like a crocodile if it were covered in matted red fur.

"Let my ship go!" I yell at the creature, surprised at the bravery in my voice.

Tiny yellow eyes blink at me from deep in the fur, like egg yolks in pools of blood.

It opens its mouth and hisses and snaps.

Then it starts climbing aboard the ship, making it list under the weight.

The rest of the creature is upright like a man, except it has a long, spiny, crocodile-like tail that thumps onto the deck, creating holes in it.

"Stay back!" I yell, holding out my sword. "I am the Goddess of Death!"

But the creature doesn't listen.

It doesn't care.

It lunges forward, the boat shaking, and I move out of the way just in time. I roll along the deck and get to my feet, close enough to drive my sword into the creature's side. The blade sinks in easily, like butter, but even though the creature cries out in pain, no blood comes from the wound.

Oh. No.

It reaches for me with a swipe of its claws, just catching the edge of my cape before I'm able to leap up on the railing and out of the way. Jumping into the river might be an option, but that thing is only going to swim after me.

My best chance to kill it is here and now.

I don't think I'm going to get many chances.

I look up and down the deck, the creature taking up at least half of it. There's not a lot of room to maneuver, not a lot of time to think.

What would kill this thing that doesn't even bleed?

It whips its spiky, reptile-like tail toward me, and I leap into the air over it, landing on its back.

The fur under my feet is coarse and slippery, making it difficult to maintain my balance, especially as the creature thrashes wildly, trying to dislodge me from its back. I cling on tight to the gross fur, my heart pounding in my chest as I try to think of a way to bring this beast down.

It lets out a roar that shakes me to my core, but I grit my teeth and stay the course. I can feel every muscle tense beneath me, every movement it makes as it throws its head back to try and snap at me.

I glance around its rotting body, searching for any sign of weakness, any vulnerability I can exploit. Most dead things will die again here and be sent to Oblivion, but the sword I drove into its side hasn't done any damage.

It bucks now, the tail swinging and taking out large sections of the railing, the wood splintering as I scramble for purchase on the creature's fur. If I don't kill it soon, it's going to sink the damn boat.

I try to move up the back toward the head, the brain the only vulnerable place I can think of. It might not have blood, but surely, it has some sort of nerve center telling it to act the way it is.

Slowly, I work my way up, nearly falling off as it tries to dislodge me, until I'm finally on its neck. I straddle it like I would a horse, my thighs squeezing tight.

It smells *so* bad.

With one hand wrapped tightly around the hilt, I raise my sword high and bring it down with all my might onto the creature's head. The blade pierces through the tough skull with a sickening crack, andhe creature lets out a guttural roar, its body convulsing beneath me.

As I pull my sword free, a strange black energy crackles around the wound, sending sparks flying in all directions, followed by heavy smoke. The creature's movements slow and then cease altogether. With a final shudder, it collapses to the deck, its ugly face gone still.

Breathless and covered in sweat, I stand over the fallen beast, adrenaline still coursing through my veins.

I think it's dead.

I hope it's dead.

But now what?

How do I get this thing off my boat? Or will it be stuck with me when I pick up the next newly dead at Death's Landing? That bell has to ring sometime, right?

But that thought fades from my head as I take a careful look around me.

In the distance, on a hill, I see another patch of earth pulsing as something moves beneath the surface. And beyond that, further still, a great boney hand comes out from the ground.

Everywhere I look, there are things, some just skeletons of men, some giants and monsters, ancient horrors that emerge from the soil, as far as the eye can see.

With clarifying dread, I know exactly what has happened.

Someone has raised the Old Gods.

And that someone is my mother.

CHAPTER 18

Hanna

THE UNCLE

The next day, Death and I sleep in a lot longer than planned. I've never been very good with jetlag, but I definitely didn't expect it when traveling across dimensions or portals or whatever you would call travel between worlds.

When we finally do rouse ourselves, it's nearly two p.m. Since we went to bed at eleven, we've had over fifteen hours of solid sleep. I suppose our bodies needed it—and who knows when our next good sleep will be.

I roll over and look at my husband.

How strange it is to think of him like that in this world.

But that's what he is.

We were married down in the crypt, and I took on the crimson crown.

I am his, no matter why he thinks I should stay behind in this world.

He had some points, of course. It's been a long time since I actually sat with my thoughts and examined what my hopes and dreams for this life were. Other than thinking about my father and his well-being, all my focus has been on surviving the Underworld and my marriage to Tuoni. Everything else just seemed like a dream I once had, something I could ponder when things finally slowed down, and I had some time to think.

Now, I'm here in the Upper World, and I'm realizing that even though this was my home and always will be, I can't let Tuoni go back without me. Perhaps it's because I love him (though he's still been careful to never say he loves me in return), or perhaps it's because I know I'm not done. There's a prophecy at stake, and I'm the daughter of a goddess—my story doesn't end here.

Is it possible that deep down, I knew I was never meant for a normal life?

I mean, I know that's what we all secretly think. We all think that maybe we really are *that* special, different in a coveted way. We grow up believing we might be some sort of chosen one no one has discovered yet.

And yet...and yet...

Here I am.

Lying naked in a hotel bed in Helsinki next to the God of Death, who happens to be a king and my husband and the man I love.

Because, fuck, I *do* love him.

With every fiber of my being.

Just watching him sleep here, in this Ikea-furnished, white-washed room so different from his black curtains and the obsidian walls of Shadow's End, I realize I will follow him to whatever world he chooses. He has my heart, every damn bit of it.

I just hope that one day, I will have his.

In the end, that's what I *truly* want.

His elusive love.

"You're staring at me," he says, his voice soft and rich with sleep, his eyes still closed.

"I like watching you sleep," I admit. It's very Edward Cullen of me.

A gentle smile forms on his full lips as he turns his head slightly, his eyes metallic in the dim afternoon light. "I slept like the dead," he says. "That was intended without pun."

I laugh and reach over, tracing the silver lines down his arms, all the way to his hand. I wrap my fingers around his, relishing the feel of his skin against mine. "Your lines haven't glowed once," I say. "I wonder what that means?"

"Perhaps no one is dying while I've been in this world," he muses.

"Wouldn't that be something? A blessing, really. That way, if *Kaaos* happens, no one will be hurt."

"Except for all of humanity inside the City of Death already," I say.

He frowns and sighs. "Yes. Except that."

"But maybe in the meantime, everyone on Earth is immortal. Can you imagine, death being put on hold temporarily?"

He purses his lips and considers it. "I wonder if anyone would notice here. I suppose not for a while, but it would be noticed in Tuonela. Lovia and Tuonen must realize something is happening. Fuck. I wish I could let them know what's happening. I hope it's not too late."

"On the plus side, at least we know that time over there is barely moving," I point out. "When we get back, we might have only been gone a day at the most."

"A lot can happen in a day if the Old Gods are raised," he grumbles. "And if Louhi resurrects her father, Rangaista, which I am sure she will, then..."

I lean over and kiss him on the cheek. "Then it's best we get started on finding our way back. We've already slept half the day away."

"That can't be," he says with a groan as he slowly sits up and I climb out of bed. "Why am I so tired then?"

"Because this world is particularly tiring," I tell him, grabbing some clothes and heading into the washroom. When I'm done washing up and getting dressed, I come back out to find him still totally naked and trying to fiddle with the Nespresso machine.

I sit on the armchair and ogle his ass for a bit while he struggles with the coffee maker. Fuck, is he ever built like a god. Strong, muscular thighs, solid round ass with just enough bounce. I just want to crawl over there on my hands and knees and bite him, lick the silver lines wherever they lead.

Yet, I know that would lead to sex, and in another world, we'd spend all day in bed fucking, but right now, we have a job to do.

So I help him with the coffee machine, promising him that once we leave the hotel, we'll stop by a shop and get him a proper cup. While it whirs and pours, I get to work on my phone.

It's damn hard not to get swept away with the internet. I know it has only felt like a few months while I've been at Shadow's End, but that's still a long time to go without checking your Instagram or Google news feed, and now, I have a whole year to catch up on.

Somehow, I stay focused. I still can't find much information about my father—the last stuff was him working at the resort before he "died." But searching through Facebook and then old emails, I was able to find out that my Uncle Osmo lives in Helsinki, working as a journalist for a local paper. My father had even emailed me his address once in case I wanted to come visit, his way of wanting to see me without any added pressure.

I stare at my father's email for a moment and the phone number in his signature. If I emailed him, would he believe it's me? If I called him, would he have a heart attack?

I decide to risk it and call him. I wanted to see him in person so he could see my face, so he could believe his daughter wasn't a ghost, but he should recognize my voice. Maybe I don't have to bother with my uncle at all.

But when I call the number, some robotic voice comes on in Finnish and then hangs up. Obviously, his number has since been changed or disconnected.

I glance out the window. Even though it's only three, it's starting to snow, and darkness is descending on the city. I'd forgotten how early the night comes here in the winter.

"I have a plan," I tell Tuoni, who by now has put some clothes on and become less of a distraction. "I tried to call my father, but I don't think his number is in service. I could email him, but I fear he'll treat it as a joke, and it will only hurt him. But I do have my Uncle Osmo's address here in the city. He's not too far. Let's get something to eat, get a coffee, and then wait until he'll probably be home from his job and pay him a visit."

Tuoni slowly nods, grooming his beard with his hands and making a small braid down the middle. "Isn't your uncle going to be shocked to find his dead niece on his doorstep?"

"He will be. He might call my mother. He might call the police. I don't want either of those things to happen. That's where you come in."

He grunts. "You want me to use my powers to influence his mind."

"Exactly. You're so good at it."

One shoulder lifts in a shrug as he finishes the braid. "I am. Let's just hope there are no dire consequences. We haven't even checked on the secretive guy to see if his mind still works properly."

Secretive guy? Oh right, the front desk clerk.

But when we leave the room and I ask the front desk clerk where to find good coffee, he's pleasant, if not bland, and there doesn't seem to be anything wrong with him that wasn't already wrong with him yesterday.

We exit the hotel and walk a couple of blocks until we come to the city's famous Fazer café. The moment we step inside, Tuoni's eyes light up like the Fourth of July. There are rows and stacks of colorful cakes, pastries, and desserts as far as the eye can see.

"We're eating here?" he asks in awe, and I have to giggle at how overjoyed he seems.

"Having cake for a meal is very Finnish," I tell him as I walk over to the counter, picking up a tray. "Besides, you get to have the best coffee this way."

Once we both decide on our cakes—chocolate for him, vanilla for me—we get two coffees, pay for it all at the register, and find a table. Naturally, everyone in the café looks over at Tuoni with interest, but they quickly look away and go back to eating in relative silence.

Both of us were hungrier than we thought, and thirsty too, so after we're done with the cakes, we grab a couple of *pulla* buns and get drinks to go—another coffee for him, while I get a hot chocolate with fat, pastel pink and green marshmallows.

"Amaranthus," Tuoni says again for the umpteenth time as we leave the café and step out into the dark city street. "Who knew coffee could taste so good?"

"Hey, the coffee you have at Shadow's End ain't half bad," I say, pulling out my phone with my free hand to look at the map and make sure we're walking in the right direction toward my uncle's apartment.

"Nah," he says with a sniff. "It's not the same. Something must happen when I have it smuggled through, or maybe my scouts aren't going to the right spots."

"Where do your scouts go?" I ask as we wait at a stoplight. I hold my arm across Tuoni's chest so he knows not to walk out in the middle of traffic again. "They aren't spat out in the Finnish wilderness, are they?"

He chuckles. "No. There is a portal underneath Shadow's End en route to the Crystal Caves. I've never dared to slip through myself, but I believe it takes the person directly to France."

"Ah," I say, walking as the hand flashes for us to cross. "That's probably where your daughter leaves from. She's talked about Paris a few times with me. Maybe she should be your scout going forward. That way, she can bring you back the best coffee, *and* she gets to go on her little adventures."

He grunts at that, but instead of looking annoyed at the idea of Lovia coming into the world and shirking her duties, he looks wistful. I can tell he's thinking about her, about Tuonen, missing them, worrying for them. I don't want to bring it to his attention, though, because he's apt to feel self-conscious.

"Here I was thinking the portal was hidden," he says, taking a sip of his coffee as we walk. "But I've underestimated Lovia too many times."

"So, when we get back, maybe Tapio's son really should be the one taking over their duties."

He glances at me with a solemn look. "When we get back, my children can have whatever the damn hell they want. I don't want to be a father who denies them anything anymore, especially not their happiness. I don't know what kind of world we're going to walk back in to, but it's not one where I have no faults. Things will change, in many ways, and for the better, when all is said and done."

"When all is said and done," I agree, tapping my cup against his.

We head toward my uncle's apartment, walking down a fir-tree lined path, Christmas lights still up on the branches. With the hot drinks in our hands and the snow gently falling around us, gathering on Tuoni's furs, the whole place looks absolutely magical.

Our boots crunch pleasingly in the snow as we carefully make our way up a slight hill, stopping in front of what should be my uncle's place, a four-story yellow building on Fabianinkatu.

"This must be it," I say, looking at the apartment directory for his name. My finger hovers on the button as I look at Tuoni. "Do you know what you're going to say?"

He arches a dark brow. "Do you?"

"I'm going to wing it," I say, pressing the buzzer.

Death scoffs under his breath. "Why am I not surprised?"

The buzzer rings and then crackles, and a man's voice comes through.

"Mitä?" he asks.

"Hi," I say in English before Tuoni leans in and says something quickly in Finnish that I don't catch.

Suddenly, the buzzer goes click, and the door opens.

"What did you say to him?" I ask incredulously as we step inside the building's dim foyer.

"I said I was his god and needed to speak with him immediately," he says, looking around. "What floor does this relative live on?"

I'm about to say the second floor when suddenly, a balding man with glasses and a kind face I recognize as my uncle pokes his head over the side of the staircase railing.

He says something in Finnish and waves at us to come up the stairs.

I'm still marveling at the fact that Tuoni was able to magic him through the intercom, and when we get to my uncle's side, I can see his eyes are glazed. He glances at me, but I can tell he doesn't really see *me*.

I'm tempted to say, "Hey Uncle Osmo, it's me Hanna, guess what, I'm not dead, I'm not a ghost, I didn't join a cult, I'm actually fine, long story", or however it would have turned out if I had winged it. But whatever Tuoni has done to him, he doesn't really see me for me, and anyway, when was the last time I physically saw my uncle? I would have been a child. I don't think he'd recognize me even if Tuoni didn't have him entranced.

I decide to keep my mouth shut and let the magic god do all the talking. My poor Finnish skills can only pick up a word here and there, but as we stand in the hallway of this old building, I get the impression that Tuoni is asking him about my father's whereabouts.

They talk for a few minutes before my uncle nods and disappears inside his apartment, leaving the door open.

I nudge Tuoni with my foot. "What's happening?"

He gives me a side-long glance and smirks just as my uncle returns and drops a pair of car keys in Tuoni's hand.

"Kiitos," Tuoni thanks him, and my uncle pats his hand and the keys a few times, nodding like Tuoni has done him some gracious favor before he goes back inside his apartment and closes his door.

"What the hell just happened?" I ask as I follow Tuoni back down the steps.

"I got ourselves a vehicle to your father's place."

"He knows where he is? Wait—we're stealing my uncle's car?"

"Clearly not. We're borrowing it. I told him he can pick it up from there in a couple of days. He thinks he's securing a place in Amaranthus by doing this."

I smack his chest. "Please tell me you're going to grant him that. You can't play with people's afterlife like that."

"It's as if you don't know who I am," he croons as we step out of the building and back into the cold, dark street. He nods at a red Saab across the street. "That's the one."

"So, wait," I say to him as we hurry across the road, "he told you where my father was?"

"Yes. He's up north. Not as far as he was before, but at a lake in the middle of a forest, living off some grid, in hiding."

"Why? Why is he in hiding?" I ask, panic coursing through me at the thought.

"I didn't ask," he says, pulling me to a stop and placing the keys in my hand. "I figured your father will explain when we find him."

"And he didn't tell you anything else?" I ask.

"He told me all I needed to know. In a few days, he'll remember where his car is, but he won't have any memory of us being here. In fact, if you were to go up and see him again, he wouldn't remember us. But we got the information we needed. So now, the question is, do we drive tonight to see your father, or save it for tomorrow?"

I ask for the address and then plunk it into my phone. It comes up as being in the middle of a national park, just below the Arctic Circle, and a ten-hour drive.

"We'll park the car by the hotel and head off early tomorrow morning," I tell him.

He gives me a broad smile, the kind that lights up his face and makes the silver in his eyes shine. "Does that mean we have time for more cake tonight?"

"Is cake another word for sex?"

He laughs. "Cake is cake, sex is sex. I will always make time for both."

The next morning, we wake up before dawn, which isn't saying much, since it doesn't get light outside until eight a.m. We didn't get as much sleep as we would have liked—yes, there was sex, and cake, but Tuoni was also up late because of all the coffee he was drinking. Who knew caffeine could affect a god so much?

We pack up our stuff and get in the car, with our little hotel coffees to go. I'm behind the wheel while Tuoni watches the sunrise and the city slowly come out of the darkness and back to life.

By the time we're five hours into the drive, I'm wishing I was the one staring out the window. It's tiring driving, even though there's not a lot of traffic on the highway, and the scenery hasn't changed much—trees, trees, more trees, the occasional moose on the side of the road, which has Tuoni marveling at how their bones aren't showing.

Another five hours, and we're driving through the dark, pulling off the main highway and down a snowy road that hasn't seen a snowplow in years. I don't know how I manage to drive the car without sliding into a ditch or a tree, but the Finnish tires seem to do a good job at keeping us safe and straight.

Finally, I spot some lights through the trees, so faint at first that I think they could be stars, except the skies are cloudy. We pull up to a cabin at the end of a lake, similar to the house I grew up in but much, much smaller.

I kill the engine and stare at the cabin, at its fading red-and-white paint and the dark roof with solar panels, its black-trimmed windows with a faint glow coming from inside, and I wonder how my dad could be here, this far off the beaten path. And why?

Perhaps this isn't even his place at all.

But then the porch lights come on and the door swings open, and my father steps out into the cold, bundling a scarf around his neck as he stares at us in wonder.

I give Tuoni a faint smile. "This is it. Let's hope he doesn't want to kill you on the spot."

I open the door and step out into the snow.

My dad comes forward a few feet, squinting at me, before pulling out a flashlight and shining it in our direction.

Then, he stops at the edge of the porch, still clad in heavy slippers, and the flashlight drops from his hands and into the snow.

"No," he says. "*Hellvete*, no. It can't be."

I smile and walk carefully toward him, not wanting to scare him.

"Hi, Papa," I say softly. "It's me."

"No," he says with a shake of his head, and with a painful pinch, I realize how much older he's gotten, even in the last year. Time hasn't been kind while I've been gone. "No, it's not...you aren't."

"I am."

I pick up the flashlight from the snow and step up onto the porch. We stare at each other for a heavy moment, so many words unsaid, and my father blinks at me, face blanching as if he's seen a ghost.

Because he's looking at one.

"Hanna!" he cries out softly, his face crumpling, and suddenly, any anger I've had towards him over his lies, over Rasmus and Salainen, all dissolve as he pulls me into a hug.

It's like I've brought my father back from the dead again.

Except I'm the one who died this time.

He holds me tight, sobbing softly, and I hold him just as tightly back.

"I can't believe it's you," he cries into my shoulder. "I thought I lost you. It didn't feel real, none of it felt real. I wanted to keep believing you were alive, that you would be found, and here you are."

"Here I am," I say. "And I have so much to tell you, so much to explain."

He pulls away, sniffling, his eyes wet as he presses his hands against my cheeks, the way he used to do when I was a kid. My heart sinks, breaks, melts, until I'm just drowning on my feet.

"I have things to explain too," he whispers, his eyes roaming my face.

"Things I should have told you a long time ago. Come on in. I'll get some tea going."

He breaks away, and I think he notices Tuoni for the first time.

I expect my father to be scared or angry seeing him, but he just stares at him and gives me a shy smile. "And who is this man who brought you to me?"

I look at Tuoni, brows raised, both of us realizing that my father hasn't just forgotten he was captured by Tuoni and held at Shadow's End.

He doesn't remember being in Tuonela at all.

CHAPTER 19

Death

THE FATHER-IN-LAW

I watch as the old man embraces his daughter, and I can't ignore the guilt that I feel, the fact that I took him from her and was prepared to keep him for good.

I'm this close to apologizing, to doing something that might resemble groveling, but then Torben Heikkinen looks at me, and he doesn't see me.

He doesn't know who I am at all.

Then, I realize that when I sent him away from Shadow's End with his memory erased, I didn't just erase the part of Hanna taking his place in the Underworld—I erased *all* of Tuonela from his existence, including myself.

In a way, it's a relief. For the time being, I can be Hanna's husband and lover, hopefully without him being too bothered by it. He won't know what I really am.

But I know that in order to find the portals back to my world, I will have to make him remember everything.

And then he'll hate me once again.

Until then, though, I am happy to play the role of a mortal.

"Papa," Hanna says to him as she gestures to me with a sweep of her arm. "This is my husband, Tuoni."

His eyes nearly fall out of his head. "You got married?" he exclaims.

At first, I think he's going to disapprove, but I suppose he's so elated that she's alive, he doesn't really care what she tells him.

"I did get married," she says.

"So, this is why you disappeared?" he asks, his puffy grey brows coming together in a frown. "You got married?"

"It's part of the reason," she says patiently. "And I promise I will explain everything. Just know that I am happy and I'm safe and Tuoni is a good man."

She gives me a secretive type of smile, and for some reason, it hits me right in the chest, her words following suit.

She's happy.

She's safe.

She thinks I'm a good man.

And somehow, *I* make her feel those things.

I swallow the strange lump in my throat, not liking these emotions that keep appearing out of nowhere. It must be the sentimental scene unfolding in front of me. Perhaps I've had too much coffee and cake, not enough sex.

She motions for me to come forward with a jerk of her chin, and I go to the trunk of the car, pulling out our bags. I have to assume he will let us stay the night, or it will be a long drive back to Helsinki.

I walk over to the cabin, and the porch groans from my weight when I step on it. Her father cowers slightly in a humorous way, a very Torben thing to do.

"You are a rather large man. Polynesian?" he asks, his eyes focusing on the silver lines on my neck.

"Mostly Finnish," I tell him.

"I see," he says. "Well, it's freezing out. Come in you two."

Hanna reaches out and gives my arm a squeeze before we follow him inside.

The cabin is toasty warm, bordering on hot thanks to a roaring fire, and it smells spicy, like cardamom and smoke. There are books everywhere, as well as a tiny kitchen with a wood stove, an old couch, and a couple of armchairs. There's a small loft up above with a narrow ladder that's about the size of one of my legs, and two doors, one that seems to lead to a bathroom, the other to a bedroom. I'm not sure where we'll be spending the night, but if I go up that loft, I will make half the cabin collapse.

"Here, please sit," he says, gesturing to the couch. "Water only boiled a few minutes ago, so I'll make us some herbal tea. Perhaps you'd like a biscuit? Are you hungry? Did you come from Helsinki?"

"Yes, to all the questions," Hanna says, sitting on the couch. I sit beside her, but there's not much room, so she's practically in my lap. That's fine with me. I put my arm around her, feeling like one of the old movies I liked to watch all the time, where a man was on a date with a woman and she brought him home to meet her family. It's strange to be living that kind of life, one so unlike my own, even if just for a minute. It's so disarming and surreal to feel and act like a mere mortal, a normal person.

There's some kind of beauty in the simplicity of it all, and none of these humans realize it.

"So," Torben says, bringing over a tray with two cups of steaming tea and a couple of flat, long biscuits. He sits down in the chair across from us, a bunch of books falling to the side and scattering to the floor. He waves at it, as if the books will clean themselves up later.

Then again, he is a Shaman. I've never seen a Shaman in his real habitat before. Perhaps I'm not so far from the truth.

"So," Hanna says, reaching for a biscuit. She doesn't eat it, just twists it around between her fingers. She's nervous. She has no idea where to start or what to say. She's going to try and wing it again.

I clear my throat. "I'm sure you're very surprised to see that your daughter is alive and well, but rest assured, she's been in good hands this entire time."

He blinks at me rapidly and then looks to Hanna. "Can I ask where you've been? Can I ask why you haven't told anyone? Hanna, dear, everyone thought you were dead. They also thought I was dead. Everyone said I had a funeral, that I had died, but that wasn't true. That never happened."

"What *did* happen?" Hanna asks, turning the questions to him already.

"Nothing," he says with a display of his hands. "I never heard about a funeral. You apparently came to visit me at the resort up north, but there was no record of you. I never saw you, I know that much."

"Was there..." she begins, weighing her words. "Was there someone else at the resort who perhaps might have lied about all of that?"

He blows his lips together. "They might have."

"Who is they?"

"Eero and Noora worked with me up north, or they did until... anyway, they disappeared. At first, I thought maybe they had something to do with your disappearance, since it seemed to happen around the same time. I searched everywhere, but no one could help..." He trails off, worrying his lip between his teeth. "You see, Eero and Noora are special people, and I thought maybe they had ways..."

"Are they why you're in hiding?" I ask.

"Hiding?" he repeats, his eyes narrowing. "Who said I was in hiding?"

"Your brother," I tell him. "He gave us his car to come and see you. Didn't you wonder how we found you?"

"Well, yes, but sometimes things just work out in mysterious ways."

He doesn't know we both know he's a Shaman. It's something he has kept from Hanna her whole life, along with his many other secrets.

"So why are you in hiding?" Hanna asks. "Is it something to do with them?"

"You're asking me all the questions," he says. "I'm the one who should be asking you."

"Then ask," she says, cupping her tea in her hands and taking a delicate sip. The way she drinks tea reminds me of a bird. My little bird.

"Alright," he says, looking between the both of us. "Where have you been? Why haven't you kept in touch? An email or a phone call would have gone a long way."

"She has been indisposed," I tell him. "And if we tell you exactly where she's been, there's a chance you might not believe us."

"You can try me," he says, straightening up and folding his hands in his lap. "I believe most things. I've seen a lot in my life."

"I'm sure you have," I say. "Shamans see more than most people ever will."

Everything seems to go still and quiet at once, even the crackle of the flames turning off, as if a switch has been flipped. That's his Shaman magic on high alert.

"Shaman?" he repeats, but his face is blank, carefully so. "I don't know what you're talking about."

"So this is how it's going to be," I say, relaxing back into the seat. "That's fine. I'll just have to make you remember a little earlier than planned."

"Already?" Hanna asks me.

"It's for the best," I tell her.

"The best for whom?" she counters.

I can almost hear her thoughts. It's not the best for her, for me, or for her father, for him to remember the tangled web we've all weaved around each other, but him knowing the truth will make the next part much easier.

None of us will have to lie, which means we can deal with the truth and get back home faster.

"What are you talking about?" Torben asks, frowning at Hanna. "Make me remember what?"

She continues to twist the cookie her hands. "Can I ask you something?"

He gives her a bewildered shrug. "Go right ahead."

"Do you approve of my husband?"

He looks at me and gives another light shrug. "I don't know the man, but if what you say is true, if you're happy and safe, then I suppose I have to take your word for it."

"Does it count if I say she also makes me very happy?" I say, and Hanna shifts beside me, shooting me a warm smile.

"Hanna would make any man happy," he says proudly. "She's the catch here, and don't you forget it. Tuoni, was it?"

"That's correct."

"Curious name," he says. "Being named after the God of Death."

I smile at him. "That's the thing, Torben. That's the very thing I want to talk to you about. That's the thing I want you to remember."

He stiffens in his chair. "What?"

I close my eyes and give my head a small shake. "I should have enjoyed having you as a father-in-law who doesn't want to kill me just a little longer."

"There's still time," Hanna says quietly, and I feel her hand on my arm.

"You know there's enough lies in your family already," I tell her.

Then I sigh and start chanting under my breath, a quick incantation, a fast unraveling of a spell. I can feel it working when the darkness inside me begins to spin, and I have to open my eyes to steady myself.

I'm already tense, poised to fight, even though Torben has never been much of a threat. So far.

He's staring at me, mouth slowly hanging more open as his eyes get wider. He gasps, his hand at his chest, and then he tries to move back so fast, the chair topples over backward, depositing him on the floor.

"Papa!" Hanna cries out, the tea spilling as she gets to her feet and runs over to him.

"Hanna!" he yells from a heap on the floor, hidden by the chair. "Run, Hanna! Run while you have the chance!"

He staggers to his knees and tries to push her along, but she stands her ground and holds him back at the shoulders.

"Papa, it's okay. I'm fine. It's fine."

"No, Hanna," he says in terror. He turns to look at me, and I remain as impassive as I can possibly. "He's here. He has come for you."

"I'm not here for her, old man," I say to him. "We're here for you."

"Please," she says, giving him a shake until he looks at her. "Everything is fine. I am fine. Neither of us are in any danger right now, I promise. Just please sit down and let everything come back to you. Let it sink in so we can explain what's happening to us, why we both need your help."

He blinks at her, mouth agape, and she squeezes his shoulders, imploring him with her eyes. Finally, he nods once, and she lets go of him. She rights his chair back up and then makes him plop down in it.

Torben looks across at me now, totally stunned.

And where moments earlier I saw a man who was only merely suspicious of my intentions, I now see a man who completely hates me.

And I can't blame him one bit.

"Torben," I say gently.

"Tuoni," he says in a rough scowl. His eyes flash, like he suddenly remembers something, and he jumps up to his feet, but Hanna is still hovering over him, pushing him back down.

"Stop," she says to him. "Just listen while we explain what's happening."

He looks to her, his expression falling. "My darling girl, you gave up your life to save mine. You freed me from his prison."

"I did," she says to him with a heartbreaking smile. "And I would do it again in a second. But you need to know that everything that has happened since has turned out fine."

More or less.

"Bah!" he cries out before he looks at me, pointing his finger. "You! You erased my memory!"

"I had to. It would have caused you too much grief otherwise," I tell him.

"But your erasure of my memory led to a different path of grief!"

"I couldn't foresee that. I did what I could," I try to explain. "I did what I thought was best for everyone."

"Papa," Hanna says to him gently. "It's okay. What's done is done. Now you remember. Now you know the truth about everything and everyone."

"Oh God," he says, his head in his hands. "I am so confused. This is too much for my old brain."

"Tell us what happened since you came back," I say to him.

He looks up at me and opens his mouth to say something, only to snap it shut for a moment. "Wait," he eventually says, a look of horror slowly coming across his brow. "Wait a minute. When you first got here, Hanna, you said he was your husband. That's not true. That was a lie, a role, wasn't it? Please tell me it was."

I exchange a wince with Hanna, which makes her father gasp.

"No," he cries out. "No, you didn't *marry* him."

"I'm sorry," I tell him, biting back a grin. "But you are, in fact, my father-in-law now."

He's about to spring to his feet again, but Hanna keeps him down.

"We didn't get married under the best terms," she tells him. "And it wasn't always easy, but it's much easier now."

His nose wrinkles. "I don't understand. How can you call marriage to the God of Death easy?"

"I don't know," she says, and something cold and calculating gleams in her eyes. "I mean, marriage is hard, isn't it? Sure, I was forced into marriage with Tuoni, but at least it was honest. At least there were no lies between us." She pauses, and I can tell she's going in for the kill. "At least Tuoni is a good husband, not one who goes off and impregnates both a demon *and* the goddess of the sun."

If I thought I felt sorry for Torben earlier, I *really* feel for him now. Granted, this is his mess that he created, and it's a big fucking mess when you consider what both of those offspring are doing right now in the Underworld. Still, it must be hard to realize you've fucked up that badly.

"What...what are you..." he begins.

"There is no point pretending with her, Torben," I warn him. "She's smart, and she's rightfully upset by your hypocrisy, as am I."

"You?" he cries out. "Why should you be upset? None of this concerns you."

I laugh, the sound dry and mirthless. "Oh, but that's where you're so very wrong. You see, it was because of your careless indiscretions that the two of us are here to begin with. We aren't in your world by choice. We stumbled here trying to find a way out of Inmost, because your dark magic daughter, the one you created and discarded with the help of my ex-wife, whom you know intimately, and your bastard, red-headed son, decided that now was a good a time as any to try and kill the both of us and raise the Old Gods."

Torben's brows go up to the ceiling, his fingers curling around the arms of his chair. "What?" He looks to Hanna, shaking his head. "I don't..."

"What are you denying?" Hanna asks. "The bastard, or the abandoned magic baby?"

He swallows, looking pained. "The bastard."

She looks over at me. I nod, giving her the floor. Since he doesn't know, he should hear it from his daughter.

"Rasmus," Hanna says to him. "Your son is Rasmus."

He blinks in shock. "No. He can't be."

"I'm sure if you look deep inside, you'll know it's true," she says gently. "Perhaps you've always suspected in some way, in your heart."

"But...how?"

I sigh and lean forward with my elbows on my thighs. "You're asking how? Allow me to explain to you how a particularly demonic woman can be especially good at seduction." Hanna stiffens at that, and I wink at her. "Fear not, fairy girl, I'm not singing her praises. Her demon ways also allow her to be adept with magic. Some magic is irresistible to a Shaman. Isn't that why you often came to Tuonela, Torben? For the magic? Well, Louhi worked her magic on you."

Fear passes over his face, distorting his features. "No."

"Yes," I tell him emphatically. "Rasmus is your son. Louhi gave birth to him thirty years ago and had him deposited in this world. And because the Creator and the Fates have a sense of humor, you took a baby created with shadow magic and deposited it in my world. Speaking father to father, you're not doing that great of a job at it, are you?"

"And what of you?" he scowls at me. "You think you're coming across as someone worthy of respect? Someone with morals? You kidnapped me."

"You were trespassing," I tell him sharply. "And perhaps I should have kidnapped you a long time ago, if not to teach you a lesson so you wouldn't mess with the gods like you have."

"You're a monster," he sneers.

"I am what I am," I counter. "Sometimes, I am a monster. Sometimes, I'm a father, a god, a king...a husband. Sometimes, I am just trying to do the right thing, and that's why we're here. Because I need to do the right thing, or else the entire world will be in jeopardy."

"And that's why we need your help," Hanna says to him. "Papa, I know you have your misgivings about what happened between you and Tuoni, with me and Tuoni, but we have to put that aside for now. We need you to take us to the portal, the one by the resort, the way I got in. We need to get back home."

He stares at her for a moment, heartbreak in his eyes. "But *this* is your home, Hanna."

She gives him a sad smile. "It will always be my home. *You* will always be my home. But I have two homes now." She pauses. "And both of them are at risk. If we don't get back there to defeat Louhi and the Old Gods, then every living being will suffer in death. We can't let that happen, no matter what. Besides, the gods and creatures in Tuonela are at risk too. What happens if they're all sent to Oblivion?"

He shrugs. "I really couldn't care."

"You'd say that even about my own mother?"

Ah. She's got him there. He goes still, swallowing audibly.

"So you know about her," he says quietly, looking over at the fire. "I guess you would have if you had learned about the other baby. Have you met Päivätär yet?"

"Not yet, and I would like to before the Old Gods decide she needs replacing."

He sighs and runs his hands over his face. Now I really feel sorry for him. He's fucked up in so many different ways, with so many different knots, it's hard to know which one we need to untangle first.

"Alright," he says carefully, his voice sounding broken. "Alright then. We leave tomorrow morning. We will need our sleep tonight." He looks up and eyes me, then Hanna. "I'll bring you to the portal, but I must warn you, it will be dangerous."

"Why?" I ask.

"Because of the reason I'm in hiding," he says with a wince. "Because I'll finally be in the open. Because there are people who want to kill me—and they'll have no problem killing you too."

CHAPTER 20
Hanna
THE NORTH

It will come as no surprise, but I barely slept a wink. Not only was there too much to think about, but my father's cabin isn't exactly built for size, nor privacy. I took the single bed upstairs in the loft, but because of Tuoni's frame (and the fact that he would probably crush the ladder), he took my father's bed, and my father begrudgingly took the couch that was too small for my husband to stretch out on anyway.

Unfortunately, my father snores like an old engine, and even the earplugs that came in the hotel's vanity kit didn't block it.

But eventually, the morning rolled around. We got up with the dawn and had coffee and more cardamom buns, packed up my father's SUV (leaving the keys in my uncle's car for when and if he comes to get it, plus a wad of euros for his trouble), and left the cabin.

In the morning light, things seem a little brighter, the land up north not so isolated or threatening as it seemed yesterday. Still, it doesn't take long for the conversation to take a dark turn.

"I need an army," Tuoni says from the back seat.

I stop trying to find a radio station and look back at him. "What do you mean?"

"We need an army to stop Louhi. She'll be taking over mine if she hasn't already. The Old Gods, the Bone Stragglers—my army will be corrupted in no time. They have loyalty to me in spades, but if they think Louhi is me, their king, they'll do whatever she says. They will usher in *Kaaos*."

My father eyes him in the rearview mirror. "Surely you have your family of gods."

"I hope," he says stiffly. "But there are only so many of us, and there are more Old Gods. We could defeat the armies, perhaps, but against the Old Gods, I am unsure. The magic used to resurrect them might be enough to protect them from being killed, and if there is a way, I don't know if there are enough of us to be a threat. Vellamo and Ahto are formidable, but I have never seen Kuutar or Hanna's mother express any interest in what happens below the sky, and my sister Ilmatar is as useless as a wet blanket. Tapio seems gentle, but I know the man can fight. But his children? Even my children? Do they have what it takes?"

I'm about to remind him that Lovia is a great fighter, but then again, I did kick her off her own riverboat. I decide not to bring that up.

"What about the giant Vipunen?" my father asks.

"He's the card I'm carrying in my back pocket," Tuoni says. "The problem is, I'm not sure what the card will say. Vipunen has always remained a mystery to me, to all of us. If he decrees that he will stay out of it and let things unfold in whatever way they need to, then he is no help to us. Just a witness to the end."

"Then you need recruits," my father says. "From somewhere else."

"Where else is there?"

My father gives him a steady look in the mirror.

"This world?" Tuoni says incredulously. "You're suggesting I bring people from this world into the Underworld?"

He lifts a shoulder and gives him a fleeting smile. "You're the God of Death. I'm sure you could arrange something. We can bring more than a few people through the portal. Perhaps make a bargain with them. You seem to like bargains. Promise them immortality, and if you can't do that, at least guarantee their return."

"No," Tuoni says. "That wouldn't work."

I twist in my seat to look at him. "Why not?"

He raises his brows at me, a gleam in his eyes. "Oh, so now you're no longer the morality police?"

"What does that mean?"

"You think I should use the powers that be to command mortals into Tuonela to fight in an army they'll most certainly die for?"

I let out a huff of air through my nose. "Look, this is war. Tough decisions have to be made."

He grins at me, both carnal and sinister, and it sends a shiver down my spine. "You're talking like a queen again, a ruthless one. You know how much I like that."

He deliberately runs his hand over his crotch, and I give my head a violent shake.

Not here, I say, pleading with my eyes. *Not with my dad in the car.*

But he just stares at me with all that molten heat, that cunning curve of his lips.

My father clears his throat. "I suppose there isn't time to find an army either way. That would take a lot of time and effort, and we need to get to the portal as quickly as we can."

I give Tuoni one last warning look and then turn around in my seat. "You're right. There's no time." I glance at my father. "And like you said, we may have dangers on this side."

"So tell me again, Torben," Tuoni says. "How did these Shamans try and kill you, and how do you know they're *still* trying to kill you?"

"I don't know if they still are, but I don't want to take that chance," he explains. "As I told you last night, I don't remember much. I don't remember when I left Tuonela. Suddenly, I was back at my cabin by the resort, waking up in the middle of the night to the sound of the door opening. It felt like I'd been asleep for days, weeks. I didn't really know where in time it was. By the time I was on my feet, Noora and Eero attacked me."

"With weapons or with magic?" Tuoni asks.

"Noora had a knife," he says, his knuckles going white as he grips the wheel. "But Eero had magic. It doesn't matter, though. They didn't get far. My own magic was far more powerful. Of course, now I know why. Though my memories of going into Tuonela for magic or to prolong my life were gone, the magic I had gleaned over the years was still in me, and it came in handy right when I needed it." He sighs. "I didn't kill them, though perhaps I should have. I merely stunned them enough for me to leave. All my instincts told me to get the hell away from them; perhaps it was you guiding me in some way, Hanna. I knew I had to go into hiding. I used a spell to cloak myself, found my father's old cabin, and watched the fallout in secret. The only person I talked to was Osmo, since he owns the cabin."

"So even my mother, the mortal one, didn't know what happened to you?" I ask.

"No," he says. "And therefore, she doesn't know what happened to you. Have you contacted her yet?"

I shake my head, my lips pressed hard together, trying to ignore the guilt.

"You probably should," he says. "Just to let her know you're alive."

"It will only raise more questions. It will only make her worry more," I say.

"Believe me, sweetie, your mother is worrying every day of her life. She is in hell with no escape. I know you had a complicated relationship, perhaps even more complicated than ours, but you are still the daughter she raised. Send her an email if that's all you can do, but make sure you do it. She deserves some sort of peace, even if she doesn't believe it."

Fuck. I know he's right. I should probably do it right now, though I'll be afraid of the reply. Maybe I'll send it just before we go into the portal; that way, I don't have to worry about it afterwards.

"Must be strange, missing a year of your life," my father comments after a moment. "I'd say the same happened to me, but I was here living it. I just didn't really know it."

"It's been a real trip, that's for sure," I admit with a sigh. "In some ways, I haven't really missed anything. The world still looks the same. Same two-faced people still in power. Same atrocities being committed. Same war. Same ignorance. Same late-stage capitalism slowly killing people."

"That's true," he says with a nod. "And none of my favorite television programs have returned either." He clears his throat and glances at me. "I think when we find the portal, me and Tuoni should go through, and you stay behind in this world. I think it's for the best."

"You and *him*?" I ask, jerking my thumb at the backseat. "Neither of you would get ten feet without trying to kill each other."

"You know I don't have to *try*," Tuoni says with a grunt.

"Okay, Yoda," I say to him as I shake my head. "No. It's not up for discussion or debate. I am needed in that world. I'm going."

"You are needed in *this* world," my father counters, raising his voice slightly, his cheeks going red. "The Land of the Dead is no place for a girl of the living."

"Even one whose mother is the Goddess of the Sun?" Tuoni asks.

"Even so."

"Even though I'm the one prophesized to unite the land? How can that world be united if I'm not there?" I ask.

"Phhfff," my father says. "I know you're special, Hanna, you truly are, always have been. But who says you're part of the prophecy?"

"Because the prophecy says the one who unites the land is the one who touches Death," I say, holding up my hand. "And I can touch Death."

I glance back at Tuoni and nod at him to take off his glove. He does so slowly.

My father takes his eyes off the road and looks back. "What are you doing?" he asks frantically.

"Don't worry," I tell him as Tuoni brings his hand forward. "Just keep your hands on the wheel and your eyes on the road."

But it's too late. The car is already swerving on the highway, my dad watching in horror as Tuoni wraps his large, warm bare hand around mine.

"Hanna!" my father cries out. "Stop!"

I can only smile up at Tuoni in response as he stares down at me with a tenderness that's absolutely disarming in the moment. Such a small thing, to touch each other like this, and yet it means so much to both of us.

"I can't believe it," my father says, looking back to the road and correcting the car. "That can't be."

"Believe it," Tuoni says gruffly before he gives my hand a kiss and then sits back in his seat, slipping on his glove back on. "But don't get any ideas. She's the only one I can touch without killing."

"Just as the prophecy says," I tell my father.

"I'll be damned," he says to himself.

"You might be," Tuoni says, "if you don't get us through the portal and back to Tuonela. How much longer is it?"

"Another couple of hours," he says, glancing at the clock.

"Then might I request we stop at one of those automobile houses that serves coffee? I have a feeling we're all going to need it."

Luckily, the next service station isn't too much further. My father fills up the SUV, and Tuoni gets his gas station coffee. He doesn't seem that impressed, but he drinks it anyway. At least it's not decaf.

Another hour and a bit later, and things start to look familiar—well, as much as they can in the monotonous land of ice and snow. I recognize the airport on the outskirts of Ivalo, then the drive I had once made with Noora. The fact that we are getting closer to her domain makes me sit up and pay attention, even as twilight begins to fall.

Everyone else in the car seems more on edge too, especially as we turn off the highway at a sign for the resort.

"So what's the plan if they're still working there?" I ask. "You went into hiding, but they may have not."

"They won't be," my father says. "I know the people there. I haven't kept in contact with them, but I know they wouldn't hire them back, not when they just disappeared like that. Things got strange after both our disappearances, Hanna. It looked badly on them that both you and I disappeared after being in contact with them."

"But you said we are still in danger," Tuoni says.

"Yes. We are. They might not be here, but at my cabin? The portal? That could be another story entirely."

The resort looms ahead of us at the end of the road, the tips of the buildings jutting out between the tall, narrow trees, a dusting of snow everywhere.

My father takes the closest entrance, one that looks like a service road, and then parks the car as far from the buildings as possible.

"Is this it?" Tuoni asks, leaning forward and peering out the window. The only light is coming from a streetlight in the parking lot a few meters away. The woods beyond are one dark shadow.

"This is the start of the walk," my father says, getting out of the car.

"I wish I could conjure up a sled to make the way easier, but the least I can do is call my reindeer."

He stands a few feet away from the car and whistles into the darkness. At first, I think maybe he's losing it a little, but by the time Tuoni and I get out of the car, throwing on our parkas and hats, I hear a shuffling sound in the forest. It grows louder and closer until suddenly, two reindeer come darting out from between the trees, heading straight for us.

"So what they say about the Shaman is true," Tuoni says, sounding reluctantly impressed. "You really are the wardens of the forest."

The reindeer look identical, and it's impossible to tell if one of them is the one I met before when they were with Rasmus. They both go to my father and nuzzle him.

"Here," he says. "This one is Sulo, and this one is Sula. Hanna, you'll be riding Sulo. Sula will carry your gear."

"Are you sure?" I ask.

Sulo comes straight over to me and nudges me with his soft nose.

"Hi," I say to him, looking into his deep dark eyes. "I guess you remember me."

"Ah," my father says. "Because of Rasmus. He was rather fond of the reindeer. If we ever get him back from Louhi's clutches, I'm sure he'll be happy to be reunited."

"First things first," Tuoni says gruffly, throwing our bags up on Sula's back and fastening the handles together so they both hang over like saddlebags. "We get to Tuonela before we talk about what happens after. The quicker we're out of any danger or disturbances on this side of the Veil, the better."

My father nods, and then everything happens quickly. I'm hoisted up onto Sulo's back, my father and Tuoni get themselves outfitted, and then we start walking off into the woods.

"I'd suggest we go to my cabin first," my father says, walking ahead of me, with Tuoni right behind my reindeer. "Perhaps have some tea and biscuits and warm up by the fire. But—"

"No time," Tuoni grumbles.

"There's no time," he says with a sigh. "It's just been so long since I've seen it. I know it's still destroyed from the fight, maybe even ransacked by the police, but it would be a lovely sight anyway. Then again, perhaps that's where Eero and Noora are hiding, waiting in vain for me to come back."

"What's their deal anyway?" I ask. "If they're Shamans, why do they hate you so much?"

"Jealousy, I suppose," he says. "I was always able to do more than them."

"Jealousy doesn't explain all that they've done," I say. "No one is that deranged, especially two of them."

"Well, perhaps they've been infiltrated by Louhi," he says. "When I knew her, she often talked about having influence in this world. She was obsessed with Shamans and their magic. That's probably why she had the boy."

"It *is* why Louhi had Rasmus," Tuoni explains. "He eventually became a weapon for her. She likes to play the long game, as they say."

"So Noora and Eero are working for Louhi," I muse as the reindeer sways back and forth underneath me. "It's hard to know who isn't connected to her."

Tuoni exhales heavily. "I know. I should have done more due diligence with her, watched her more closely instead of looking the other way and wishing she'd take a wrong step into the Star Swamp."

"We've all done things we regret, things we could've done better," my father says tiredly. "I suppose the only good thing about hindsight is the ability to apply it to the future. Oh, would you look at that!"

I'd been staring at the lantern on the back of my father's belt and the way it has been casting shadows over the snow, so when I look up to follow my father's gaze, I gasp.

The northern lights are dancing above the treetops, casting the sky in slow moving shades of green and purple, twinkling stars appearing in the inky depths beyond.

"My stars," I hear Tuoni, honest awe in his voice. "Is this the aurora borealis?"

"Yes," my father says back at him. "You've never seen them before?"

"I'm not sure they exist in Tuonela," he says. "And if they do, that sky has been covered by clouds for too long for anyone to notice. At least, it was that way until I met Hanna."

It's my father's turn to grumble. "I have to admit, I don't think I'll ever get used to the two of you together in any way, shape, or form. It's not...natural."

"Oh, but it feels very natural," Tuoni says in a knowing tone, and I give him a look over my shoulder to not get weird again.

Thankfully, the conversation is dropped after that. We continue to walk through the forest under the northern lights for another hour, maybe two. My nose is starting to freeze, and I know I'll need to stop soon to warm up. Maybe going to my father's cabin first would have been a better idea.

All you need to do is get to the waterfall, get through the portal, and then you'll be in the land where you won't feel so frozen.

And it's not long after I have that thought that my father comes to a stop.

"We're getting close now," he whispers. "The river is just over there, the one that comes from the waterfall. Both will be frozen right now, but we're almost there."

We keep going, the path between pines getting narrower until suddenly, it opens up. Under the glow of the lights and the moon and the lantern is the frozen waterfall, just as I remember it last time.

"What is this?" Tuoni asks as my father comes over to me, gesturing for me to get down.

"It's the entrance to the portal," he explains as I climb off the reindeer and land in the snow. "Right behind that frozen waterfall. This is where we leave the reindeer. Come now, grab your bags. No sense going into the other world without a change of clothes."

Tuoni grabs the bags off the other reindeer, and both animals turn to run off into the forest, more than ready to get out of here. Weird vibes, I suppose. My father is already walking ahead, and I shuffle through the snow to catch up. At least by walking, I'm getting a little more warmth into my body.

But as we come along the ledge leading to the waterfall, my father suddenly stops just behind the sheet of frozen water.

"Dear God, no," my father whispers.

"What is it?" Tuoni booms, walking over to stand beside him.

I hurry forward and look around them to see what they're staring at.

In the dim light of my father's lantern, I can see the remains of what once was a tunnel. Dirt and rock flow out of the hole, creating a mound that nearly touches the ceiling. There's no way to get into that tunnel, not unless you had several days and an excavator.

My father sighs. "The portal is gone."

CHAPTER 21

Lovia

THE UPRISING

I *need to get the fuck out of here*, I think, looking around me at the Old Gods rising from the earth. *I need to get help.*

The only problem is, the dead crocodile beast on the boat is kind of weighing things down more than I'd like. Would it be quicker to go back upstream with the boat? Logic says it would be safest, but I also feel like I'd be a sitting duck, especially if I had to go past that giant elk monster.

I decide to take my chances on land. At least I can run fast.

I manage to steer the boat to the side of the river that doesn't seem to have a lot of dead things reanimating, and then I grab my sword and jump off the boat. I head into the tree line where the forest comes down on the slopes of the mountains and take cover beneath the canopies, letting the cedars shield me from view of any Old Gods who may decide to pop up along the riverbank.

I start heading back to the City of Death. It will be a long walk, but it's closer than the Hiisi Forest, and once there, I can hopefully find the Magician. My end goal is to make it back to Shadow's End, but with all that's happening—dead people, Old Gods, and Bone Stragglers rising—I can't count on my father being there. He wouldn't let any of this happen.

Which means something really has happened to him, I think. *My mother must have gotten her claws in him somehow. But how? How is that even possible?*

Tears spring to my eyes, but I angrily brush them away with the heel of my palm. There's no use thinking about this now. I can't let my emotions run away on me. When they do, I can't think, can't act, and I need to do both of those things right now.

I keep walking beneath the trees, relishing the smell of the cedar keeping the stench of death at bay. Every now and then, a Bone Straggler pops up through the ground, but I make quick work of them with my sword. I do it silently, so as not to draw any more attention to myself. I can defeat them one or two at a time—thankfully, they are easier to kill than the Old Gods—but if a bunch of them got wind of me and started to attack at once, that would be a different story.

Eventually, I reach the dock, where I tie up to walk to the City of Death. It's been destroyed, giant footprints left behind in the light dusting of snow. They look like they belong to a rabbit, if rabbits were ten-feet tall, and unfortunately, that might be the case.

I look around, expecting the giant rabbit to come out to get me, or that deer beast, or some other creature of cosmic horror, but it seems totally deserted. I take a closer look at the giant bunny prints and see skeletal footprints join up with it, along with other weird tracks. All of them are pointed south in the direction of Shadow's End, as if all the resurrected beings have been called there through some internal messaging system.

Gee, that's not unsettling at all, I think.

Still, I can't afford to let my guard down, especially not as I'm about to make the long, desolate track to the City of Death, where I'll be completely exposed to assailants.

So, I start running. The further inland I get, the more worried I get. The despairing thoughts keep jutting into my brain, wanting me to spiral out of control. Where is Tuonen in all of this? Is he safe? If my mother somehow infiltrated Shadow's End, would she actually hurt him? I'd like to think she wouldn't, but I also know my brother. He's got a good heart underneath that blasé attitude, and I know he'd do what he could to stop our mother if she was intent on doing something devastating.

What would she do then? Would she choose her son over her ambitions?

Fuck, I hope so.

I give my head a shake as a fine drizzle starts to fall. Clouds roll in, dark and low, the air eerily still. Though the snow is gone and I'm in the sand of the rocky desert, the mist makes it seem like I'm walking into infinity.

Then, out of the grey, comes a shadow.

I stop, my hand at my sword, and watch with bated breath.

From a distance, it's hard to say how big the figure is—could it be a monster?

But as it gets closer, I realize it's the size of a tall man, and it's not a walking skeleton either.

It's a man in a cloak.

The Magician.

"Loviatar!" he calls out to me, walking quicker now, and I run a couple of steps to meet him.

He stops in front of me, holding me by the elbow with his velvet gloved hands as I stare into the void of his face, at the spinning galaxies and shooting stars.

"I thought you would be dead by now," he says. His normally calm and serene voice is panicked. "The Inmost dwellers have taken the city!"

Fuck.

"What happened?" I ask.

He shakes his head. "I don't know. I should know, but I didn't see this coming. It had been so long since you brought me another dead that I went inside the gates to see if I could find out what was amiss. All I saw were the Inmost Dwellers running to the Golden Mean. Someone said they had all been let loose."

"By who?"

"I don't know, but I know it wasn't your father."

"No," I say grimly. "It wasn't him."

"It was Louhi," he says. "Perhaps not by her physical form, but at least indirectly. That much I know."

"And she's awoken the Old Gods," I tell him. "I've seen it with my own eyes. That's what I was coming to tell you. There hasn't been any dead to transport, but I decided to head down anyway, and that's when I saw them. They started rising out of the ground, like half-dead monsters, creatures I'd never seen before—the Bone Stragglers too."

The Magician doesn't say anything for a moment as two moons seem to spin around where his eyes should be. It gives me the impression of a computer processing or, more likely, a universe of information being searched.

Finally, he says, "Shadow's End has been compromised then. The City of Death has collapsed. We must head to our next allies."

"The Forest Gods," I say. "I think the way might be clear. From all the footprints and tracks I saw, it looks like the Bone Stragglers and the Old Gods are heading to Shadow's End."

"How were you able to get to me without being harmed?" he asks.

I show him the tear in my cape. "I have this for a battle wound. I was only attacked by one of the Gods and a few Bone Stragglers. The skeletons I can easily deal with in combat. The weird beast thing was harder to take down. I had to plunge my sword into its brain, but it worked."

"Good to know there's a way to defeat them."

"Do you have any combat training?"

He shakes his head, and I swear I see a shooting star curve up where a smile might be. "No. I'll need you to protect me."

I grin at him, glad to have purpose and something to keep my mind off my family. "I will gladly protect you."

"We should start going now," he says, glancing over his shoulder. "I don't know how long those city gates will hold, but I don't want to be here when they fall. All I know is that our problems will be a lot worse."

"All hell will quite literally break loose," I say under my breath. "Come on."

We start back the way I came. I wish I had an extra sword I could give to the Magician, but if he doesn't have any fighting training, then I don't think it would do him much good. On one hand, I don't see why anyone, including my mother, would bother with him. On the other hand, he's been sending centuries of people to the pits of Hell, so he's the first person they're going to want to kill. I wouldn't be surprised if Ethel Bagley was the first one out of the gate and coming for him.

On that note, I pick up the pace so we can put as much distance between us and the City of Death as possible.

We run and run, ducking through the trees, following the river, until my legs feel like they're going to give out. Eventually, the forest and mountains subside, and we end up walking along the Gorge of Despair. Occasionally, a Bone Straggler will appear from nowhere, running toward us, but the Magician smartly steps out of the way and lets me do all the fighting, lopping off their skulls left and right.

But all the swordplay and running has left me tired, with barely enough strength to cross the last hurdle before we reach the Hiisi Forest: The Liekkiö Plains.

This is my least favorite part of Tuonela, and the one I get through the fastest when on the boat.

"What is this place?" the Magician says as we come to a stop so I can catch my breath. He's looking along the horizon at the large expanse of dry, red soil and the few scraggly bare trees that reach into the smoky air like grasping, dark fingers.

"The Liekkiö Plains," I tell him. "Surely you've heard of them."

He glances at me from the side, and suns grow round in the center of his face. "The murdered children."

"Yes," I say grimly. "The murdered children. Once upon a time, long before you became the Magician at the gates, the spirits of murdered children gathered here on the plains to roam for eternity, their bodies forever on fire, creating the smoke and mist you see here. According to the stories, anyway."

A faint wailing punctuates the air, and I can't help but shiver.

"They are Old Gods themselves," he says warily. "Would that not mean they'll turn on us?"

Oh fuck.

I didn't think about that.

"Yes. Well, I guess our little break is over then." I take a deep breath, trying to find strength and courage. I usually consider myself quite brave, but there's something about these dead children covered in flames that gives me the creeps—and it's not just because children give me the creeps in general. "Come on. We're almost there."

We start running again, as fast and quietly as possible, our feet barely making a noise against the crumbly dry ground, though the wailing of the children gets louder and louder.

"Over there," the Magician says, pointing at the smoke, where a couple of bodies emerge. They're tiny skeletons, half-rotted so you can still tell they were human children at some point, their mouths open in a never-ending scream, their bodies in flames. They spot us and start walking toward us quickly.

"My father told me they bite," I tell him, taking my sword in my hand. "It's best we not put that to the test."

I move my legs faster now, and the Magician effortlessly keeps up, even in his heavy robes. More children emerge from the smoke, running unnaturally fast.

This isn't good. This isn't good at all.

Straight ahead, I can see the tops of the trees that make up the Hiisi Forest, where the children can't cross through the protective wards. If we can make it there before the children, then we'll be safe.

Providing the same old rules apply.

I'm about to tell this to the Magician when I hear a sharp *thwack*, and suddenly, an arrow appears, slamming into the galaxy void that is the Magician's face.

I stop and scream, watching as the Magician sways on his feet and then falls backward onto the dirt, the arrow sticking right out of his face.

I whip around in the direction the arrow came from, my sword raised, prepared to see one of the murdered children with a bow in their hands.

But instead, I see a man standing between us and the flames.

Dressed in all black.

His smile depraved.

His hair red.

"You must be my sister," the man says. "It's a pleasure to finally meet you."

CHAPTER 22

Hanna

THE PASSAGE

"Maybe we're not in the right spot?" I say, trying to find hope in the situation. "Maybe there's another frozen waterfall with a portal underneath it?"

My father puts his head in his hands and shakes it. "No. This was the main portal."

"Something must have happened here," Tuoni says, looking around at the dirt mound piled outside of the tunnel. "An earthquake? Do those happen here?"

"Sabotage," my father grumbles. He looks up at us with fire in his eyes. "This was the work of Noora and Eero. They wanted to make sure I could never come back."

"But that doesn't make sense," I say. "Wouldn't they want or need to use the portal at some point? There has to be another one, maybe nearby."

My father sighs. "Yes, there is, but..."

"But what?" Tuoni says gruffly. "If there's one near, you must take us there immediately."

"It opens up at the bottom of the Great Inland Sea," he says, and I'm suddenly remembering something. In the grotto, the little mermaid, Bell, had told me about a portal at the bottom of the sea. It must be the same one.

"What's the problem?" Tuoni asks tiredly.

"The problem is, not only will we get wet, but I'm not a god like you. Hanna might be half-goddess, but I don't know if that means she can breathe underwater."

"She's done it before. All it takes is a bit of magic," Tuoni says with a wave of his hand. "I can bestow the same magic on you. Besides, you're a Shaman. Surely, you know a spell or two. You probably know far more than I do. I can learn spells, but I can't create them. That's something you do."

"I don't know of any spells to help me grow gills," my father says. "Which means I'll have to trust that you won't let me drown at the bottom of the sea."

"Are you still coming with us?" I ask him. "Wouldn't it be better for you to remain on this side, where it's safe?"

He raises his chin in determination. "If you think I'm going to let you waltz off with Tuoni to the Underworld alone, you need to get your brain examined. Of course I'm coming with you."

"Papa, I can't lose you again."

"You won't." He eyes Tuoni. "So as long as the God of Death is as noble as you seem to think he is."

I look at Tuoni, and he nods. "I will protect you both. You have my word. Now please, show us to the other portal. The clock on this side is ticking."

My father sighs heavily, his shoulders dropping. "Alright, but I'll have you know that it's a much longer, narrower, darker tunnel. Sometimes, there are strange creatures in there that bite your ankles. It's really not preferable, but if we don't have a choice..."

"We don't have a choice," Tuoni says gravely.

"Alright, follow me," my father says, squeezing past me under the waterfall and out into the open.

"Aren't you going to call back the reindeer?" I ask, following in his footsteps, Tuoni behind me.

"There's no real point," he says. "It's not that far, another hour walk from here. Hopefully, I won't get lost along the way." He brings out a compass from his coat pocket and squints at it under the lights from the aurora borealis.

I'm even more cold and tired than I was before, and Tuoni rummages through his duffel bag and takes out some protein bars we got from the service station and the three of us chew them down, followed by Finnish chocolate and a bottle of cola. It gives me just enough energy to continue on.

It also gives me enough strength to email my mother.

"What a talent," Tuoni says from behind me. "The ability to type on your phone and walk at the same time."

I can't help but smile to myself. "All humans have this ability."

"Not me," my father says ahead of me.

"All *young* humans," I clarify as I finish typing the email. It's basically a couple of paragraphs, telling her that it's really me, that I'm fine, and that she doesn't need to worry. I told her I met a man and we're happy together, that she can show this to the police if she wants, but I'm not coming back home. I also added in a bit about my father. I made it seem like I hadn't heard from him and hoped he was okay. That way, if any suspicion falls on him again, it won't seem like he had anything to do with my disappearance. Knowing my mother, she won't put any effort into looking for my father, and I can't really blame her, knowing what I know now.

I press send and put it away in my coat, knowing it won't survive the swim through the sea and that it wouldn't work in Tuonela anyway. I assume. Either way, I hope I've given my mother peace of mind. It's for the best that I won't get to see the aftermath.

"I think we're getting close," my father says in a whisper.

We slow down as we walk along a narrow passage through the trees and come to an open clearing. The northern lights are still doing their dance, illuminating a rocky outcrop on the perimeter of the snow-covered field.

"There," my father whispers as he comes to a stop.

"Where?" I ask, standing beside him, trying to follow his gaze. "The rocks over there?"

He nods. "We slip on through the cracks. See that dark fissure? It goes straight down for a bit before it levels out. It's like caving."

"Oh great," I mutter. I've watched *The Descent* one too many times.

"Will I need to be coated in some sort of oil to fit in there?" Tuoni asks.

"Let's hope not," my father says and starts walking as Tuoni grumbles something under his breath about this world being too small for him.

We cross the field and stop at the pile of rocks. The fissure looks barely wide enough for Tuoni to squeeze through. Beyond it is darkness, blacker than the void, and a cold wind comes shooting out of it. To my surprise and relief, it smells like the sea.

"I'll go in first, since I know where I'm going," my father says. "Tuoni, bring up the rear."

"Are you sure?" Tuoni asks as my father starts to lower himself through the crack. "I can't imagine getting lost down there."

"You'd be surprised," he says, wincing as he squeezes through. "Don't want to make the wrong turn."

"Wait a minute," I say just as my father's head nearly disappears. "Have you actually gone through the portal this way? You said not breathing underwater was, you know, an issue for you."

He gives me a sheepish look. "I'll tell you the truth, daughter: I've walked to the end of the tunnel. I saw through the Veil and the sea beyond. That, plus the little ankle biters in there, was enough for me. I decided to stick to the other portal after that."

Then, his grey head slips away into the darkness.

"Papa?" I cry out softly. "Are you still there?"

"Yes," he says, his voice echoing slightly. "The rocks down here act like steps. I'll get down to the next one to make room, and then I'll tell you to follow."

"Okay," I say uncertainly, looking over at Tuoni. Not going to lie, I'm a little apprehensive. The portal at the waterfall was one thing but slipping through rocks in the ground was never my idea of fun.

"You'll be fine," Tuoni says. Yet he's frowning, his eyes focused elsewhere. He breathes in deeply through his nose, his nostrils flaring.

"What is it?" I whisper to him.

"I don't know," he says slowly. "Torben?"

"Yes?" comes his voice, further away and more muffled now. "Just made it to the second rock. You can come down now, Hanna. Plenty of room and...what's that?"

"What?" I ask him, my heart starting to race.

"Hello?" my father calls out from below. "Is there someone there?"

Oh, fuck no.

"Papa, who's there? What's happening?" I glance back at Tuoni, but his attention seems elsewhere.

Silence follows. My heart thuds loudly in my head. Then, my father coughs. "I don't know, I thought I saw..." He trails off. "Hello?" he calls out again. "Who is there, please? Oh God, Hanna, I'm coming back up, I—"

Everything goes silent.

I go closer to the fissure, trying to see inside. "Papa, what—?"

"Hanna, duck!" Tuoni yells, and I look up just in time to see a man launching himself off the rocks above me, about to land on my head.

I dive to the ground just as Tuoni leaps forward and the tackles the man to the snow.

At the same time, I hear my father yell, "Hanna! Hanna, they're here! Run! I'm—"

My father breaks off into a scream that sounds like it's swallowed by the cave.

"Papa!" I scream, trying to get to my feet again.

I don't know what to do. I watch as Tuoni fights this man bundled in reindeer skins, and I figure it's no contest, except that the man has a knife that seems to operate without being held.

As if by magic.

And I realize who this man with the long grey beard is.

Who *they* are.

Eero.

I'm betting inside that cave, it's Noora who has my father.

Eero throws his knife around, nearly cutting into Tuoni several times, and I know I have to figure out who to help. Tuoni is the God of Death and can handle himself, but after what Salainen did to him, I know he's not invincible. My father has handled Noora before, but in a cave like this? Was it luck the first time?

But before I have a chance to squeeze between the rocks and go after my father, I watch as Eero slips up and gets too close, and Tuoni grabs the old Shaman by the throat. He lifts Eero in the air, much like I've seen him do before, but this time, he spares the man no mercy.

I watch as Tuoni snaps Eero's neck right in half with a sickening crack. Eero's head hangs off his body like a flower from a broken dandelion stem.

I don't have time to react.

I swallow the scream building inside me and manage to yell at Tuoni. "Throw me his knife!"

But Tuoni throws Eero several feet away instead, as if he were a shot-putter, and then picks up the knife and runs over to me, motioning for me to get out of the way. I do, my body moving automatically while my brain tries to deal with what it just saw—an actual human being killed in front of me—and what needs to be done.

Tuoni brushes past me and manages to squeeze through the cracks into the cavern. From the darkness, I hear my father yelling, Tuoni's grunts, and a woman's scream, all of them echoing into one awful crescendo.

"Do you need help?" I yell, wishing there was something I could do. I look around for a weapon of some sort. Damn it, we should have held on to one of the swords!

I go to the duffel bags and wonder if Tuoni's mask, which he still has with him, can be weaponized somehow.

But out of the corner of my eye, I see something moving.

I suck in my breath and look over at the field where Tuoni threw Eero, wondering if the northern lights are manipulating me into seeing things, but they aren't.

Eero's body is moving.

His leg is twitching.

Is it possible for the body to be in death's throes right after having its neck snapped in half?

Maybe...

But then an arm moves.

Then the other arm.

Slow, deliberate movements.

And then I watch in pure horror as Eero slowly sits up, his head hanging off him.

I scream.

"Hanna!" I hear Tuoni yell from inside the cave.

But I can't take my eyes off Eero, watching as he slowly gets to his feet, his head swinging back and forth, and his eyes—oh God, his eyes—they're *watching* me.

I'm going to vomit.

"Tuoni!" I scream, still unwilling to take my eyes off the zombie. "Eero isn't dead! He isn't dead!"

I hear rocks scraping behind me and turn around to see Tuoni climbing out of the fissure, dragging a dirty-looking woman out with him. He throws her to the side, where she lands in a heap in the snow, a knife in her throat, blood staining the snow red.

Noora.

It would be another traumatic sight to witness, but so far, it doesn't hold a candle to Eero, who is slowly shuffling across the field toward us, his mouth snapping and making gurgling noises.

And now, Tuoni sees him too.

"What the fuck?" he breathes. "Is this magic? How can Shaman magic defeat the God of Death?" He looks down at Noora and quickly takes off his glove, grabbing her bare hand. "If this doesn't kill her, nothing will."

But then Noora's eyes fly open.

She opens her mouth, and blood pours out, gathering around her, and her hands try to grab the knife from her throat.

She's not dead either.

Fuck, fuck, *fuck*.

I look at Tuoni, my mouth dropping open. "No one dies!" I cry out. "We were right! No one can die while you're in this world!"

"Well you better get your butts to the Underworld then!" my father yells, poking his head out of the cave. He looks at Noora, then Eero, eyes growing wide. "Now!"

Quickly, Tuoni grabs the knife from Noora's throat and stabs her in both eyes, her eyeballs exploding like red grapes.

"There," he says, putting his hand on my shoulder and pushing me toward the cave. "That should at least slow her down."

I nearly choke trying to stop the vomit from coming up as I'm forced down between the rocks, slipping into the cave, my feet dangling into nothingness.

Until someone grabs my legs.

I let out a muffled cry before I realize it's my father helping me down to the next rocks. "Are you okay?" he asks me.

"Are you okay?" I ask back.

He brings out his flashlight, his face bruised but otherwise fine. "I am if you are."

Am I?

My husband just snapped a man's neck in half and then stabbed a woman in both her eyeballs, I want to say, but I guess I'll just wait for that trauma to pop up later at a completely innocuous time.

He pats my shoulder and then helps me climb down a few more rocks while Tuoni quickly comes in after me.

"We need to move," Tuoni says. "The faster I'm in Tuonela, the quicker they will die for good this time. And I don't want them going through the portal with us."

My father nods and hurries off. "This way."

I follow quickly, Tuoni close behind me. The tunnel goes down for a bit, but then as it levels out, the walls start to get narrower, until my shoulders are brushing against them. The light from my father's lantern shows nothing but black dirt walls, and even then, it seems to be swallowed up by the darkness.

"I'm sorry you had to see that," Tuoni says from behind me. "I didn't mean to get so violent."

"Yes, you did," I tell him. "You're the God of Death. That's what you do. And if I'm the Goddess of Death, I better get used to it."

Not that I could ever get used to *that*.

"Good girl," he says under his breath. "I think you're become more and more suited to me with each passing day."

I smile faintly at that. As much as I love it when he calls me a good girl, though, I can't let myself think about anything until we get out of this cave system. The longer I'm down here, the more I'm starting to panic. How much longer until we reach the sea? What if Noora and Eero go into zombie mode and run after us? How do we stop them from killing us down here if they themselves can't be killed?

I suppose we might not be able to be killed either, but there's no way I want to test that theory out, not here.

"How much longer?" I ask my father, trying to keep the fear out of my voice.

"Not much more," he says. "I know it's a long slog, but we should be—"

He breaks off just as a low rumble starts to sound, the walls and ground shaking.

"What's happening?" I cry out.

"A cave-in!" Tuoni yells.

"It's them," my father cries. "They're making the tunnel collapse. Hanna, run! We're almost there!"

My father reaches back and pulls me forward, pushing me past him. I start running, my father and Tuoni right behind me. The light from his lantern swings back and forth, my figure casting shadows on the rocks as we race along.

Dirt and rocks from the ceiling begin to fall, the ground still shaking, and yet, up ahead, I see it: a strange kind of glow.

"That's the portal and the sea beyond! Keep going!" my father yells from behind me.

I run faster now, small rocks hitting my head as I go, and the portal gets closer and closer. It's as if someone put a sheet of plexiglass at the end of the tunnel with an aquarium on the other side.

Tuonela.

Almost there.

Almost...home.

"Keep going!" my father yells again. "Run right through it; you'll be fine!"

But then the rumble gets louder, the earth shaking so hard, I fall to the ground, and a large rock lands on my leg.

I cry out in pain and hear my father and Tuoni yelling.

The lantern light goes out.

I scream for them, but the rumble of the cave is too loud, and I know it's going to bury us all.

"Keep going!" I hear Tuoni's voice carry out. "Hanna, keep going!"

I get to my feet, limping along, and then run a few feet more until I'm pushing through the portal's veil, the sensation like pushing through a bowl of jelly.

And then suddenly, I'm sucked through the rest of the way.

Submerged underwater.

Turning around in the sea just in time to see the portal behind me collapse.

Trapping my father and my husband inside.

"No!" I scream, but the sound is muffled by the sea as water pours into my lungs.

My husband had the magic that would let me survive this journey.

My husband is now buried in a tunnel at the bottom of the sea.

I'm starting to drown.

I do what I can to twist around and kick back down to the portal, to try and push through the veil, but my hands barely sink in, and all I see on the other side is dirt, like there was never a tunnel at all.

And then, my vision starts to fade.

My lungs burn, and I have no air. All I want is air, to breathe.

All I want is to live.

But I won't live.

Because everything goes black.

CHAPTER 23

Lovia

THE HALF-BROTHER

I stare at the man, blinking, as he walks toward me on the Liekkiö Plains.

The smoke swirls around him, the flaming children in the distance coming closer and closer, but he doesn't pay them any attention. All his attention is on me.

"Rasmus?" I say, my grip sweaty as it tightens around the hilt of my sword.

He grins at me. In some ways, he looks like a mere mortal, one I could easily picture being Hanna's half-brother. That would be their father's side.

But then there's a glint in his eyes that doesn't seem all that mortal to me. Wicked, perhaps a little deranged—that would be our mother's side.

Considering he just put an arrow through the head of the Magician, there's no doubt he's Louhi's son through and through.

Now I have to figure out what he wants from me, and fast.

"You should put down the sword," he says, still approaching me like I'm a wild animal. "That's no way to treat family."

"You are no family of mine," I tell him, moving the sword from side-to-side, flashing the metal at him. "Now, stay back if you know what's good for you."

"I know very well what's good for *you*," he says, reaching back and grabbing a bow from his quiver.

"I'm pretty sure your beloved mother would disown you if you were to kill me," I tell him, flashing him the sword again.

"I'm not going to kill you," he says. "Just disarm you."

"You will never disarm me," I growl back.

"Let's try and see." He sets the arrow into his bow and aims it at me.

I don't have much time to react. The arrow flies through the air, and I raise my sword, my body moving faster than I thought possible.

The arrow collides with my sword with a *ting!* before flying off to the side.

Rasmus frowns, not expecting that, but he's quick too, already loading another arrow. It fires at me, my sword deflecting the shot again just in time.

Then, it fires again, and I deflect it again, all while he's slowly walking toward me, all while I'm slowly walking back. I don't dare look over my shoulder to see if I'm about to stumble, nor to see how far I have to go to get to the safety of the Hiisi Forest. With the Magician still lying there, arrow to the face and motionless, I feel a deep sense of futility for the first time—like I truly am alone in the world, at least in this one, and no one is going to come and save me.

I told the Magician I would protect him, and I didn't.

I don't even think I can protect myself.

"I can stop, you know," Rasmus says. "All you need to do is put down the sword and come with me, sister."

"I'm not going anywhere with you," I counter just as he fires another arrow at me, which I block just in time. Damn it, how many of them does he have?

"That was never an option," he says as he raises his arm in a dramatic fashion and points at me. "*Saada*!" he commands.

Suddenly, all the flaming murdered children wail again in unison, their tiny mouths snapping as the inhuman, haunting sounds fill the air. They start running toward me. There must be at least twenty of them, and at first, I think I might be able to stay and fight them off, but then I look over my shoulder and see how close the forest is.

I take my chances. Once past the wards, I'll be safe.

I turn and run as fast as I can, knowing that though the little fire spirits are fast, they are still children, and I'm faster, with a head-start.

Thwack.

I hear the arrow at the same time I feel it.

My right leg explodes in pain, as if it's been torn off at the knee, and I collapse to the ground in a heap, rocks cutting my palms as I try to break my fall, red dirt smearing up my elbows.

I try to hold back a scream, but it comes out as an anguished cry. I am in pure agony; I can barely breathe through it, and I know if I don't ignore it, it will become the death of me.

I twist around and look at my leg, at the arrow sticking out of my calf, the blood dripping onto the dirt. Right behind me is the swarm of flaming children coming to kill me, and behind them, the figure of Rasmus striding through the dark mist.

No, I can't die here.

I grab my sword and manage to get to one knee, turning around to face the children. The closest one to me, a little girl with missing eyes and teeth and roaring flames for hair, jumps at me. I swipe my sword across her while she's in mid-flight, severing her body in two.

Another child flings themselves at me, and I quickly bring the sword across their neck, moving just in time to do the same to another. I try to get to my feet, but my leg howls in pain, and I have to drag it across the dirt to get more distance between me and the Liekkiö, unable to use my sword in close combat.

More come at me now, jumping onto my shoulders, pulling my hair and bringing me down to the ground. I kick and scream, flames burning me, and I watch in horror as Rasmus appears just a few feet away, the arrow in his bow nocked and aimed right at my head.

"I'll call them off," he says with an acidic smile. "You just have to come with me."

I grind my teeth together and growl in response, knocking a child's skull off their body with a throw of my elbow, the flames licking my skin, glancing down to kick another one that's grabbed hold of my foot in the face.

But when I look back up, Rasmus is no longer holding the bow.

And he's no longer alone.

There's someone behind him, holding an arrowhead, the sharp point pressed against the side of Rasmus' neck, enough that it has drawn a trickle of blood.

The hands are gloved, the arms robed.

The Magician!

His galaxy face appears just behind Rasmus.

"Didn't you know that you can't kill the universe?" the Magician says.

Rasmus snarls and tries to twist away from the arrow's tip, just as another child skeleton lunges for me. I kick the kid in the chest, breaking ribs and sending them backward while Rasmus tries to fight the Magician off.

The Magician moves back, waving his hands in a sweeping manner, and suddenly, long, pale tendrils shoot out of the ground at Rasmus' feet and wrap around his legs with startling ferocity.

Rasmus yelps and tries to move after the Magician, but the tendrils move like lightning, snaking up his legs, around his waist, to his arms, holding him in place.

Mycelium, I think just as another child hurls itself at me.

But now, the Magician is coming toward me, waving his arms in an outward manner as more of the mycelium reaches outward from the earth, wrapping around the Liekkiö until they're entirely covered in a throbbing network of fungi fibers. The mycelium shoot inside their skulls like a living nightmare, choking the incessant screams right out of them.

Then, the Magician comes over to me and reaches down, grabbing me by the elbows and hoisting me up to my feet.

"Loviatar, are you alright?" he asks me, hands firmly on my shoulders. I swear, if he wasn't holding me, I'd probably crumble.

"I was supposed to be the one protecting you," I tell him feebly.

"You can pay me back," he says. He looks down at my leg. "Best to leave that in for now. If I pull it out, you'll lose more blood."

"I'm the Goddess of Death," I whisper. My title sounds so weak. "It can't kill me...can it?"

His face swirls, crescent moons forming where his eyes should be. "Take nothing for granted anymore. The Tuonela we know and love is gone. We'll get you to the Forest Gods; they'll have something to help you. This much I know."

He looks over at the children taken over by the fungi, and then to Rasmus, still held in place on his feet, the mycelium strands wrapped around him all the way to his nose. He stares at us with a mix of broken anger and fear, both emotions cycling on his brow while he's breathing hard through his nose.

"How did you do that?" I ask the Magician. "Command the mycelium?"

A shooting star flits across the lower half of his face.

"There are some things I can do. The mycelium network is strong, and so is my network. They listen to me, and I listen to them, and occasionally, they will help if it suits them. I suppose it suited them today."

"What do we do with him?" I say, nodding at Rasmus.

"We could leave him here," the Magician says, to which Rasmus lets out a muffled cry. "See how long a half-God will last in this place. But I think he needs to come with us."

I grunt at that, not too enthused about having him along. "He seems like a liability."

"He could be, he could be," he muses. "Or he could help us."

"Do you really think he's going to help us?" I ask, putting my hand on my hip, though the movement puts more weight on my leg. I wince at the sharp pain.

"We could make him. I realize that sounds like a threat, but these times deserve threats. The other gods, *our* gods, they could make him. You might be able to make him, too. Otherwise, he's leverage."

"Do you really think Louhi will care if he lives or dies? He hasn't been in her clutches very long. I'm her daughter, and she was willing to have me killed." I say that so easily, as if it doesn't secretly wound me inside, as if I'm not burning up at my own mother's betrayal. "I think we could kill Rasmus and it wouldn't change a thing for her."

"Are you sure about that? She's hung onto him for a reason. Rasmus might play a part in our lives we're unsure of yet."

I squint at the universe of his face, watching the spinning moons as they orbit planets. "How much do you know? What is it that you're not telling me?"

"There is much I am not telling you, Loviatar," he says to me, his voice kind. "But that is only because it would be too much for your mind, even the mind of a goddess, even one as sharp as yours. Not all knowledge is helpful or good for everyone." He pauses and runs his hand down my arm to my hand and gives it a squeeze. His gloves are soft, his grip strong and surprisingly warm. "But I can tell you that what has started can be finished. We just need to keep going, and having Rasmus might help us more than hurt us in the end."

Though his words are cryptic, they still bring comfort. At least he's still alive and by my side. I've never been very sure if I can truly trust the Magician—my cynical nature combined with his ambiguous persona doesn't help—but I think I finally do.

If this is truly the end of our world, I guess you should probably trust someone in your last days.

"Alright," I say. "How do we do this?"

Still holding my hand, he leads me through the forest of frozen fungi children and over to Rasmus.

"May I have your sword?" the Magician asks.

I hand it to him, and he takes it, hacking away at the mycelium around Rasmus' feet. They glow in response and then shrink back into the earth.

"Don't worry, this doesn't hurt them. They'll just re-network," he says before handing me back my sword. Then, he unravels a few tendrils around Rasmus' neck until they resemble a leash and gives them a sharp tug.

Rasmus stumbles forward and falls to his knees, where he remains. From his muffled screaming, I can't tell if it's in pain or protest.

The Magician gives the strands a yank. "Come on. Make this easier on yourself. If not, I have no issues dragging you to the Forest Gods. Either way, you're coming."

Rasmus refuses to move. To be fair, I don't think getting to your feet is an easy task when you're bound like a mummy.

The Magician just shrugs and starts walking. The mycelium holds, as if a metal chain, and Rasmus is dragged in the red dirt behind him. He makes it look as easy as dragging a cart.

I keep pace with the Magician, occasionally looking behind me at Rasmus with his face full of dust and dirt, until we finally come to the invisible ward between the Liekkiö Plains and the Hiisi Forest.

"Let us hope the Forest Gods still exist as we know them," the Magician says as we step through.

CHAPTER 24

Hanna

THE SUN GODDESS

Water.

Everything is water.

My eyes, my hair, my mouth, my nose.

Water.

My lungs breathe in water, water moves through my body, and I feel like I'll never stop drowning.

I'm floating, I'm sinking, I'm caught in a current.

In the back of my mind, I think about dying, that this could be death, and then I realize there's something about death that appeals to me.

Not dying.

But Death with a capital D.

The God of Death.

The man I love.

He's floating in a vision of blue, his eyes glowing like pewter stones, like lightning strikes, and I'm swimming to him through the void. I am drawn to him, this man who has brought me to life in so many different ways and will bring me back to life again.

But as I move through the water, through the nothingness, as thoughts of Oblivion are carried past my head, I realize that Death isn't here.

He hasn't come for me.

And neither has dying.

My hands reach out into the blue void, and they strike something solid but soft in return.

But this isn't my Tuoni.

It is, however, someone.

In the darkness, in that blue nothing, I feel hands wrap under my arms, and then I'm being pulled up from the depths.

My life flashes across my eyes, but I can't grasp any of it. It's like watching a movie in fast forward, just images and clips. Me and my father on the dock at the lake, me sitting on the floor after dance class crying. Me moving into my suite on a sunny day in Los Angeles, me walking through the portal with Rasmus. Me being thrown in an oubliette. Me growing wings in the middle of Inmost.

Me and Death in a restaurant bathroom.

Me and my father hugging on a snow-covered porch.

A tunnel collapsing.

A tie severed.

I open my mouth to scream as the memories come flooding back, just as the sea floods into my lungs again, and then I'm rushing to the surface and bursting through into the cold air.

"Breathe," I hear a woman's delicate voice at my ear. "You can breathe."

I open my eyes, blinking wildly at the grey sky above just in time to see what looks like a bony pterodactyl fly overhead, disappearing into thicker clouds.

I gasp, my lungs burning, and water comes churning out. There's a hand at my back, a fist pounding me, until I cough up all the swallowed sea.

"There," the person says sweetly, and I look beside me to see a beautiful girl with long green hair and scales along her hairline.

Mermaid.

She's a mermaid.

My brain feels so puny, it's hard to put anything in the right order.

"It's okay," another voice says, this one achingly familiar.

I look down to see a doll-size mermaid with an iridescent white tail swimming in front of me.

Bell! I think. *This is Bell.*

"You're looking at me like you don't recognize me," Bell says. "Don't tell me you have another little mermaid friend. Do I need to worry about her? There can only be one."

I can't tell if she's making a joke or not. Everything is moving *so* slowly.

"Don't worry," Bell says. "Madra and I have you. When I heard someone was using the portal, I didn't know what to expect. The last thing I thought I would see was you floating there. You gave me a heart attack. I got Madra to help you to the surface."

I nod slowly, coughing again, and look around. We're treading water maybe a hundred yards from a snow-covered shore, tall trees beyond it. It looks different somehow, and there's something off-putting about it, but at least I know where I am.

Tuonela.

"What about Tuoni?" I manage to say, my voice hoarse. "My father? Did you see them?"

Both mermaids shake their heads.

"No," says Bell. "They didn't come through with you. We would have seen them if they did. They're still on the other side. What happened?"

"There was a cave-in. The tunnel. They told me to run. I thought they were right behind me and then..."

Oh God, please let them be alright. I'm not as worried about Tuoni in the tunnel—I'm pretty sure that god can punch his way through a wall with his bare hands—but what about my father? If he was hurt, if something happened to him...

But he can't die. Even if he was hurt, he couldn't die.

I let out a shaking breath. At least there's that. As long as Tuoni remains on that side, no one on Earth is dying. That means they'll both have Eero and Noora to deal with, but I have no doubt Tuoni will deal with them in a most gruesome way.

"I am sure they are fine. There are always other portals," Bell says in a soothing voice. "They'll find their way back." Then, her expression turns crestfallen. "Though I'm not sure they'll want to come back to this world."

I swallow hard, looking again at the shore. It's only now that I really see. The snow isn't just snow: there are mounds and mounds of white bones everywhere.

In the middle of all the bones, sitting on a long grey log, is the Goddess of the Sea, Vellamo, her head in her hands and a shattered crown of coral on her head.

"What happened?" I whisper to the mermaids. I've never seen Vellamo look anything but cool and stately. Even though I'm far away, I can tell she's absolutely broken. I know that feeling all too well.

"We don't really know," Bell says quietly, swimming around in anxious circles. "It was such a blur when it happened. We were in a grotto when we were attacked. Creatures came from nowhere, swarmed us—giant creatures, monsters, ones I had never seen before. Vellamo commanded us to leave while she called in her sea serpents, and Ahto took control of the water. We came here, and still, the monsters were everywhere, coming up from the bottom of the sea..."

"The land was full of skeletons," Marda says in a musical but melancholic voice. "They were all walking south. Bone Stragglers, but hundreds of them. Then, Vellamo came." She exchanges a mournful look with Bell, her shoulders sagging. "She was carrying..."

"She was carrying Ahto's body," Bell says, and I gasp.

"He's dead?" I cry out, my gaze going back to Vellamo, still motionless on the shore.

My brother-in-law is dead? This will destroy Tuoni.

"Yes," Bell says sadly. "She was so distraught. She said it was one of the Old Gods. Then, she went on shore and killed every skeleton she saw."

I immediately start swimming for shore, suddenly feeling strong enough. Madra pushes me along every now and then, since my clothes are weighing me down, and Bell keeps up pace beside me.

Finally, I reach the snowy shore and stagger out of the sea, each step heavy and water-logged.

Vellamo still doesn't look up until I'm standing right in front of her. I can see where the coral in her crown has cracked in various places, the missing pearls. Her seaweed gown is ripped and torn, bloody in places.

"Vellamo?" I whisper.

She looks up at me slowly, eyes bloodshot, tears streaming down her face.

A broken goddess.

A Goddess of Grief.

She opens her mouth to speak, but no sound comes out.

I drop to my knees in front of her and take her hands in mine. They're surprisingly cold, considering I'm the one who just emerged from the sea.

"I just heard," I tell her. "I just heard what happened to Ahto. I am so sorry."

She stares at me for a moment, slowly blinking. "Tuoni?" she manages to say, her normally deep and smooth voice cracking. "Where is he?"

"He's stuck. He's okay—I think he's okay—but he's stuck on the other side."

Her thin brows knit together. "The other side?"

"The Upper World."

"What were you doing there?"

"We were bested by Louhi and Salainen, the girl who looks like me. Louhi has taken over Tuoni by way of his Shadow Self. The two of them locked us in Inmost with the intent to replace us, to act as imposters on the throne."

"And raise the Old Gods," Vellamo says flatly. "Which they did."

"Salainen killed Tuoni." Her eyes go wide. "Briefly," I add quickly. "He came back to life. Somehow, I brought him back. I don't know how, but I did discover that I can touch him and live, and that my mother is Päivätär. So maybe that has something to do with it."

"So Tuoni is alive," she says carefully, her tone dull. "And you are the prophesized one. I figured as much. Too bad you figured it out too late."

I swallow hard and give her hands a squeeze. "I am so sorry. When we escaped Inmost, we ended up in the Upper World. We tried to get back here as quickly as we could."

"I am unsure of what could have been done," she says, looking away. "These Old Gods...they have the power to kill the new ones. It shouldn't be possible. Ahto should be alive with me, standing here beside me, figuring out what to do. Instead..."

"Instead, you have a half mortal girl," I say. "I know. It isn't fair. It's not fair in the slightest. I didn't even think it was possible for anyone to die here while Tuoni was outside of the realm, but I am devastated to hear that's not the case."

"You thought no one could die here?"

"Because no one can die in the Upper World, so as long as he's on that side."

Her brows raise. "Oh," she says, wiping her tears away with her thumb. "That might explain why I haven't seen Lovia or Tuonen with the ferry. They usually cross the sea several times a day."

"Have you seen them at all?"

She shakes her head. "No. I haven't seen anyone, just these damn Bone Stragglers. I killed every one of them that crossed my path."

"With your bare hands?"

She gives me a weak smile and pulls out a pearl knife from between her breasts, tucked away in her bodice. "Not quite."

I slowly get to my feet, the cold starting to set in. Bell and Madra are at the water's edge, elbows on the shore, watching and listening. I look around, but I can't see where Ahto's body would be.

"I didn't want to burn him in case Tuoni could bring him back to life," she says quietly, picking up on my thoughts. "I didn't want to bury him in case he was raised like the Old Gods were. I tied rocks to his feet and brought him out to the middle of the sea. That's the best place for him."

I nod. I'm cold, soaking wet, and I have no idea what our next move is, but I feel I need to try and take some of that burden from Vellamo. She may be a goddess, but she is grieving her husband, which means I need to take the reins. We can't just sit here forever.

"Did you want to have a service for him?" I ask her delicately.

She squints at me. "A service?"

"A funeral. A ritual. To say a few words."

She shakes her head and slips her knife back into her bodice. "No. I have said words and will continue to say words each day for the rest of my life. If I see your husband again, perhaps then we will share our words with the rest of the family, but not now." She straightens up, towering over me. I'm a tall girl myself, but her posture and stature puts her well over six feet. "Now, we must avenge him."

I can't help but grin at that. It might look a little maniacal.

"I was hoping you would say that," I tell her with an appreciative nod. "Okay, so what do we need to do? Most importantly, if you killed the Old Gods, how were you able to do it?"

"It happened so fast," she says, adjusting the crown on her head. A tiny sea cucumber pokes out from a crevice in the coral, then retreats. "My sea serpent ripped them all in half. That's how we killed them."

"Can your sea serpents come on land at all?"

"No, but there are things in this land that listen to us, to the New Gods. Things as powerful as a sea serpent."

"Things like what?"

"Giants, for one."

"Like Vippunen?"

She scoffs. "No. Much smaller, but still giants. They live in the deep moss pockets between the Star Swamp and the Hiisi Forest, along the coast of the Outer Sea. They keep to themselves, but they will rip apart anyone when provoked."

"When provoked, or when asked to?"

She lifts her shoulder in a delicate shrug. "Guess we'll find out."

"What about us?" Bell asks from the water.

"What about you?" Vellamo says, crossing her arms. "If you think I'm going to take you with me, I don't have any room left in my bodice."

"But we have to be able to do *something*," Bell says.

"Yeah," Madra chimes in. "All my sisters of the sea want to help. Use us."

"Watch the portals for Tuoni," Vellamo says.

"And my father," I add.

Vellamo sighs at that, giving me a pained look. "The Shaman?"

"Please. They're together," I explain. "He's helping."

"Very well," Vellamo says tiredly. "Bell, Madra, watch the portals for

Tuoni and Hanna's father. If you see any sea serpents or the Kraken, send them down river as far as they can. Better yet, tell them to take the Ice River to the Outer Sea, then go down towards Shadow's End. When it comes to pass, I think that's where we'll be fighting this war. That's where we will need all our allies and friends."

"What about the Forest Gods?" I ask. "Tapio, Tellervo, they were with us at the Bone Match."

"I believe Tapio is in the forest and safe for now," she says, closing her eyes briefly. "As soon as we gather the giants, that's where we will go. Tapio has power over all the animals in this realm. We'll need each one of them on our side, and we can't afford to lose anyone else."

With a sorrowful wave, she says goodbye to Bell and Madra. I almost walk away, but then I run over to the water's edge and pick Bell up out of the water, holding her out in front of me the way I used to do to my American Doll as a kid.

"I would take you with me," I tell her, "but I lose things easily."

She lets out a tiny, melodic laugh. "That's okay. I have a job to do now."

"Stay safe," I tell her, about to lower her back into the water.

"Wait," she says, and I pause as she turns around in my grasp to look up at me with hopeful eyes. "Can you yeet me? Been a long time since you did that."

Now, it's my time to laugh. "Okay, but I have to let you know that no one says *yeet* anymore. You sound dated."

"Maybe in the Upper World," she says with a raise of her chin. "Here, I'm a trendsetter."

I can't argue with that. I take Bell to the side and throw my arms forward like I'm tossing a bale of hay. Bell goes flying through the air, landing in the water in a perfect swan dive.

Madra gives me a hopeful look afterward, and I shake my head. As if I could pick her up.

"Don't get any ideas," I tell her.

She pouts and then dives under the water, swimming after Bell.

I turn and walk back to Vellamo, who is staring at me completely unamused.

"The mermaids like you," she says.

"Well, I did set Bell free from Shadow's End, so that helps. Now, which way do we go?"

She nods straight ahead, and we walk into the sparse forest. Every now and then, I'll come across a dead Bone Straggler with armor and weapons. I gather up a short sword, a dagger I slip in my boot, and a shield that isn't too heavy to carry. Who knows when this thing will come in handy?

Vellamo isn't much for talking, so we walk in silence through the mostly-empty forest. I know she's going through a range of emotions, that she'll talk when she feels like talking. As for me, I'm trying not to think about what might have happened to my father and Tuoni. Instead, I'm trying to think about what they would have me do in this situation. I know they'd want me to ally myself with one of the gods or Tuoni's relatives. I think Tuoni would want me to find out where his children are, and then he'd want me to figure out the best way to take out Louhi and Salainen.

But where does my mother come in?

"Vellamo," I say quietly.

She's walking a few feet ahead and only vaguely glances at me over her shoulder. "Mmmm?"

"I told you my mother is Päivätär, and you didn't seem all that surprised."

"No, well, I knew you had goddess blood in you. Everyone at that meeting did; that's why we were trying to figure out who she was."

"Päivätär and Kuutar were the only ones not there."

"You have more fire in you than you have coolness," she says. "I figured you were a daughter of the Sun Goddess, not the moon. Have you since discovered any abilities that aren't normal for a mortal?"

"I was able to grow wings and set my body on fire," I tell her. "But I haven't been able to do it since."

"Being able to fly is a nice asset. Are you sure you couldn't give it a go?"

"I don't know if I'd be able to fly even if I could sprout wings on command," I say, ducking under a tree branch with red berries hanging from it.

"What a pity," she says under her breath. "You could fly ahead and tell us if we're going the right way."

"What?" I say, coming to a stop. "You're saying we're lost? How?"

"My dear, my mind is not working like it usually does," she says in a measured voice, and I immediately feel guilty. She stops and turns to face me. "Perhaps it is best we stay here for the night. It will be dark very soon."

I look around. We're in a small clearing surrounded by trees with red berries. There's no snow here like there was by the sea, which means we're getting closer to the Hiisi Forest, but the ground looks cold and uncomfortable.

"Do you have anything to light a fire?" I ask her. "I'm rather wet."

She looks me up and down. "I'm sorry. I don't know what it's like to be dry."

I decide to leave her be and set up a little bed for myself, laying down the shield as protection from the ground and adding some fallen leaves and moss on top. Then, I curl up into a very wet, uncomfortable ball. I'm reminded of when I first came into the world, when Rasmus snuck me in. Where is he now? Carrying out murders for his mother? Did she bend and break him until he was hers?

While I think, I absently watch as Vellamo gathers sticks and logs and starts placing them near me, building a fire. Considering she's the antithesis of fire, it's rather nice of her to be doing this for me. Still, I don't have any matches. All of that was left behind in the duffel bag.

Unless...

I start pulling out all my items from my coat pockets—a protein bar, some Haribo gummy bears that have come loose, a couple of wet and wrinkled euros, a hair scrunchie, and my cell phone.

Vellamo has been staring at all of them with interest. I toss the cell phone to her.

"It's wet and it doesn't work, but if you wanted to just look at it," I explain as she catches it.

"You think I'm some sort of magpie?" she says, tossing the phone back after giving it a cursory glance. "What are those colorful blobs?"

"Gummy bears," I tell her. "Have some. They're the best brand."

She comes closer and peers at them. "They look like tiny sea slugs."

"I'd say they probably taste better, but with you, I don't know."

She takes one from me and puts it in her mouth. Her face immediately looks shocked. "Oh," she says. "They are sweet. And chewy. Like sugary sea slugs."

Way to ruin gummy bears for me.

"Have the rest," I say, handing them to her. "Sorry about any pocket lint. Don't mistake it for seasoning."

She eagerly takes them and starts eating. I look back at my meager findings—nothing to light a fire with. Unless I took apart my phone? But even if I did suddenly turn into MacGyver, I don't think anything could produce a spark wet. I know physics aren't really a consistent thing down here, but still.

Vellamo goes to the other side of the pile of wood and crouches down, taking out her knife and scraping it against a rock. "This goes against all my instincts, but I'm fairly certain this is how you make a fire like the dry folk do."

I sit up closer, watching her, waiting for a spark to appear.

And then suddenly—surprisingly—the logs all catch fire at once.

"You did it!" I cry out happily, already feeling the warmth. "I didn't even see a spark."

Vellamo stares at the blade and the rock. "I didn't create a spark. I didn't do anything. The logs, they just—"

She looks up at me from across the fire, and then she looks above me, her mouth dropping wide open.

Her face starts to glow with an otherworldly light, just like the rest of the forest, the berries on the branches burning like little stars, as if the sun has just risen.

"Hanna," Vellamo says in a low voice, slowly getting to her feet.

I look over my shoulder to see what she's looking at in such astonishment, and my whole world turns to shining, blinding white light.

"Hanna, your mother is here."

CHAPTER 25
Death
THE TUNNEL

For the second time in a very short period, I came close to dying.

Unlike the first time, though, I didn't actually die, but it was pretty damn close. Well, as close as it can be when you're stuck in a world where death has taken a vacation.

Worst vacation I've ever had.

The cave system collapsed on us. I had a feeling it might once I learned that Noora and Eero couldn't be killed. I figured they would try their magic to bring it all down on us as a last resort, which is one of the many reasons why we needed to make it through the portal while we could.

Part of the cave struck my shoulder and then took out Torben, and the last thing I saw before it buried us was that Hanna had made it through the Veil, swimming in the sea.

I can only hope and pray that Vellamo or one of the mermaids down there find her and bring her up to the surface, or that her Goddess mother has been watching over her this whole time. It's possible that Hanna really does possess the ability to breathe underwater like I do; it's just never been put to the test before.

I refuse to think of any other scenario. If I do, I might never recover.

"Tuoni," Torben says from beside me. "My daughter."

I reach over and brush the dirt from his beard. Luckily for me, I can see just fine in the dark. "She'll be fine," I tell him. "She made it to the sea."

"But she could drown."

"She'll be fine," I tell him again adamantly. "We have to work on getting ourselves out of here first. Can you try to dig through the rubble behind you?"

I watch as he tries, but he immediately gives up. "There's pure rock behind it. I can't lift it up."

The ground shakes again at that, more dirt falling from the ceiling.

"Come on," I tell him. "We won't be safe until we do something about the Shamans."

"What the hell can we do about them if they won't die?" he says.

"I'll chop them up into many different pieces," I tell him, "and scatter them in the woods. They aren't zombies; they can't come back together again. They'll just be alive in different bits."

"That's diabolical," he says with a gasp.

"That's the only way we'll be able to survive this and get to Hanna. You don't want to give up on your daughter, do you?"

"Of course not, but what can we do?"

"We take care of the first problem at hand before we take on the second one and then the third. First, let's see if we can make our way back to the surface. We don't know if the whole tunnel collapsed or just here, where it counted. Then, I dismember the Shamans, and then, we get back to Tuonela and Hanna."

He stares at me, clearly not believing anything I'm saying.

"I am a god, Torben," I remind him. "I have advantages mortals don't, and I don't give up easily. Now, come on."

I turn around and start digging my way through the dirt and rocks that come up to my waist, trying to clear a path for Torben to follow through. It's slow going, with some boulders hard to squeeze past, but eventually, we make our way out of the rubble and back into the regular tunnel.

"From now on, we'll be as quiet as possible," I tell him in a hush, brushing the excess dirt from my body. I reach down and pull out the knife from my boot, the very one I used to stab Noora's eyes out. If we're correct in thinking no one can die while I'm here, then we're about to get a very unpleasant surprise once we make it to the surface.

Soon, light starts to faintly glow at the end of the tunnel, and we're below the rocks that lead out of the fissure. I can see a slice of the northern lights still dancing in the far away sky.

Then, I see a silhouette of a head.

Hear a gurgling cry.

Feel sticky wet liquid drop on my face.

Her endless blood.

"They're waiting for us," I mutter to Torben. "Stay behind until I give you the all clear, or until I think your magic might come in handy."

I take a deep breath, stick my knife in my mouth, and quickly start climbing up the rocks.

Noora is already at me by the time I reach the surface, her hands grabbing my hair and trying to bash my head against the rocks. I push forward, the strength of a god no match for hers, and then burst out on the cave, throwing her off me.

She screams, blood spraying from her open throat as she does so. Eero tackles me from the side, as I predicted he might.

He doesn't take me down, his strength from earlier thwarted slightly, perhaps from using all their magic to try and take down the portal, or because his head is hanging on by a thread. I swing him around, and he goes flying into the snow, though this time, he gets up much quicker.

I take my knife out of my mouth and wave it in front of them, wishing I had my sword for this.

"You really want to do this?" I ask them as Noora gets to her feet as well, walking blindly toward me. "Do you really want to live in the agony of a thousand pieces while you dream of death? You won't be able to die until I return to my kingdom. Perhaps if you play nice with me and tell me where the next closest portal is, I can at least show you mercy, mercy that you most definitely won't receive when you step into Inmost."

Noora laughs, more blood spraying, and even though she can't talk, I have a feeling I know what she's laughing at. I have no doubt they were waiting in the tunnels in the event that we showed up, sent there by

Louhi or one of her many minions. They know there is an uprising happening in Tuonela, and Louhi has probably promised them a seat at the table. They don't fear death either way.

And therefore, I must show no mercy.

I go for Noora first, grab her by the hair and bend her neck back even more. I take the knife and start sawing through her flesh and muscle and bone as quickly as I can.

Meanwhile, Eero is running forward to stop me.

"Torben, you're needed!" I yell toward the cave, keeping the knife working through the cartilage in her throat until I meet the bones of her vertebrae.

Out of my peripherals, I see Torben appear from the cave and start running toward Eero. He throws out his hands, and I see a green spark before Eero goes flying backward. I really need that man to show me his magic tricks.

I quickly finish up, severing Noora's head before tossing it far away over the rocks, where it lands with a thump. Then, as her headless body squirms beneath mine, I quickly cut off her hands and then kick her in the side until she's down.

Still squirming, though. Still won't die.

How awful, I can't help but think. I'd never realized how death can be such a mercy, how the whole world would descend quickly into chaos if no one could die, if everyone could suffer indefinitely.

With those thoughts in my head, I turn to Eero, who is pushing himself up off the ground. I go over and kick him in the head, the impact knocking his head clean off.

Torben screams at the sight, then turns to the side and vomits.

But I'm not done. Instead of the hands this time, I cut off Eero's feet, severing them at the ankle so he can't walk, and I kick him again for good measure, hoping he'll learn to just stay down and play dead.

I turn back to Torben, feeling breathless myself. "That should take care of them. I could cut them into more pieces, but I think this should suffice. Without their heads, they won't know where they're going anyway."

Torben still looks a shocking shade of green, though that could be the glow from the northern lights. He vomits again, wiping his beard with the back of his hand.

"I don't know what to say," he says in a ragged voice.

"I do," I say, going over to where we had dropped the duffel bags earlier in our haste. "That a world without death isn't a world worth living in."

"Or that the God of Death is as sadistic as I thought."

I glare at him. "Or that the God of Death has to make hard decisions sometimes in order to help the greater good. And your daughter, Hanna, she's the greatest good of all. Now, let's figure out how to get back to her. Are you sure there are no other portals around here?"

He shakes his head. "No. The one at the waterfall would be easier to dig out than this one, though."

"That could take weeks," I point out gruffly, my impatience getting the best of me.

"But you yourself said that time behaves differently over there," he says. "And we might have weeks. First things first, though, we'll consult my Book of Spells and see if there's anything there. Sometimes, you can make a portal appear through magic alone, though I've never tried that myself."

"Where is your spellbook?" I ask him.

"Back at my cabin. At least now I know these two won't be waiting there for me."

"Do you have coffee there?"

He rolls his eyes. "Come on."

He starts walking off across the field, and I follow. Even though I know we have time, I still want to get out of here as soon as possible. I need to get back to Hanna. She's over there unprotected. I know her mother and Vellamo and the others will do what they can to help, but I feel no one has her best interests at heart like I do. No one cares about her like I do.

If anything should happen to her, it would be no different than having my heart and soul chopped up into pieces and scattered in a field. I would be in agony for all of eternity, with no death to provide relief.

Don't even entertain the idea, I remind myself. *Hanna will be fine. You have to believe that, or none of this is worth doing.*

We walk through the trees, the journey seeming longer this time. The irony that I'm stuck here in the Upper World with my father-in-law is not lost on me.

"Say I do find a portal in the book," Torben eventually says. "Then what?"

"Then, we go through the portal, find Hanna, and then we'll be back in Tuonela."

"Yes, but then what?"

"We take on Louhi and the Old Gods."

"But how?"

"You are a man of many questions."

"Of damn good questions," he says, glaring at me over his shoulder. "How are you planning to take her on? How are you planning to defeat her and win back the throne?"

"Well, I suppose I'll kill her—chop off her head and the rest of her into little bits, since I'm good at that now. You kill the queen, and the hive will die."

"No, that's not true," Torben says. "If the queen dies, it's every bee for themselves. The rest of the females will start reproducing. I've had hives before; it turns into chaos until you get a new queen, and not all hives will accept the new one. Either way, they lay eggs birth males and the whole colony dies, since the males don't do anything."

"So I was right. Kill the queen, and the hive will die."

"Yes, eventually. Unless a new queen is introduced and they take to her." There's a weighty pause. "This Salainen."

"The magic baby you created? Yes, I suppose she could become the new queen, but I'll just kill her too."

"But she killed you," he reminds me. "It was Hanna who brought you back to life. What makes you think you can kill her?"

I grumble, not liking this scenario.

"And don't say it's because you're the God of Death," he quickly adds. "I'm tired of hearing it."

"I'm tired of a lot of things. What if *you're* the only who can kill her?"

Torben goes silent, seeming to consider it. "I suppose that makes sense. Hopefully, it won't be put to the test."

Fuck. What if my father-in-law is the key to all of this? Wouldn't that be something. Of course, I don't tell him that. I wouldn't want it to go to his head.

"But even if you were to take out Louhi and Salainen," he goes on, "the hive will descend into chaos. The underlings will fight back. No Inmost Dweller wants to go back to Inmost. They'll want to stay free, and they'll fight you with everything they've got, even if the queens are gone. How are you going to deal with them? You're outnumbered."

I shake my head, noticing that snow is starting to fall in the forest. I'll be frozen solid by the time we get to his cabin. "I'll figure it out," I tell him, hating that I don't have an answer yet.

"I think you already have," he says. "We talked about you building an army here. The only issue was there wasn't any time. Now, we have time. Whether we need an excavator to clear out the portal tunnel to Death's Landing, or I need time to create or locate another portal, you have time now to do some recruiting."

I stare at the back of his head as we walk. I can't even begin to wrap my head around it. Sure, I could probably find some people and command them to fight for me, and I could probably grant them some sort of reward in return. Perhaps not immortality, but I could get them a spot in Amaranthus if it still exists.

But where would I find these people who know how to fight? How would I gather all of them without attracting any attention?

"You know, Finland has mandatory army training," Torben says. "Our army during wartime is nearly two hundred thousand soldiers strong. Even with current conscripts, you're looking at twenty thousand people, easily."

"Are you suggesting I go to the nearest army base, magic my way in, and command all the soldiers to fight for me in the Underworld?"

Torben looks at me over his shoulder and nods, a glint in his eye. "That's exactly what I'm saying."

"That almost seems too easy," I say, weighing the options carefully.

"Oh, I'm sure it won't be easy at all," he says. "And there are major moral and ethical implications of brainwashing the free mind and using them to fight for a cause that doesn't directly affect them. But as you've said about having to make tough decisions...this might be one of those decisions. This might be the only way you'll be able to defeat Louhi, Salainen, the Old Gods, and the Bone Stragglers."

I find myself nodding, though I'm having a hard time coming to terms with it.

With the truth.

The battle for the afterlife will happen in the Land of the Dead.

But it's the mortals who might end up saving the world.

THE END...for NOW

Because the fourth and final book, Goddess of Light, is slated to release November 2024 (date may change) and you can preorder it now at your own peril.

The novella God of Death is still coming in 2024.

I'll have some teasers and excerpts from these for my REAM subscribers. Also feel free to follow me on IG, Tik Tok, Threads, my newsletter, etc. if you want to stay updated (I've also been posting lots of Underworld Gods art...and I'm due to post a NSFW art piece of Hanna and Death for my newsletter soon!)

AND I've included a short story about Tuonen if you'd like to turn the page...

Tuonen: Son of Death

An Underworld Gods Short Story - Previously published as part of the Bookish Box's Winter Anthology

There's a bell that rings when someone has died. It's located on the pebbled shores of Death's Landing, a place where the newly dead end up, confused and shrouded by fog. Despite the confusion, most people know on some innate level that they are dead and that they are to ring the bell to continue their journey to the afterlife, even if they have no idea what exactly this afterlife entails.

But some people, like Aven Morris, are so completely against the idea of death, particularly *their* death, that the bell doesn't even appear to them. Every single cell in their body tells them that they are alive, that there's been some mistake. They can't even remember the last moments of life on the other side, anything that led to their death. To them, one minute, they were living as usual, and the next, they're standing on a misty shore, black water gently lapping the rocks, wondering how the hell they ended up there.

In those cases, the lack of acceptance doesn't change anything. The bell doesn't need to ring for the ferryman, because the moment someone dies, Tuonen and Lovia, the son and daughter of Death himself, feel it in their bones. It's an internal alarm that will forever sound for them, a scar of responsibility to the Finnish Underworld, the land of Tuonela.

So, while Aven Morris stood on the shores in disbelief, Tuonen, who was on ferryman duty that day, knew he had to pick someone up and bring them to the City of Death.

Unfortunately, Aven's death happened during a game of *Pukata*, one of Tuonen's many vices. While Tuonen and his sister, Lovia, shared the duty of ferrying the newly dead down the River of Shadows to the afterlife, Tuonen did everything he could to distance himself from his job. Sometimes, that included gambling on games of Pukata with the dead of the Golden Mean on the very days he was supposed to be working.

"Fuck," he swore, feeling that alarm sound through his body. A second later, his opponent's ramfrog headbutted his ramfrog off the table. The frog fell to the ground, its tiny, exposed bones shattering into pieces. Other than their heads, the frogs were especially fragile.

"I win again!" said Harald Drumsheller, grinning at him with missing teeth. He held his hand out and wiggled his fingers, indicating payment, while scooping up his winning ramfrog with his other hand. The ramfrog peered at Tuonen with a haughty look, two large black eyes underneath a massive bare skull with curled ram's horns, before a long tongue slid out, tasting the air.

Tuonen grumbled and shoved his hand into his coat, pulling out a small bottle of frostberry liquor and handing it to Harald. Tuonen enjoyed gambling in the Golden Mean, the middle ground in the City of Death. Beneath it were the dark and disgusting tunnels of the Inmost (what most mortals would consider Hell), where the horrible people went to live among monsters. Above was Amaranthus, a nirvana or heaven. Most people, however, weren't entirely pious and good, nor evil and malicious. Most people ended up spending eternity in the Golden

Mean, a place that was comfortable at best and bearable at worst. It was here Tuonen related to people the most, where the gambling was always easy. After all, in Amaranthus, they already had everything they could ever want.

In the Golden Mean, the most popular things to bargain for were alcohol, which was scarce at times. Even the dead still had a need to get drunk.

"Lucky for me, I have to go anyway," Tuonen told Harald, getting to his feet.

"Aye," Harald said, breaking the bottle's seal with glee while his ramfrog leaped to the table. "The dead never stop coming, do they?"

"Never," Tuonen said grimly with a shake of his head. Death was the only thing certain in all the worlds and would be so for an eternity. Though Tuonen was an immortal Lesser God and didn't view time the way most mortals did, he avoided thinking of living his life, just like this, for eons to come. It made him want to tear his hair out at the monotony of it all.

Tuonen left the Golden Mean through the twisting streets of the city, through a series of checks and gates until he was outside the main walls, which stretched for miles up into the ever-present clouds of Tuonela. He went to the dark river, got in his ferry boat, and set out toward Death's Landing. Tiny snowflakes began to fall from the charcoal clouds, dusting his coat, and Tuonen wondered what set his father off in a foul mood. Snow was ever-present in the north, but near the city in the south, it was rare, unless his father, Death himself, was feeling particularly miserable. His moods controlled the weather, after all.

The boat glided through the dark waters with increasing speed, the way it did when Tuonen was late to pick someone up. The boat didn't communicate with him, but even so, it seemed to be autonomous and committed itself to the job more seriously than Tuonen often did.

To Tuonen, there was no rush. Time often behaved strangely in the Underworld, especially where the newly dead were concerned. Though countless people and creatures throughout the universes died every second, their entry into Tuonela was slow and controlled. Whether it be Tuonen or Lovia, they were constantly going back and forth between Death's Landing and the city, transporting the dead one at a time (though sometimes more if they happened to have died together).

In the case of Aven Morris, Tuonen didn't know anything about them, except that the bell hadn't been rung, which meant he might be dealing with a special case. Sometimes, he liked the challenge of dealing with mortals who didn't accept that they were dead, but on this day, he wanted things to be easy, just so he could go back to his game against Harald and try another ramfrog.

It wasn't until the boat left the snow-packed drifts of the Frozen Void and cut through the fog toward Death's Landing that the belligerent dead revealed themselves to Tuonen.

It took him a moment to realize he was staring at the most beautiful woman he had ever seen.

Aven wasn't feeling like herself. In addition to the fact that she was standing on a strange shoreline, enveloped by a deepening mist, when moments earlier she had been...well, *not* there, she felt like she'd been drugged. In fact, as she tried in vain to make sense of her new situation, she was certain that her slow thoughts, a sense of disassociation, and feeling of being completely empty inside (*as if someone removed my lungs and my heart*, she thought absently) were because she was drugged. Someone somewhere must have slipped something in her drink.

But had she been drinking? What had she been doing moments before this all happened? What had happened, anyway? She couldn't remember, and the more she tried, the more her past seemed to slip away. She lived in London...didn't she? She had a flat in Shoreditch, she ran an animal shelter with her best friend, she had trained as a classical pianist before...before...

No, she thought to herself. *That's what they want. They want you to forget where you came from. That's what this place is, a place to erase your memory and yourself.*

That thought frightened her. Until that moment, she hadn't really been afraid, just disoriented, but now, she felt her pulse quicken, and it gave her the smallest bit of comfort.

If I have a pulse, then I have a heart, and I'm not empty after all.

She straightened up, her Reeboks slipping slightly on the pebbles, and tried to think. It was like her brain was wading through porridge.

Who am I?

Where am I?

All this time, the constant lapping of the black water on the pebbles hadn't ceased, became nothing but white noise in the background, but now, there was a new noise: the sound of water splashing, rhythmic, getting louder, closer.

A dark shape came through the white mist until Aven had to blink at what she was seeing.

A large open ship, similar to ones Vikings would have used to cross the north seas, slid into view, its hull scraping loudly along the pebbles.

Aven took a step backward as a figure came forward to the bow of the ship.

Fear struck her like tiny lightning strikes as she felt the figure's eyes on her, shrouded by the thick mist.

"You didn't ring the bell," a deep male voice said. The words fell over her spine like warm water, the first pleasurable feeling she'd had since she'd arrived.

"The bell?" she repeated.

The figure raised its arm and pointed to the spot beside her, where a large iron post was stuck in the rocks, a bell hanging off it. She hadn't seen it before.

"Ring it," the man said.

Aven felt herself reaching for the bell but then stopped herself. The world seemed to turn upside down for a moment, and then she narrowed her eyes at the man. "Why?"

"It is Death's Bell," he said. "You ring it so the ferryman can take you to the afterlife."

"But I'm not dead," said Aven. She was drugged, yes, and totally confused, but she wasn't dead. How could she have even died? She would have remembered that.

The flat in Shoreditch, five floors up with no lift, *that* she remembered, lugging her groceries up with burning thighs.

She didn't remember dying.

The figure shifted, as if anxious. "Even if you don't ring the bell, it won't change the truth."

"Who are you?" she asked.

"The ferryman," he replied.

"Do you have a name?"

There was a pause before the man jumped off the boat, landing in the knee-deep water. Here, she could finally see what he looked like. He was tall, stupidly so, and broad-shouldered. He took up so much space, it reminded her of the time she had gone to California and walked beneath the redwoods, feeling their power and strength and age, and she wondered how she could feel that now. He was spectacularly, almost inhumanely, large, but his face didn't come with the feeling of depth and wisdom she had felt when she was humbled by those trees. He was beautiful, but he was young. Only his eyes hinted at something deeper.

"Tuonen," he said. "I am the Son of the Death. And whether you want to believe it or not, nothing changes the fact that you're dead."

Son of Death, she thought. She wanted to laugh; she knew she would have under other circumstances, but somehow, the title felt right. He looked maybe a few years older than her, in his late twenties, and he had the thick, shiny black hair, high cheekbones, and haunted eyes that anyone cosplaying Death would have. But it was also in his presence, his smell, his energy, that seemed to envelop her with each passing second, that made her think of a forest in autumn.

She had the distinct feeling he could make her do anything he wanted.

Again, a lightning strike of fear, something telling her that maybe she should turn around and run.

But before she could, she felt herself reaching for the bell again and giving it a ring. The sound was so loud and jarring, it made her teeth clack together. Then, everything flipped around, like she was trapped on a negative of film passing through a shutter, and when she blinked, she found herself on the boat.

"The more you fight it, the harder it will get," Tuonen said from behind her.

She whirled around, though it felt like her body was moving underwater, and spotted him at the back of the boat. He was sitting casually, one leg up, leaning against the knee and eating an apple. Something about eating an apple always struck Aven as the epitome of casual, and here, she especially didn't trust it. It was like Tuonen was wanting her to let her guard down.

Then again, she got on the boat somehow, and she didn't think it was of her own accord. Her guard was down already.

"Where are you taking me?" she asked, noticing that the boat was moving fast enough through the black water that a cold wind was blowing back her hair. There was nothing but mist for as far as she could see, though snowflakes were starting to fall from above, adding to the haze.

"To the City of Death," Tuonen said before swallowing. "Where the Magician will tell you where in the city you will spend your afterlife."

"A magician?" she asked. "You're the Son of Death and you don't even know?"

"I'm afraid I know nothing about you, not even your name."

Don't tell him. Giving him your name will give him more power, she thought.

But still, her lips were moving.

"It's Aven."

I'm in serious trouble, Tuonen thought. Despite everything he was doing to play it cool, he was one hundred percent enamored with this woman.

"Aven," he repeated, letting her name sink in richly, like chocolate on the tongue. She had a name, a powerful one at that. He didn't always know the names of the dead he was transporting—most of the time, he didn't care to ask—but he knew her name meant something to him. What, he had no idea. And why he was so smitten with her already, he didn't know. After all, he had seen millions of beautiful humans cross his path into the afterlife, and none of them had any hold on him the way Aven seemed to.

Ridiculous, he thought to himself. *She doesn't even look all that special.*

But while he finished his apple, staring at her, trying to find flaws, he couldn't. Back in the Upper World, she would have been considered pretty. Beautiful, even. Her features were large—brilliant blue doe eyes, a wide full mouth, strong nose, round jaw, high forehead—but put together, they made him think of ancient goddesses that past worlds would paint: a memorable, commanding face. Her shiny dark hair fell around her shoulders, and she was wearing sneakers and a navy-blue dress littered with snowflakes as the boat glided toward the Frozen Void. Though her skin was as pale as milk, he surmised it was probably summer back where she was from, and he was grateful for it, since her body was exquisite.

"Where are we?" she asked, breaking eye contact with him to look around. Damn. It was like he was spellbound.

"Tuonela," he said. "The Land of the Dead."

"Tuonela?" she said, looking puzzled. Then, she looked to him with raised brows. "You mean in Finnish mythology?"

He shrugged. "Many call it that, but it is not myth. It is fact." He paused. "Most people haven't heard of this *mythology*, though. It's always about Hades and the Greeks..."

"I studied it in school," she said, and a look of awareness came over her face as she remembered. "Yes, I went to university. In London. I went to Queen Mary."

Tuonen frowned. When people first died, they remembered bits and pieces of their previous life, but as the journey progressed into the

Underworld, they quickly forgot. When they reunited with their loved ones (though that wasn't always the case, depending on which part of the city their loved ones were in), they knew who they were, recognizing their soul and spirit, but the mundane details of life slipped away.

It was strange that Aven still remembered. The resistance she had to being dead was stronger than Tuonen thought.

"You lived in London?" Tuonen asked. He knew he shouldn't, was already cursing himself for doing so. He wanted her to forget, not remember.

"*Live,*" she corrected him, taking a seat on a bench. "I still live there."

Tuonen smirked at her stubbornness. He waved his hand at the snowy banks of the shore as they came into view. "And this? What do you make of this? If you still live in London, how are you here?"

She looked at the snow as the boat glided past, the river a stark, inky black against all the white as the snow started to fall harder.

"And you may have noticed, it's snowing," Tuonen said. "Which is normal in the Frozen Void, where it's always winter, but you're only wearing a summer dress. You don't wonder why you're not cold?"

She shook her head and brushed the snowflakes from her arms. "I'm dreaming. Or I'm drugged."

"Okay," he said, playing along. "Let's just say you are dreaming or someone drugged you. Back in London, right? Can you tell me what you did the day before all of this happened?"

Aven rubbed her lips together in thought. It was obvious it wasn't coming easily to her.

"I can't," she eventually said. "But that doesn't mean anything."

"What else do you remember about your life?"

She gave him a look of surprise. "Everything. Why wouldn't I?"

"Do you still go to school?"

She had to think about that. "No. I don't. I graduated with a degree in history. It was useless."

Tuonen laughed. "My father always says that education is never useless."

"It is when you don't end up getting a job in your field."

"And what job did you get?"

She blinked, feeling resistance. "I...I don't remember. But later, I opened a shelter. For dogs. I love dogs, I wanted to help the strays..."

Part of Tuonen's heart pinched. Helping animals—that was admirable. She would be going to Amaranthus for sure.

Which meant he would probably never see her again. While Tuonen had free reign in the city, he never went to Amaranthus. He left the good people alone. Their world was happy and pure and he, being the Son of the Death, was a blot on their light. They didn't like to be reminded at all that they were dead, and his dark personality and energy would violate everything they deserved in that world.

"How old are you?" he asked.

"Twenty-five." She said this without hesitation.

He smiled. "And you opened your own animal shelter? To save dogs? I know that, in your society, to do that by the age of twenty-five is most impressive."

She shrugged. "It's my calling. It was hard, but I did fundraising, I saved up. I did what I could to get the money to open it, and it's still hard. It's emotionally taxing, constantly trying to get these dogs a home, to raise awareness. It's a twenty-four seven job, but I couldn't do anything else. If I don't do it, who will?"

Another pinch in Tuonen's heart. Who would take up her role now that she's dead?

"So when you say I'm dead, well, I know that can't be true," she continued, a spark in her blue eyes. "I can't die. I have so much life ahead of me. I have so much left to do. I have my parents. They need me. My mother is recovering from breast cancer, and my father is blind. They depend on me. I have my dogs; I need to keep giving them homes. I have...so much to give. I know that dying wouldn't be fair to me, to anyone, to the world."

Tuonen nodded slowly. The more she said, the deeper he felt himself falling, like the hold she had on him was deepening. For a moment, he actually feared she was a shaman and had tricked him, as the shamans often did when they snuck into Tuonela in search of treasures and magic.

But she wasn't a shaman. She was just a girl with a lot left to live for.

For the first time in his existence, Tuonen felt bad that Aven had died. In fact, he started to think there was some kind of mistake.

But the Creator never made mistakes, or so they said. When your time was up, your time was up, and there was nothing you could do about it.

Except I could do something about it, Tuonen thought. But the thought itself was dangerous, because the *Killerling* would come for her if he let her live, not to mention selfish. Yes, he felt Aven had a lot left to live for, but if he let her go back to the Upper World to continue her life, she would leave him.

She will be going to Amaranthus anyway, he reminded himself. *She's going to leave you no matter what. Besides, she is not part of your role here. She is not meant to be yours.*

He sighed, rubbing his hand over his jaw. "Do you remember how you died?"

She stared at him, snowflakes gathering in her eyelashes, making her look ethereal. "I didn't die."

"Do you remember your last moments?"

She shook her head. "Stop it. I didn't die. I'm dreaming. This is just a dream." She raised her arms, the snow melting on them. "See? I'm warm-blooded. The snow melts, and I'm not cold in the slightest. I'm dreaming. I *know* I'm just dreaming."

Tuonen swallowed hard, knowing that the more he asked about how she died, the more she would finally realize the truth. He walked across the boat toward her, and she stiffened at his approach, a trace of fear on her brow.

He reached down and grabbed her by the elbows. Her skin was as warm as she said it was and tantalizingly soft to touch. His eyes closed briefly, taking in the feel of her, and he breathed deep, his nose filling with her floral scent, so unlike the stark white world around them. She smelled like spring, like everything he wasn't. She was life, he was death.

He pulled her to her feet and held her in place as he peered down at her. She stared up at him with round eyes and took in a shaking breath. "How did you die, Aven?" he asked.

She worried her lip between her teeth. He wondered what she tasted like—another reason he needed her to accept her death. "I didn't die."

"How did you die?"

She shook her head. "No. Stop saying that. I'm alive. I'm in bed, I'm at home, I'm dreaming."

"What did you do before you went to bed? Tell me."

"I...I..." She trailed off, looking away in frantic thought. "I was crossing the road..."

Now they were getting somewhere. "You were crossing the road?"

The line between her brows deepened. "I was crossing the road, heading toward work," she said in a faint voice. "There was a potential adopter coming to see one of the senior pit bulls we had, Aria. The sweetest dog. I had worked for so long to get Aria adopted, and finally, someone had seen her pictures and fallen in love. I was so happy; the poor old girl was finally going to get a home. Then..."

"Then?" he pressed, squeezing her arms lightly.

"Then I...I crossed the road. And then I was here..."

"Something happened to you in the middle. What was it?"

She swallowed audibly, tears starting to well in her eyes. "I don't want to know," she whispered. "I don't want to think about it."

He felt bad but he pressed on. "You were crossing the road. Which road?"

"Shoreditch High Street," she said.

Then, her eyes grew wider, and tears flowed down her cheeks like a river spilling over its banks. "I was crossing the street, and I heard the horn. It came from nowhere. I remember the bus driver's face and..."

And just like that, Aven remembered her death.

She crumbled into Tuonen's arms, the realization overwhelming.

Tuonen was surprised at first, at the way Aven fell into him, like he was seeing the life drained out of her in that moment. But then his arms went around her, and he held her tight, feeling every emotion roll out of her and soak into him.

This had never happened before. He'd never seen any of the dead cry over their own death or at being in the afterlife. Then again, none of them fought against the very notion of their death as hard as Aven did.

"I'm dead," she wailed, sobbing uncontrollably. "I'm dead."

"It's okay," he said to her, his voice shaking slightly, unnerved by her emotion. "You will adjust quickly. Everyone does."

"No!" she cried out into his coat. "I will not adjust. I can't die. I can't." She looked up at him, the sorrow on her face breaking his heart. "My parents. My mother, my father. My friends. The dogs. I can't leave any of them, don't you understand? They need me. I need them. I can't let them go. I can't leave them in the world without me."

"You will forget them soon," he said. "You will probably be put in Amaranthus. That's heaven, you know. Nirvana. That's the place everyone wants to go, and you're lucky enough to warrant it. In Amaranthus, you will want for nothing. You will feel no pain, no sorrow, no grief. You will be happy."

"And what if I'm not?"

"Then that would mean you're in Inmost, and you certainly don't deserve that."

She shook her head, the tears spilling. "I have so much life left. I'm only twenty-five! I'm just getting started. This can't be the end for me, it can't. There was so much I wanted to do. I wanted to make a difference in the world, I wanted to find my purpose...I wanted to fall in love."

Tuonen's chest felt tight at that admission. "I'm sorry."

She pulled away and turned her back to him. "I will not die," she said under her breath.

She started running down the length of the ship, and before Tuonen could reach her, she jumped over the side into the River of Shadows.

The water was shockingly cold, which was strange because Aven hadn't felt any of the falling snow or icy temperatures until that point.

But when she sank under the dark water, it chilled her to the bone.

In some ways, it woke her up.

She was dead. She had died, been hit by a bus crossing the road on the way to work, and for a split second, she saw the vision of her bloody and crumpled body beneath the front of the bus, bystanders gathered around her, yelling.

But that wasn't enough to stop her. She wasn't just going to accept her death. She was going to do everything she could to fight it.

If she could escape Tuonen, the Son of Death, if she could get back to where she came from, maybe she could find her way back to the world. After all, it wasn't like he was transporting a prisoner. She had a feeling everyone else who died never put up a fight.

So she kicked toward the surface until her head broke through.

She gasped for breath, thinking how interesting it was that she was dead and yet still had to go on breathing.

Then she started swimming for shore, as fast as she could go.

There was a splash behind her, and she knew Tuonen had jumped in the river after her, but she had to keep going. She had to try.

She had too much left to live for, even dead.

The shore came quickly, but the snow that gathered on the banks of the river were high. She tried to climb out, but the snow fell in around her. Still, she kept going, pulling herself out of the water, feeling more frozen by the second, then moved as quickly as she could through the packed snow until she was on her feet.

She knew Tuonen was behind her, knew that with his long legs and his strength and the fact that he was an immortal God of sorts, he would catch her soon, but she kept on going, as fast as she possibly could, one foot in front of the other. She didn't even know if she was running in the right direction; there was only snow as far as she could see. Off in the distance, there seemed to be a herd of white reindeer, only they looked rotted, and she could see their bones through their fur.

Land of the Dead, she thought to herself. *This can't be my future.*

Seconds after that thought, she was tackled from behind.

Tuonen pushed her into the snow and then flipped her over on her back, pinning her arms down with his hands. She stared up at him, at his otherworldly face, at the white snowy sky behind him, the way he looked like a black stain against it.

And yet there was something so beautiful about it all, something beautiful about him.

Beauty in death.

Beauty and death.

"What are you doing?" Tuonen snarled at her, and for once, she saw fear in his eyes. "You can't do that."

"I'm trying to go back," she said, struggling for a moment before she realized it was completely useless. He was impossibly strong. "I'm trying to live."

"You could have died again," he said, a harsh gleam in his eyes. "If you die again in this land, you will be sent to Oblivion, where you float in darkness for eternity."

She blinked in shock for a moment, her stomach sinking. "Well I didn't know that!" she sniped.

"Now you do," he said. "And if you try anything again, I may not be able to save you. There are monsters in the water that will consume you, creatures on this land that will tear you to pieces. There's my mother, a demon, and my father, the God of Death, and they don't mind handing out punishment to stragglers."

Desperation welled up inside her. "Please, Tuonen, you have to let me go."

He gave his head a stiff shake, his jaw tense. "I've never let anyone go. That isn't for me to decide."

"But you can," she said. "I know you can. You have that power. You can take me back to where you found me. Isn't there a way back?"

Oh, please, tell me there's a way back.

From the hesitant look in his eyes, she knew there was.

"Tuonen, please," she said again. "Take me back. Let me live. I have so much life left, so many other lives to change. There must have been some mistake, I shouldn't be here. If you let me live again, let me see my parents, let me save those dogs. I'll...I'll do anything. I'll make any bargain. I promise."

Now she had his attention. He adjusted his grip on her wrists. "What kind of bargain?"

"I don't know," she said, feeling hope swell through her. "Whatever it is you want, as long as I can go back and live my life."

He seemed to think that over, shifting his jaw back and forth. "I could get in trouble," he eventually said. "I would have to strike a deal with the *Killerling*."

"Who is the *Killerling*?" she asked.

He sighed and then got to his feet, quickly reaching down to pull her up beside him. "They are the ones who hunt those who refuse to die," he said. "There aren't many of you, but there are enough. If I let you go back to live your life, they will come for you, even if I tell them to leave you alone. They will try and kill you, drag you back here, and there's nothing I can do about it."

She didn't like the sound of that, but she would have to take her chances. "I can deal with that."

He studied her for a moment, his gaze roaming her face. She could have sworn there was affection in his eyes, as if he felt something for her. Something soft. "But nothing comes for free. Your death is still owed, and I am still to bring you to the City of Death, no matter what. I can only give you so much more time—if the *Killerling* don't find you first."

"I will take any time you can give me," Aven said desperately.

He nodded carefully at that, licking his lips. "Okay. Then I will try to be fair. You are twenty-five now. You have a mother and father who need you. You have animals that depend on you. You need time to continue making a difference in the world. I will give you until you're forty years old."

"Forty," Aven said softly. Forty used to feel so far away, and yet now, it was unbearably close.

"That's all I can give," he said. "It's enough time to change the world, I think, in whatever way you can. I will lead you back to where you came, and you will pass through a tunnel and through the rocks to emerge in the wilderness, somewhere in Northern Finland. You will return to your past life, and your death will be erased."

She couldn't help but grin, a smile so wide, it nearly hurt her face. "Thank you."

His eyes were cold in response. "But when you turn forty, you will have to come back here. You will have to die. That is, if the Killerling don't hunt you down before then."

"Okay," she said, extending her hand to shake on it. "I accept."

His mouth curled up into a wicked smile. "You haven't heard the bargain, Aven. A bargain means there's something in it for the both of us. There's something in this for me, too."

She narrowed her eyes at him warily. "And what is that?"

"When you return, you won't be going to Amaranthus. You won't be going to heaven."

Her heart twisted. "Where will I be going?" she asked fearfully.

His eyes glimmered as they focused on her mouth. "You will belong to me. I am not losing you to a place I cannot go. If you accept this deal, it means that when you die, you will be living in Tuonela. Not the City of Death, and certainly not Amaranthus."

Oh shit. She wasn't entering some marriage bargain, was she?

"You want me to be your…wife?"

"I want you—that's as much as I know," he said. "And when you're mine, I will not be letting you go. Not again. Not after this time."

Now she had food for thought. She could go on and live her life for another fifteen years, but then she would die again and be bond to the Son of Death for eternity?

He watched her carefully as she tried to make a choice.

The pull of her life back in London was fierce, and the urge to live was stronger than anything she'd ever known.

"And you're sure you'll want me at age forty?" she said.

He let out a soft laugh. "You mortals are so preoccupied with aging. At forty, you will be at your most beautiful, Aven." He reached forward and placed his hand at her cheek. His touch made her feel like there was a lightning storm inside her. "And I can't wait to see it."

Then, he leaned in and kissed her lightly on the lips, the lightning intensifying until she felt like her body was lit up and glowing. Her eyes fluttered closed, succumbing to the feeling.

Maybe it won't be so bad, she thought. *I'll be forty, and he'll still look like he's in his late twenties.*

Tuonen pulled away, and the light faded. He took her hand in his and shook it firmly.

"We have a deal, then," he said with darkened eyes.

Power flowed from his palm to hers, and she knew she was being bound to this bargain, that there would be no escaping it.

But she also knew that the moment she walked through into her old life, the moment she truly escaped and was alive again, she was going to spend the rest of her life trying to cheat death, no matter the cost.

And from the wry look in Tuonen's eyes before he led her to the boat and took her back to Death's Landing, she knew he knew this too.

He was up for the challenge.

Acknowledgments

This book was a very long time coming. Thank you to each reader who has shown me such grace and patience. I struggled for a time, not just through the throes of my mental health, physical health, grief, and other problems, but because I wasn't sure where I wanted the story to go.

Actually, let me clarify that: I KNEW where I wanted it to go, I just wasn't sure how to get there. I am a plotter by nature, and when it comes to my books, I know (more or less—I'm always open for improvisation as I write) what will happen in each chapter and how to get to "the end." However, with a series, I'm a little more open. I know how it will end, but I am not always clear on how it will get there.

Luckily, even though I know the years spent with this book were annoying for the reader (and honestly, a burden to carry for me—I do hate letting people down), the time did make me realize I knew where the series was going and also HOW to get there.

It made the delay worth it. In my eyes, anyway. You may or may not agree, but for me, I am glad that the way out of Inmost led into our world. If I had pushed and forced this book when I was supposed to, that never would have happened, and this book and series just got SO much more epic and exciting because of it.

When I was a kid, one of my favorite movies was Crocodile Dundee, particularly when he went to NYC. I wanted the spirit of that in this book, and I hope it delivered.

Most of all, I hope you had fun. Death and Hanna's relationship continues to deepen and become more real, and I really can't wait for that God to tell her he loves her! I'm also excited to see Hanna and her mother, to see how Torben and Death get on with their plans, to know how Tuonen is, and also...am I the only one suddenly intrigued by

Lovia and the Magician? Another thing that wasn't planned, but I sure am liking them together.

Also…will Hanna ever pay back that guy for stealing his car?

Goddess of Light is book four and the final (and longest) book in the series, and it's coming in November (…providing my schedule allows). Either way, it's coming, so buckle up!

Wow. This was a long acknowledgment without really thanking anyone?

Big thanks to Laura, Hang, Lauren, Michelle, Sandra, Kathleen, Mikayla, Catherine, Alexa, and Scott.

Then, I must thank my Ultimate Book Lover subscribers from REAM:

Breena, Mariana, Nicole, Krista, Judith, Meaghan, Kaeori, Kylie, Katlyn, Rachael, Diana, Coral, Kandace, Julie, JennX, Amy Tiffany, Betty, Syd, Sarah, Letretia, Veronica, Melissa, Jana, Nikki, Laura, Alex, Brittney, Terrill, Meg, Kila, Ally, Lara Croft, Sabrina, Shelby, Shek, Lauren Veronica, Shery, Rachel G, Laura Annis, Bee, Tammy, Chandra, Liz, Brooke, SM Andrews. Thanks again for being such fab supporters, it means so much!

About the Author

Karina Halle is a screenwriter, a former music & travel journalist, and the New York Times, Wall Street Journal, and USA Today bestselling author of River of Shadows, The Royals Next Door, and Black Sunshine, as well as 80 other wild and romantic reads, ranging from light & sexy rom coms to horror/paranormal romance and dark fantasy. Needless to say, whatever genre you're into, she has probably written a romance for it.

When she's not traveling, she and her husband split their time between a possibly haunted, 120-year-old house in Victoria, BC, their sailboat the Norfinn, and their condo in Los Angeles. For more information, visit www.authorkarinahalle.com

Find her on Facebook, Instagram, Pinterest, BookBub, Amazon, and Tik Tok.

Also by Karina Halle

DARK FANTASY & GOTHIC ROMANCE

River of Shadows (Underworld Gods #1)

Crown of Crimson (Underworld Gods #2)

City of Darkness (Underworld Gods #3) - 2023

Black Sunshine (Dark Eyes Duet #1)

The Blood is Love (Dark Eyes Duet #2)

Nightwolf

Blood Orange (The Dracula Duet #1)

Black Rose (The Dracula Duet #2)

A Ship of Bones and Teeth

Hollow (A Gothic Shade of Romance #1)

Legend (A Gothic Shade of Romance #2)

HORROR ROMANCE

Darkhouse (EIT #1)

Red Fox (EIT #2)

The Benson (EIT #2.5)

Dead Sky Morning (EIT #3)

Lying Season (EIT #4)

On Demon Wings (EIT #5)

Old Blood (EIT #5.5)

The Dex-Files (EIT #5.7)

Into the Hollow (EIT #6)

And With Madness Comes the Light (EIT #6.5)

Come Alive (EIT #7)

Ashes to Ashes (EIT #8)

Dust to Dust (EIT #9)

Ghosted (EIT #9.5)

Came Back Haunted (EIT #10)

The Devil's Metal (The Devil's Duology #1)

The Devil's Reprise (The Devil's Duology #2)

Veiled (Ada Palomino #1)

Song For the Dead (Ada Palomino #2)

CONTEMPORARY ROMANCE

Love, in English/Love, in Spanish

Where Sea Meets Sky

Racing the Sun

The Pact

The Offer

The Play

Winter Wishes

The Lie

The Debt

Smut

Heat Wave

Before I Ever Met You

After All

Rocked Up

Wild Card

Maverick

Hot Shot

Bad at Love

The Swedish Prince

The Wild Heir
A Nordic King
The Royal Rogue
Nothing Personal
My Life in Shambles
The Royal Rogue
The Forbidden Man
The One That Got Away
Lovewrecked
One Hot Italian Summer
All the Love in the World (Anthology)
The Royals Next Door
The Royals Upstairs

ROMANTIC SUSPENSE

Sins and Needles (The Artists Trilogy #1)
On Every Street (An Artists Trilogy Novella #0.5)
Shooting Scars (The Artists Trilogy #2)
Bold Tricks (The Artists Trilogy #3)
Dirty Angels (Dirty Angels #1)
Dirty Deeds (Dirty Angels #2)
Dirty Promises (Dirty Angels #3)
Black Hearts (Sins Duet #1)
Dirty Souls (Sins Duet #2)
Discretion (Dumonts #1)
Disarm (Dumonts #2)
Disavow (Dumonts #3)

Printed in the USA
CPSIA information can be obtained
at www.ICGtesting.com
LVHW032001160724
785208LV00002B/4

9 798869 277084